Then he returned to the storage area, found a hammer and used the claw end to puncture a hole in one of the remaining cans. The combustible liquid dripped from the shelf to the floor, forming a pool. He pushed several more containers on top of it, then carried the puncture can with him, backing out of the storage area into the office, leaving a wet trail behind him.

He stopped at the door to the alley and pulled a book of matches from his pocket. The trail would act as a fuse, burning across the carpet to the explosive cans in the closet.

Hurrying back through the lab to the steps, the Executioner struck a match and dropped it. The ancient wood caught fire, the flames growing slowly as he raced to the office.

Mack Bolan's back was to the alley door when he struck another match and dropped it into the trail of alcohol that led to the storage area. He turned, grasped the knob of the door and opened it.

A feeling of utter shock and surprise washed over him.

Behind the door that should have led to the alley was a solid brick wall.

STONY MAN™

DEADLY AGENT

A GOLD EAGLE BOOK FROM

W◍RLDWIDE®

TORONTO • NEW YORK • LONDON
AMSTERDAM • PARIS • SYDNEY • HAMBURG
STOCKHOLM • ATHENS • TOKYO • MILAN
MADRID • WARSAW • BUDAPEST • AUCKLAND

DID YOU PURCHASE THIS BOOK WITHOUT A COVER?
If you did, you should be aware it is **stolen property** as it was
reported *unsold and destroyed* by a retailer. Neither the author nor
the publisher has received any payment for this book.

*All the characters in this book have no existence outside the imagination of
the author, and have no relation whatsoever to anyone bearing the same
name or names. They are not even distantly inspired by any individual
known or unknown to the author, and all the incidents are pure invention.*

*All Rights Reserved including the right of reproduction in whole or in part
in any form. This edition is published by arrangement with Harlequin
Enterprises II B.V. The text of this publication or any part thereof may not
be reproduced or transmitted in any form or by any means, electronic or
mechanical, including photocopying, recording, storage in an
information retrieval system, or otherwise, without the written
permission of the publisher, Eton House, 18-24 Paradise Road,
Richmond, Surrey TW9 1SR*

*This book is sold subject to the condition that it shall not, by way of trade
or otherwise, be lent, resold, hired out or otherwise circulated without the
prior consent of the publisher in any form of binding or cover other than
that in which it is published and without a similar condition including this
condition being imposed on the subsequent purchaser.*

DEADLY AGENT © 1995 by Worldwide Library

® and ™ are trademarks of the publisher

ISBN 0 373 61898 0

25-1200

*Printed and bound in Spain
by Litografia Rosés S.A., Barcelona*

DEADLY AGENT

PROLOGUE

Plzeň, Czech Republic

As the door swung open Jonine Hammersmith smelled death.

She and Nigel Bentley followed the informant through the entrance into a dimly lighted hallway. The door swung shut again. Hammersmith noted the cold concrete walls as they moved toward a steel stairway at the end of the hall, the near-silent tapping of their rubber-soled walking shoes sounding overly loud. Behind her, Bentley's anxious breathing seemed equally loud. She took a deep breath, willing herself to relax.

As they started down the steps, Hammersmith's hands moved to her waist pack. Holstered in a secret Velcro-secured pocket at the back of the pack, she felt the reassuring hardness of the Beretta Model 21. The little .22 long rifle pistol, complete with sound suppressor, was the favored assassination weapon of Israel's Mossad. It didn't have the type of firepower Hammersmith preferred, but it was quiet, and the woman hoped it would throw a red herring into the game if she was killed and the enemy found the gun.

Another long corridor waited at the bottom of the

steps. The light faded further as they crept on, and Hammersmith reached into the waist pack to produce a small penlight. Pushing the switch, she aimed the thin ray ahead.

The informant halted in his tracks and twirled to face her, his face a mask of horror in the glow. "No lights! Not yet!"

Hammersmith killed the beam. They moved on.

A moment later, a hand reached out in the darkness, stopping her. Bentley bumped softly into her back, then the scratching of a key searching for a lock in front of her echoed through the hallway. The sound was replaced by the soft screech of another steel door swinging open.

Subdued light met Hammersmith's eyes as she stepped into the room. In the faint glow, she saw long tables covered with test tubes, petri dishes and other laboratory equipment. Against the far wall, a large glass window sparkled faintly in the dim light. To one side was a short metal staircase that led up into some other area of the split-level underground compound.

The faint sound of voices drifted down to them.

The informant grabbed her by the shoulders, and pressed his face close to hers. "Wait until we get there," he whispered in heavily accented English. "Shine your light only long enough to be sure. Then we must leave." He paused, then for emphasis added, "Hurry."

The squeaks of their walking shoes seemed even louder as the informant led Hammersmith and Bentley through the maze of lab tables and machines to the window. Stopping in front of the glass, Hammersmith glanced to the frightened man, who nodded.

The British MI-6 agent flipped the switch on her penlight once more. She felt her mouth fall open in horror as she followed the beam through the window.

On the other side of the glass, Hammersmith saw a fifty-by-fifty-foot steel chamber. Several dogs and cats, now dead, had been tethered to the floor. Over the animals heads, spray vents were visible in the low ceiling.

"You have seen it, now—" the informant whispered.

Hammersmith grabbed his arm, silencing the man. One more second. That was all she would need. Her report would have to cover all that was visible inside.

As the flashlight moved to the side, the beam passed what appeared to be the legs of a chair behind the dead animals. Hammersmith felt her heart stop as some deep unconscious understanding sent chills up her spine. She heard Bentley gasp behind her.

Strapped to the wooden chair, his eyes still opened wide in the terror of impending death, was the body of a man.

What the informant had told them was true.

Sudden footsteps on the metal stairs shook the British agents from their shock. Hammersmith turned automatically, her hands fumbling with the Velcro enclosure on her pack. She looked up as her fingers found the butt of the Beretta.

A man wearing a uniform marked Jablonec Security reached the bottom of the steps and flipped the light switch.

Bright light suddenly flooded the laboratory, momentarily blinding Hammersmith. As she drew the Beretta from her pack, she saw the uniformed man go for the automatic pistol holstered on his hip. At the same time, she heard a second set of feet on the stairs. From the corner of her eye, she saw Bentley jerk his own .22 from the waistband of his slacks.

Hammersmith had already fired five shots by the time the uniformed man cleared leather. The tiny .22 rounds coughed from the Beretta, stitching a pattern of red dots across the khaki shirt in a three-inch group over the heart. The guard dropped to the floor as the second set of uniformed legs started down the stairwell.

To her side, the British agent heard the muffled report of Bentley's weapon. Two rounds ricocheted off the concrete wall next to the stairs as the second guard dropped into view, a CZ-75 9 mm pistol gripped in both hands.

Hammersmith swung the Beretta frantically toward the man. The suppressed .22s wouldn't be heard above. But if *he* fired, the 9 mm bullets would sound like nuclear explosions against the concrete walls. She pulled the trigger twice, sending a pair of rimfire rounds from the barrel of the Beretta into the guard's shoulder. He fell to his knees as Bentley pumped three more .22s into his belly.

Hammersmith raised the tiny automatic and sighted down the barrel at the guard's head. Her own finger pulled back as the explosion threatened to deafen her in the confines of the laboratory.

The .22 caught the guard squarely between the

eyes. He fell forward on his face, but not before he got off a shot that drilled past Hammersmith and slammed into her partner.

The Beretta locked open, empty.

Hammersmith twirled toward Bently as he fell to the floor. She caught a glimpse of the informant's stunned face, then her eyes focused on her partner. Half of his face had been blown away. His eyes stared fishlike into space.

Hammersmith had no time for sorrow. Footsteps pounded down the stairs. Grabbing the informant's arm, she dragged the man back across the room toward the door. He bumped frantically into her, knocking her face-first into the concrete next to the door and bloodying her lip. Recovering, she pulled the man through the door, down the hall and up the steps.

A moment later, they were outside and racing into the night. As they ran, one question raced through Jonine Hammersmith's mind above all others: would whoever was responsible for the underground killing chamber believe Nigel Bentley had acted alone? Or would they realize that the West knew what was going on and step up the project that, until now, Jonine Hammersmith had prayed was only rumor?

CHAPTER ONE

South Pyrenees

Mack Bolan, a.k.a. the Executioner, wearily massaged the tight muscles at the back of his neck as he boarded the C-17 cargo plane piloted by Stony Man Farm's ace flier, Jack Grimaldi. He knew a tense situation was brewing, otherwise Hal Brognola wouldn't have called in Phoenix Force to mop up the big warrior's last mission, which had involved Basque terrorists kidnapping a young U.S. citizen. After a hasty briefing from Yakov Katzenelenbogen, Bolan had sprinted across a mountain meadow toward the waiting aircraft.

Grimaldi nodded a greeting and pushed the control as the Executioner dropped into the copilot's seat. The plane taxied forward across the pasture.

Bolan lifted the radio mike from the console and thumbed the button. "Stony One to Base," he said, then leaned back against the aircraft's copilot seat and closed his eyes as he waited for the message to pass through the scrambling device, bounce off the satellite and end up in the U.S.

"We read you, Striker," Barbara Price replied a moment later. "Everything go all right?"

"It went. The ambassador's boy is safe—tired and worn out, but safe."

"Hal will pass the word on to the President. Let me get him on the line. He needs to talk to you."

Bolan dropped the mike to his lap as he waited. He heard a series of clicks and buzzes on the other end as Grimaldi lifted the plane into the sky. Then Hal Brognola's familiar voice came over the airwaves.

"Striker, we need you in the Czech Republic."

Bolan remained silent, settling into his seat for the briefing he knew was about to follow.

Brognola cleared his throat. "You remember the Biopreparat program?"

The warrior felt the hair on the back of his neck stand up. Designed to perfect biochemical warfare by developing plagues that would resist Western antibiotics, the Biopreparat had been a top-secret Soviet research project of the seventies and eighties—in direct violation of the 1972 treaty. "I remember it, Hal," he answered. "It was supposed to have been shut down by Yeltsin."

"The operative word there is 'supposed,'" Brognola replied. "Yeltsin did kill the project, but somehow it's come back to life in the Czech Republic. At least something's going on. Exactly what, we don't know yet."

"Where's all this coming from, Hal? The Company?"

"In a roundabout way. It's really from the British. A snitch took two of their MI-6 operatives to an underground aerosol-dissemination testing facility in Plzeň last night.''

''How did *we* get in on the deal?''

Brognola sighed. ''MI-6 contacted the CIA for help. The director went to the President, who decided he'd rather have us than the spooks. The Man told them not to get involved, that it sounded like a wild rumor to him. Then he called me.''

Bolan frowned. ''So why not just send in a team of blacksuits and wipe this dissemination chamber off the face of the earth?'' He referred to the Stony Man regular troops who lived and trained at the Farm. They could handle a situation like that without involving specialists such as Phoenix Force, Able Team or himself.

''Call it a hunch, Striker, but if there's one of these dissemination chambers still operating, there might be more. And we don't know where they are.''

The Executioner answered his own question. ''And if whoever's behind this deal learns for certain that we're on to him, he'll move the sites. What little Intel we have will go right down the drain.''

''Right.''

''So I take it you want me to get into this chamber, find out what's going on and locate any other similar sites?''

''Right again. Grab a chute from the back. You're jumping near Plzeň. Jack's got the coordinates. One of the MI-6 agents—Hammersmith's her name—will meet you. She speaks fluent Czech, and knows computers and the area.''

Bolan paused. Brognola had said two British agents

had seen the dissemination chamber. Yet only one was picking him up.

The Executioner knew the answer to his next question before he asked it. "Where's the other MI-6 agent?"

"Nigel Bentley? Dead."

Prague, Czech Republic

STRONG CAVENDISH tobacco smoke and the lively chords of "Dance of the Comedians," from Smetana's opera *The Bartered Bride,* filled Joseph Ryba's parlor. The fragrance of the tobacco filled his nostrils, and the sweet aftertaste of cherry *kalache,* his mouth. He pulled another draw from the long stem of the hand-carved Alpine pipe, then set it on the table next to his leather chair.

The gold chains that adorned the pipe, linking the stem, bowl and carriage, tinkled as they struck the wood. Ryba smiled. As young men, his grandfather and great uncles had been professional pipe makers, carving a meager existence from the business as they carved the briar that became the smoking pipes. Then had come the late-nineteenth-century migration of Czechs and Slavs to America, and Frantzen Ryba's brothers had all boarded steamers bound for New York, moving eventually across the new country to settle in Kansas and Oklahoma. Only Joseph's grandfather had remained behind, continuing to carve the pipes that were now sold in tobacco shops the world over.

Ryba lifted the pipe again, watching the dying

smoke curl from the bowl. The initials *F.R.* had been sculpted into the front of the bowl, then inlaid in solid gold to match the chains. The pipe, more than one hundred years old now, had been well taken care of by Joseph's grandfather, then his father, and now himself, and Ryba had hoped someday to pass the antique on to his own son.

A sudden twinge of melancholy flooded Ryba's chest. That day would come, but not as he had once hoped. His wife, Eva, was unable to bear children, and the pipe would have to go to one of the bastards he had fathered. Or course the love he had once felt for Eva had fallen along the wayside years ago, to be replaced by the lust he now felt for his mistress. He would have preferred to live with Marja.

And one day, when the time was right, he would.

A soft knock echoed through the parlor from the door to the hallway. "Come," Ryba said, setting the pipe down again.

Karl, resplendent in his black waistcoat and red sash, stuck his head inside the room. "Mr. Schoevenec is here as requested, sir," the servant announced.

Ryba straightened the tail of his purple smoking jacket. "Send him in."

A moment later a squat, blocky man in his late fifties entered the room and stood at attention. Ryba remained seated, indicating a couch across from his chair. He studied Petre Schoevenec as the visitor's stumpy legs carried him to the seat, the sight reminding him again of his grandfather.

Frantzen Ryba had always been quick to point out that the Ryba family was Czech, not Slovak. Only the purest of Bohemian blood ran through their veins. The Slovaks, on the other hand, were a mongrel race whose bodies probably contained as much barbarous Hungarian DNA as it did Bohemian.

Petre Schoevenec was such a hybrid, and belonged in the new Republic of Slovakia. But after the bifurcation of Czechoslovakia, many Slovaks who had been relocated under Communist rule chose to remain in the Prague area. Some, like Schoevenec, had even found office during the blind reign of socialism that had ignored the inherent superiority of some races over others. And until a racial cleansing could be undertaken as was being done in Bosnia, men like Joseph Ryba would be forced to endure animals like Petre Schoevenec.

"So, Petre," Ryba said without introduction. "What have you learned?"

Schoevenec cleared his throat nervously. "Little more than we informed you of last night. The body of the man has still not been identified."

"And what of the guard he killed?"

"The bullets in the body were .22 caliber. Probably of Western manufacture, although the criminologists say they cannot be certain. A Beretta pistol in the same caliber was found next to the dead man."

Ryba leaned forward. "A .22 is a small bullet, is it not?"

"Yes."

"Used primarily for hunting small game, or for assassination because of its low noise?"

"That is correct, Mr. Ryba. The Israelis are famous for its use."

"So then am I to believe that the man who broke into the laboratory was an agent of the Mossad?"

Schoevenec shook his head. "I think not. I suspect the weapon was used to confuse us."

"Did this man act alone, or were there more agents who escaped?"

"We do not know," Schoevenec admitted. "One of the guards thought he heard footsteps in the exit hall, but when he opened the door, no one was there. It is impossible to know."

Ryba sat back against the chair, picked up his pipe and pulled a gold lighter from the side pocket of his smoking jacket. "There is a test, I believe, for bullets. Ballistics?"

"Yes. The rifling marks from the bullet can be compared to those made by the barrel of a weapon."

"Has that been done?"

"They are doing it now."

Ryba held the lighter over the pipe bowl and sucked deeply on the stem. The tobacco crackled in the silence. "If the bullets match this man's Beretta, we will learn nothing. Only that the dead man killed the guard. But if they came from a different gun…" He let his voice trail off.

"Yes," Schoevenec finished for him. "We will know that other agents were present and saw the laboratory and dissemination chamber."

Ryba sucked silently on his pipe, watching the smoke float toward the ceiling. Finally he said, "When will you know?"

"They should finish their testing later tonight."

"Inform me immediately."

"Yes, sir." Schoevenec stood, taking the cue.

Ryba let him get halfway to the door before stopping him. "Where is Skrdla?" He watched Schoevenec's shoulders tighten at the mention of the name.

"Bulgaria. He is taking care of a small problem."

Ryba knew what that meant. "When does he return?"

Schoevenec shrugged. "It will depend. But I should think another day or two."

The Czech rose from his chair and walked to meet Schoevenec, towering over him like a tall tree over a scrub bush. "If you discover that more agents were present, order Skrdla to track them down and kill them," he said softly.

"And if he has not returned?"

Ryba sighed. "Need I remind you in addition to being the minister of the interior, I am the leader of the Autonomy Party? And your position as director of state security might well be in jeopardy if it were learned that you had assisted me so often in the past in a…shall we say, unofficial role?"

"I am well aware of the consequences if we are discovered. I only inquired concerning your wishes if Skrdla is delayed."

Ryba felt the anger rush to his face as he looked down at the big forehead on the little Slav. The sooner he carried out his plan, the sooner he could start with phase two and begin cleansing the world of stubby little men like Schoevenec. "I want any other agents who saw the chamber dead. And if Skrdla is not available, *do it yourself.*"

CHAPTER TWO

Above the Czech Republic

As the C-17 neared its destination, Bolan tapped several buttons on the control panel. An aerial photo of the terrain just north of Plzeň appeared on the computer screen. Squinting at the shadows, the Executioner studied the valley where he was about to meet Jonine Hammersmith. "You see it?" Barbara Price asked over the radio.

"Affirmative. Looks like it's about halfway between Plzeň and some little village on the Berounka River."

"That's it," Price confirmed. "Plasy's the name of the village. Good luck, Striker."

Bolan dropped the microphone to the console. "How much time, Jack?" he asked.

"Five, maybe six minutes," the ace pilot replied.

The Executioner nodded, rose to his feet and returned to the cargo area. He slipped into the parachute and oxygen tank. When he slid the cargo door open, his ears popped.

"Ten seconds, Striker," Grimaldi informed him.

"Got you, Jack." He slipped the oxygen mask over

his face, counted down the numbers and leapt from the aircraft into the clouds.

Bolan pulled the rip cord almost immediately. The chute shot out over his head, blossomed and jerked him upward. Still blinded by the white billowy mist, he began to drift slowly earthward.

Desiring to enter the Czech Republic with no "paper trail," the Executioner had decided on a High Altitude High Opening jump that would allow him to first locate the valley north of Plzeň, then Para-Sail toward it at a height where he wasn't likely to be spotted.

The clouds parted suddenly, and the rounded green plateau of Bohemia appeared far below. Far in the distance, no matter which way he turned, Bolan saw the high mountain peaks that separated the region from Moravia to the east, Austria to the south and Poland to the north. The dark Bohemian Forest, about which countless fables and fairy tales had been written, was visible to the west, separating the Czech Republic from Germany.

Bolan reached up, his hands closing around the canopy toggles, his eyes locked to the tiny spot that had to be Plzeň to the north. The wind at his back, he faced the canopy against it, slowing his speed and letting it blow him over the city.

The Executioner watched the lights of the famous beer-making city begin to turn on as dusk fell over eastern Europe. He felt somewhat naked, his only weapon the Cold Steel Magnum Tanto knife.

The mission he was about to embark upon would call for the most delicate of clandestine maneuvers, and uppermost in his mind was the fact that if who-ever was behind the revival of the Biopreparat program learned of his interest, all might be lost.

The combat knife bore no serial number or markings, and was distributed widely around the world. But the Desert Eagle and Beretta were both of limited production and definitely "Western" designs. If they were dropped or abandoned in battle, they wouldn't point a definite finger to the West, but there was no point taking chances. The Executioner had decided to use traditionally Eastern Bloc weapons that wouldn't be associated with the U.S. or her allies.

As the city disappeared beneath and behind him, Bolan began to drop closer to the ground. Spotting the smaller village ahead in the quickly fading sun-light, he counted three miles back toward him and sailed for the spot.

The small valley lay right where it had on the computer screen.

The Executioner hit the ground running and turned a fast 360 degrees, searching for curious eyes. The valley was deserted. Jerking in the chute, he pulled a foldable entrenching tool from his pack and buried the canopy in the soft ground. He was returning the small shovel to his pack when the sound of a car engine met his ears.

Bolan sprinted behind a lone tree in the center of the valley, drawing the long blade as he took cover. Peering around the edge of the bark, he saw a yellow Fiat pull to a halt at the top of the rise. He waited.

A moment later, a small woman with bright red hair stepped out of the car. She wore blue jeans, walking shoes and a blue nylon Windbreaker. A royal blue belt pack was buckled around her waist, and a camera case strap hung from her neck.

Bolan resheathed the knife and stepped out from behind the tree. It had to be MI-6 agent Jonine Hammersmith.

No real tourist would look that "touristy."

Hammersmith smiled as he approached, and the Executioner noticed the swollen upper lip. An injury from the escape the night before? If so, she'd gotten off lucky. The woman was in her mid-thirties and had a pleasant, pretty face. But her eyes looked tired, sad, like they'd seen too much violence in too short a time.

"Nice valley," Hammersmith commented as Bolan stopped in front of her.

"Any tigers around?" Bolan asked.

"Doubt it. They're all in Detroit."

"With the Lions," the Executioner said, completing the code.

The woman extended her hand. "Jonine Hammersmith. Call me Jonnie."

"Pollock, Rance," Bolan told her.

"I've got presents for you in the car," Hammersmith said, turning on her heel, "and I've been instructed that you'll be calling the shots."

Bolan didn't answer. He followed her to the Fiat, watching her cover the distance in smooth, graceful strides. It was hard to tell with what she was wearing, but she appeared to be in good shape—not always the case with intelligence officers. Their jobs rarely demanded top physical conditioning.

But the Executioner's did. And if this petite British

lady was along for the duration of the ride, it was important that she be able to keep up.

He took a seat on the passenger's side as Hammersmith slid behind the wheel. She reached over the seat, grabbed the handle on a large suitcase and pulled it into the front. "Merry Christmas."

Bolan took the suitcase, sending a second glance Hammersmith's way as the woman twisted the key in the ignition. She couldn't tip the scales at more than a hundred pounds, and the suitcase had to weigh at least twenty-five. Yet she had handled it with ease.

The warrior filed the information away, along with his speculation on her physical conditioning.

The British agent threw the Fiat into reverse, backed away from the valley and started back across the bumpy grass to the road as the Executioner opened the suitcase. Inside, wrapped in oil paper, he found a Hungarian FEG PJK-9HP, a clone of the time-honored Browning Hi-Power. He dug deeper, unwrapping the plastic paper from a 7.65 mm Skorpion vz/62 full-auto machine pistol.

Beneath the guns lay extra box magazines and cartons of 9 mm and 7.65 mm ammunition, all of Eastern European manufacture. Bolan broke open the boxes and began loading as Hammersmith turned onto the highway that led back into Plzeň. "What are you carrying?" he asked the woman.

Hammersmith patted her left armpit under her Windbreaker, then pointed to her belt pack. "I've an H&K P-7, and .22-caliber Beretta with silencer."

"You know how to use them?" the Executioner asked bluntly.

The woman turned long enough to give him a dirty look. "I do."

The sun finally dropped below the horizon, casting the green farmlands of Bohemia into darkness as they drove the final few miles into Plzeň. Bolan sat back against the seat, closing his eyes. He liked Hammersmith. She seemed to be a serious, no-nonsense agent intent on doing her job for God and the queen. She had risked her life in the underground test chamber and, according to the report, had killed one of the guards.

The Executioner opened one eye and stole a glance at the short red hair that framed the smooth skin of her face. Jonnie Hammersmith wasn't hard to look at, either. She exuded a certain hard-soft quality—she appeared to be professional without giving up any of her natural femininity.

Bolan got the feeling she'd come through in a crunch, be there beside him with both pistols blazing when it hit the fan.

He closed his eye again. And it *would* hit the fan. Soon.

"I reserved a room for you at the Continental," Hammersmith said as they topped a rise in the highway and the lights of Plzeň appeared in the distance. "Would you like to go there and get settled in?" She didn't wait for an answer. "Or, my apartment is closer. You could freshen up—"

Bolan shook his head. "Let's go meet your snitch. Then we're going back to the dissemination chamber."

Plzeň, Czech Republic

"THAT'S HIS VAN," Hammersmith announced as they walked past the parking lot just off the old cobblestone street in downtown Plzeň. "It belongs to the research lab." She reached up and slipped her arm through the Executioner's as they neared the gray stone building.

Along with the weapons, Hammersmith had furnished Bolan with a nylon Windbreaker that matched her own. He caught a glimpse of the British woman on his arm as they passed a storefront window. With the twin Windbreakers and Hammersmith's belt pack, they looked like the typical foreign vacation couple who'd decided to check out the Plzeň nightlife.

The Telc Disco was in a basement below a crystal factory, three blocks off Plzeň's Old Town Square. It mixed old-world charm with American rock and roll, the sum of that addition coming out to be an establishment no different than thousands of others all over Europe. The large dance floor, complete with multicolored strobe lights and a twirling mirrored ball, was in the center of the room surrounded by small tables, chairs and booths.

Silent movies projected onto the four walls told their own stories in bits and pieces as the lights flashed by. Small bars stood in each of the four corners, the bartenders behind them serving wine and spirits as well as the many varieties of pilsner beer that had put the otherwise mundane city on the map for more than four hundred years.

Still wearing his white lab coat, Vincent Hlupnek

sat alone at a table near the wall, a foaming glass of beer in front of him. He looked nervously toward the door as Hammersmith led Bolan inside.

They took chairs at the table as a waitress in faded blue jeans and a Princeton University tank top appeared. "Two more Urquells," Hlupnek shouted over the music, and the girl headed back toward the bar. Turning back to Bolan and Hammersmith, he held the tail of his lab coat with both hands and said, "Please, you will excuse my clothes. I was sent to pick up supplies and came straight from work. I must return soon."

Hammersmith nodded, then introduced Bolan as Mr. Rance Pollock. Bolan shook Hlupnek's hand, at the same time taking a quick glance around the disco.

It wasn't yet ten o'clock, but already the place was filling up. The clientele was primarily the twenty-to-forty crowd, more intent on themselves and who they might go home with than they were on the conversations of two tourists and some guy in a white coat.

Bolan turned his eyes back to the informant. "You work at...at the place?"

Hlupnek nodded. Taking the cue, he said only, "I am a research scientist."

"So why are you helping us?"

A look of shock came over Hlupnek's face. "It is not obvious? People will die."

Bolan didn't answer. Hlupnek was presenting himself as one of the rarest of all animals—an honest snitch, a man whose motive was simply to help mankind. He wasn't working off a criminal case, he wasn't being blackmailed, and according to Hammersmith he wasn't even on MI-6's payroll. As far as Bolan could see, the man had everything to lose and nothing to gain—until you thought about the dead man in the test chamber and realized that Vincent Hlupnek was smart enough to know it could have been him.

The waitress brought two more glasses of pilsner. Bolan gave her some money and waved away the change. "Why did you take the job in the first place?" he asked.

"Under false pre…pre…"

"False pretense?" Hammersmith offered.

"Yes. They give me false pretenses. Say I am to do research to discover new cures for disease. Anthrax, they say, and tularemia."

"So what made you realize that wasn't the purpose behind your work?" Bolan continued.

Hlupnek shrugged and looked down at the table. "It is hard to explain to one who is not scientist. But there are ways you work to find cure for disease, and other experiments to find way to make disease worse. You understand?"

Bolan nodded. He'd decided to trust the man. His gut-level reaction was that Hlupnek was on their side. And sometimes guts were all you had to go on.

The Executioner sat back in his chair as a song ended and the disk jockey spoke in Czech over the sound system. "We've got to get in there," he said.

Hlupnek shook his head vigorously. "Impossible. The Deliverance Squad—they are masquerading as the security guards, I think—have changed the locks.

I have not yet been issued a key. A new alarm system—"

"I'm not talking about the test chamber itself," Bolan interrupted. "I've seen dead animals and men before. There's nothing I can learn in there that we don't already know." He paused, glanced around, then continued. "What I need is records, documents, that sort of thing. I want to know if this is the only lab, or if there are others. Surely there's an office of some type on the grounds."

"Of course..." Hlupnek said hesitantly. "There is a record room and office just off the research library. But it is kept locked, and I do not have the key."

"We can worry about that bridge when we come to it. You do have access to the library, don't you?"

"Of course. I do much research. But how do I explain your presence?"

"You said you had to pick up supplies?"

Hlupnek's face took on a puzzled look. "Yes. A shipment of lab equipment that has come in from Prague. Why?"

"How big are the boxes?"

Hlupnek stared at him, then held his hands out shoulder width.

"Do the guards know what you're picking up?"

"Of course not. It is none of their business." His face grew even more curious.

"Great," Bolan said. "Let's go."

Hammersmith stood up next to him, an elfish grin on her face. She'd already guessed what the Executioner had in mind.

Hlupnek hadn't. "What—" he said as he rose slowly to his feet.

Bolan took his arm and led him toward the exit. "If they ask you what you're bringing in, Vincent, you better tell them it's office furniture."

"THE DRIVE WILL TAKE approximately twenty minutes," Hlupnek called from the driver's seat as he pulled the van out of the parking lot and started down the street.

Inside the large cardboard box, Bolan glanced up to the corner where the tape had torn away from the flap. A tiny shaft of light glowed through, highlighting Jonnie Hammersmith's crimson hair. They lay side by side facing each other, newspapers packing them in like giant pieces of china. The MI-6 agent's head rested against the Executioner's chest, her perfume wafting up to his nostrils in the confined space.

He didn't know what the brand of perfume was, but he couldn't say he didn't like it.

The van bumped along over the cobblestone streets of Plzeň, then the sounds of traffic died down as they left the city proper. Hammersmith finally broke the uneasy silence, looking up into the Executioner's face with the same impish grin he'd seen before. "We've got to stop meeting like this," she said. "People will become suspicious."

Bolan smiled. "What we've got to stop doing is talking," he whispered. "Desks and office furniture don't say much."

The van bumped on. The warrior rested his arm on Hammersmith's side, reflecting on the vulnerable position they were in. If he was wrong about Hlupnek, the guards would mow them down easily.

Finally the van slowed, then turned again and halted. "I must get the guards to help me unload you," Hlupnek said, and Bolan took note of the nervousness in the Czech's voice.

The van door opened, then closed. The sound of footsteps on concrete faded into the distance.

Bolan and Hammersmith waited silently, their breathing the only sound inside the box. The MI-6 agent shifted slightly, and her breath blew gently into the warrior's neck. He felt a stirring in his lower abdomen, the response cut off by the creak of the van's rear door opening. Hlupnek's voice penetrated the cardboard, followed by two more voices speaking Czech. A moment later, the box was shoved out the door and tipped onto what Bolan assumed was a dolly.

The movement threw the warrior back at a forty-five-degree angle, and Hammersmith tumbled into him face-to-face. The Executioner reached out, wrapping his arms around the woman to steady her.

They had to remain still inside the box. Hlupnek had been instructed to tell the guards he was bringing in a desk if they asked, and desks didn't bounce around inside the carton.

Hammersmith circled her arms around Bolan as the guards pushed the box forward across the concrete. The British woman's face dug into his throat as she grasped tighter, doing her best to keep from shifting with the rocking movement of the dolly.

They stopped, then heard the sound of a key entering a lock. A moment later, they were moving again, bumping over a threshold. A short outburst of Czech curses met their ears, then they rolled more smoothly down what sounded like a tiled hallway.

Another door opened, a few more words were exchanged, then the box was wrestled off the dolly and lowered to the ground.

Bolan found himself facedown on top of his companion. A door closed and footsteps retreated down the hall. A moment later, the tape was ripped away from the lid.

The Executioner climbed out, reached down and pulled Hammersmith out. He squinted, letting his eyes adjust to the light. They were in a library, all right. Floor-to-ceiling bookcases lined the walls, with more shelves creating a labyrinth through the middle of the large room.

The Executioner pulled the box out of sight behind a bookshelf. Hlupnek held his finger to his lips, then motioned for them to follow him. He led the way to a steel door at the rear of the room. "Please hurry," he said urgently. "The guards make unscheduled rounds. They could return at any time."

Bolan nodded, then turned to the door, studying the lock. He had come prepared for anything, and what he saw now was a double-sided disk tumbler lock. Kneeling, he pulled a slim black leather case from his rear pocket and unzipped it to reveal a set of four double-sided picks.

"What should I do while I wait?" Hlupnek asked.

"Research," Bolan whispered over his shoulder. "Somewhere near the front." Hlupnek walked off as the Executioner lifted one of the picks and went to work on the tumblers.

Hammersmith stood watch until the lock snapped open. A moment later, they were inside the record room and closing the door behind them.

File cabinets stood against the walls. In their center, the Executioner saw a small personal computer. Next to it, on a table, were several file boxes containing floppy disks.

Hammersmith moved quickly to the computer and turned it on. Bolan hurried to one of the file cabinets and slid open the top drawer. Just as he'd expected, the records were kept in Czech. He joined the British agent as the computer finished warming up, watching her call up the menu on the hard drive, then drew the FEG Model 7P, an identical copy of the Browning Hi-Power manufactured locally, and moved to the door to stand guard.

Bolan cracked the door and pressed an ear into the opening. Far at the front of the room, he could hear Hlupnek moving about the shelves. Behind him, he heard Hammersmith tapping the keyboard, wading her way through the tedious task of checking the entries on the hard drive.

Fifteen minutes later, Hammersmith rose from her chair and joined Bolan at the door. "This system is more complex than I'd anticipated," she whispered. "They've got entry codes and traps that have to be circled."

"So this isn't the only test lab?"

"Hardly. So far, I can tell you this—this is a three-part operation. There are other research centers like this one that keep perfecting the diseases to resist antibiotics. They appear to be concentrating on anthrax. Phase two is the production plants where the manufacturing and packaging takes place. Last, we have 'launch' sites. That's where the diseases will be dispersed when they decide to use them.''

"How?" Bolan asked.

"I don't know."

"Have you gotten any of the sites pinpointed yet?"

Before Hammersmith could answer, they heard the door at the front of the library open. A person hidden behind the tall bookshelves entered the room and spoke loudly in Czech.

Hammersmith rose on her toes, whispering into the Executioner's ear. "Why are you here so late?" she translated.

Hlupnek's voice drifted back over the books.

"He said, 'I have my work, you have yours,'" Hammersmith whispered.

There was a grunt of disgust from the front of the room, then the door closed again. Bolan followed Hammersmith back to the computer. "Let me have your .22," he said.

The British agent ripped the Velcro-closure on her belt pack and handed him the sound-suppressed weapon. Bolan returned to the door in time to see Hlupnek hurrying toward the office.

"*Please*," the Czech begged. "We must leave. They are getting suspicious."

Bolan nodded. "Go back to the front." He turned back to Hammersmith.

"How much longer?"

The agent leaned back and sighed. "I've broken through and gotten a list of the research sites like this one."

"Have you read it yet?"

"I haven't had time. But I've come up with something else that might be of value."

Bolan waited.

"The name Joseph Ryba keeps coming up. Ever heard of him?"

The warrior shook his head. "No, but we'll get on it. You close to the production and launch sites yet?"

"No. The codes are far more complex. Simply put, I'm stumped. Even if I had a hundred years, I'm not sure I'd be able to break through."

Bolan paused. Turning to a cabinet next to the computer, he knelt and opened the door, rummaging through until he came across a box of new floppy disks. "Format some of these and copy the hard drive. We'll take it with us."

"All right," the woman said. "But like I said, I don't know if I can ever break into—"

"Don't worry," Bolan assured her. "I know someone who can."

The warrior turned back to the door as Hammersmith carried on with her task. He slipped through the opening and made his way silently to the front, where he found Hlupnek taking notes at a table, an open book in front of him. Catching the Czech's eye, he motioned him behind a shelf. "We're almost done. You'll have to tell the guards they sent the wrong desk. Have them carry us out again."

"They'll never believe it."

"They'll have to," Bolan answered. "There's no other way out."

Hammersmith had finished by the time Bolan returned to the record room. The Executioner helped her pile the diskettes into a box, and they went back to the library.

Five minutes later, they were again facing each other inside the box. Hlupnek left to get the guard, then returned. Hugging each other again, Bolan and Hammersmith were lifted onto the dolly, rolled out of the building and lifted into the van. Moments later Hlupnek pulled the van out of the parking lot and onto the street.

CHAPTER THREE

Carl "Ironman" Lyons gripped the Calico M-950A machine pistol in his right hand as he slid the 50-round helical drum into the well above the receiver. The side clamps snapped around the drum with a satisfying click.

The leader of Stony Man Farm's Able Team slid the bolt back, then let it slide forward again. Though he couldn't see it happen inside the weapon, he knew the first of the blue-nosed 9 mm Nyclad hollowpoints now rested in the chamber.

Lyons felt the surge of adrenaline flood his veins as he looked quickly from Rosario "Politician" Blancanales on his right to Hermann "Gadgets" Schwarz on his left. Both men gripped the larger version of Lyons's strange-looking weapon—Calico M-960A submachine guns.

But the subguns didn't carry the same 50-round drum. Their longer oblong magazines held an even hundred Nyclads.

Schwarz and Blancanales nodded their readiness. Lyons lifted a combat boot, kicked and the front door of the two-story house swung open.

Then he hit the doorway in a half crouch, his eyes

making a lightning-fast 180-degree sweep of the entryway—a large living room to the right, a door across the room that led to some other part of the house, what appeared to be a parlor to the left and a staircase straight ahead.

A floor plan of the terrorist safe house hadn't been provided, so assignments couldn't be given in advance. But the men of Able Team had followed Lyons too long for that to be a significant problem.

Without being told, Schwarz entered the parlor. Blancanales took the living room.

Lyons sprinted to the foot of the stairs. He was three steps up when the man aiming the AK-47 dropped from the ceiling and didn't break stride. Bringing the Calico up, he fired from the hip and sent a 5-round burst of the blue-nosed man-stoppers splattering into his target.

Subgun fire from both ends of the first floor told Lyons that Schwarz and Blancanales had engaged the enemy as well. He raced up the steps, dropping the front pistol grip of the machine pistol and grabbing the banister as he reached the landing. He had pivoted around the rail and started toward a darkened hallway when the second man dropped from the ceiling.

Wearing a striped T-shirt, and sporting a spotty brown beard, the man held an AK-47 identical to the first.

Six 9 mm rounds burst forth from Lyons's weapon this time, with the same result.

Lyons turned back to the hallway. Dark. Too dark. Anything could be waiting. Flipping his index finger forward, he hit the button at the front of the Calico's trigger guard and the miniflashlight mounted to the frame shot a thin stream of light down the corridor.

Empty. Two doors in the walls. Another at the end of the hallway.

Lyons crept cautiously forward. His combat skills had been honed to a razor's edge long before he joined the men of Able Team. In Vietnam, he had learned the art of jungle warfare. As an LAPD cop he had been educated in the carnage of the streets. Terrorists, he knew, fell somewhere between the two styles of fighting, having learned the deadliest skills of both disciplines. In the woodlands, terrorists made use of the same foliage the Vietcong had used for concealment. In the streets, the took they same hostages that any crack-head or would-be bank robber might happen onto.

Which brought Lyons back to the present. They might not have received blueprints of the house plans from Stony Man Farm, but Able Team *had* been given Intel, and that Intel had assured them that the terrorists had taken hostages.

A dark form appeared suddenly from a doorway off the hall. Friend or foe? Lyons swung up the Calico, centering the figure in the beam of the flashlight. In a thousandth of a second, he saw the gray turtleneck, the revolver and a look of focused hatred on the face. Using the flashlight as a sighting device, he pulled the trigger.

Another eight rounds shot from the Calico. The first hit the man on the upper right-hand portion of the chest. Lyons drew the weapon to his own right, stitch-

ing a line to the terrorist's left and nearly cutting the
man in two.

Throwing his back against the wall, Lyons cut the
flashlight beam as the light suddenly came on in a
room off the hall. He sidestepped carefully toward the
open door, his rubber-soled combat boots barely au-
dible. As soon as he reached the opening, he dropped
to a squatting position, then peered slowly around the
edge of the doorway.

A terrorist with long black hair and an earring stood
in the corner. One arm encircled the neck of a frightened woman. The other pressed the barrel of a
.45-caliber Colt Government Model to her temple.

Closer, but still against the wall, a second, older
man with gray hair held a man in a similar deadly
embrace. His weapon of choice was a long stiletto.

Long bursts from the M-960s in the hands of the
other Able Team warriors sounded on the floor below,
as Lyons pulled his head back into the hall. Taking a
deep breath, he flipped the Calico's selector to semiauto. Then, after another measured inhalation, he
swung around the corner into the bedroom.

Lyons hammered a double-tap of semiauto fire into
the face of the man behind the woman, the first round
drilling a third eye, the second smashing into the
bridge of his nose.

Swinging the Calico to his right, he squeezed the
trigger once more, catching the second terrorist in the
throat with his third Nyclad and dropping the next into
his chest.

The firing from the first floor died down momentarily as the echo of Lyons's rounds faded within the

room. He squinted briefly at the man and woman who had been held hostage only seconds before.

They stared back emotionless, frozen by shock.

Lyons grinned as he flipped the selector back to full-auto. Spinning on the balls of his feet, he leapt back into the hall just as two figures seemed to spring up out of the floor. Both wore turtlenecks and aimed Heckler & Koch MP-5 submachine guns in his direction.

The Calico chattered again as the former LAPD cop clipped a figure eight of autofire back and forth between the two hardmen, shearing their chests into tattered scraps.

He had just let up on the trigger when a closet door swung open farther down the hall. Another figure seemed to float out in the semidarkness.

In one swift movement, Lyons raised the Calico and flipped on the miniflashlight. His trigger finger was moving back when the light caught the glimmer of silver on the blue uniform. The face above the badge wore the same strange lack of emotion he had seen on the hostages.

Lyons eased off the trigger, shouldering the police officer out of his way as he raced to the door at the end of the hall. Bouncing the light beam off the wall, he looked down at the top of the Calico's drum mag. Portals were cut next to the numerals 50, 37, 23 and 9. The holes were dark through 23. Brass gleamed through the aperture marked 9.

He had somewhere between nine and twenty-three rounds remaining. Around fifteen he'd guess, if he hadn't lost count. More than enough to take out at least one or more of the enemy. But this was no time to take chances. He had a feeling the "grande finale" waited behind the closed door.

Flipping the catches to the sides of the Calico's mag, Lyons lifted the drum out of the well and shoved it into his waistband. Pulling the extra-long drum from the off side of his shoulder rig, he slipped it into the well, under the guide lips and snapped it down.

Another pull of the bolt handle and this time the Calico had a hundred rounds of Nyclads, ready and waiting.

Footsteps pounded up the stairs behind him. Lyons swung the machine pistol around, dropping the front post sight to the center of the corridor. A half second later, the familiar silhouettes of Schwarz and Blancanales came into view.

Lyons held a finger to his lips and pointed to the door.

The two warriors slowed to a walk, their weapons in assault mode.

As soon as they flanked him, Lyons kicked. The aging wood creaked, squealed, then splintered as the door flew from its hinges to sail into the room.

The men of Able Team went in low.

Three terrorists circled a smallish man wearing glasses and a three-piece suit. Three more aimed weapons at a uniformed cop tied to a chair. One man, clutching the rear pistol grip of a Thompson subgun in one hand, stood next to the window. On the other side of the window was a short stocky terrorist aiming a double-barrel 12-gauge shotgun their way. Between them, the two men each held one arm of a four-year-old girl.

Other men and women, both friend and foe, lurked in other nooks and crannies of the room.

Lyons started the party, firing a 3-round burst high into the forehead of the man with the Thompson. No sooner had the last 9 mm cleared the Calico's barrel than he swung the machine pistol over the little girl and onto the shotgunner. Four rounds peppered into the squatty man's neck and face, ending the threat to the child.

Schwarz opened up on the men holding the cop, tapping a short burst of autofire into the three men as Blancanales concentrated on the trio guarding the businessman. Lyons swung his weapon toward another of the bearded terrorists in turtlenecks as a cop came sliding down out of the ceiling.

Suddenly the room was quiet. Then footsteps pounded up the stairs behind them and came down the hall.

Leo Turrin, Stony Man Farm's longtime undercover expert and training director, strolled into the room behind them. Next to him was John "Cowboy" Kissinger, Stony Man's chief armorer. Turrin held up the stopwatch in his hand. "Two minutes, 16.4 seconds," he said. He looked up at Lyons. "Not bad for new weapons. I haven't scored the targets yet. Hit any of the good guys?"

Lyons's mind flew back to the paper hostage targets in the bedrooms, the cops who had come out of the doorways and dropped from the ceiling, and especially the little four-year-old girl whose paper face still looked at him from between the shredded remnants of her two abductors. He shook his head.

Turrin turned to Schwarz and Blancanales. Both men shook their heads.

"Good," Kissinger said, stepping forward. "Then let's get down to the real reason behind this training exercise. How'd you like the Calicos?"

Schwarz smiled like a ten-year-old boy who'd just unwrapped his first .22 rifle on Christmas morning. "They're great. I've still got…" He looked down to the portals on his drum. "At least twenty-three rounds left. Without ever having to reload."

"Between thirty-seven and fifty," Blancanales said.

Schwarz grinned. "That's 'cause you don't shoot as fast as me," he quipped.

"No, that's 'cause I don't *miss* as much as you."

Kissinger turned to Lyons. "How about you, Ironman? Want to give these new guns a try?"

Lyons nodded. "They've definitely got their place. Of course, a 9 mm isn't ever going to do the job of my 12-gauge Atchisson, but—"

"They've got a prototype for a 24-round shotgun in the works," Kissinger interrupted.

"But in a situation where you need lots of firepower," Lyons went on as if he hadn't heard, "and aren't likely to have time to reload, I doubt if you can beat these babies."

Kissinger smiled. Lyons knew the Stony Man armorer had been impressed with the Calicos' small size and capacity since they'd first come out. He'd given both the subguns and machine pistols complete tune-ups before turning them over to Able Team for field-testing, and the weapons' victory on the training course had been a conquest for Kissinger, as well.

"Okay," Cowboy said. "We've still got a few other models to check out. There's a concealable subgun, a couple of carbines—"

He was interrupted as the walkie-talkie on Leo Turrin's belt suddenly squawked. "Stony Man Base to Stony Man Five. Come in, Five," Barbara Price's voice said.

Turrin unclipped the radio and held it in front of his face. "Go ahead, Base," he answered.

"Affirmative, Five," Price said. "Is Able One with you?"

"Sure thing." Turrin handed the radio to Lyons.

"Go ahead," Lyons said.

It was Hal Brognola who answered this time. "How'd the new shooters work, Ironman?"

"No problems."

"Good. Grab your boys and get back here on the double. You're about to test the Calicos out for real."

Blue Ridge Mountains, Virginia

STONY MAN FARM WAS one of the best-kept secrets in the United States government. Few people were aware of its existence.

Set in the Blue Ridge Mountains, Stony Man appeared to be—and was—a working spread with all the trappings of a modern farm. There was the large main house, a tractor barn and several outbuildings. The field hands in overalls who worked daily about the grounds helped to complete the desired image.

Indeed, Hal Brognola thought as he ordered Able Team in from the training ground, the privacy of the Farm lay not in the inability of anyone to find its location. It lay in the fact that it went "seen but unnoticed." Day after day, year after year, Stony Man Farm hid in plain sight.

Brognola let up on the microphone button. He was director of the Justice Department's Sensitive Operations Group, and he did exactly what that title implied—directed missions that possessed world-shaking consequences should they go wrong.

The big Fed glanced down as his wristwatch. By now, Able Team should be loaded into the van with Leo Turrin and Cowboy Kissinger and be halfway back to the house. Turning to the glass wall between the Mission Control Room and Computer Room, he saw Aaron "The Bear" Kurtzman. At the top of his wheelchair ramp, the computer expert's fingers flew across the keyboard in a near blur.

Even before it had all come in over the MI-6 computer modem in Prague, Kurtzman had gone to work on the coded files Bolan and Hammersmith had acquired at the research lab. Time was of the essence, but right now, Brognola needed Stony Man's computer wizard in the War Room for the meeting that would determine the course of the mission.

Still watching through the glass, he tapped the intercom and lifted the phone receiver.

Kurtzman didn't move toward the phone at his side. His hands continued to fly across the keyboard as he twirled toward the glass. Brognola pointed toward the elevator in the far corner of the Computer Room. Kurtzman nodded, grabbed the sides of his wheelchair and started down the ramp.

Brognola wore more than one hat, having worked his way upward in the U.S. Department of Justice over the years. That position had been the catalyst that found him also playing the role of liaison to the White House. Working directly with the President, he stood prepared at a moment's notice to shield the Man from the political fallout that would occur should a Stony Man mission go sour.

So far, all ops had been successful. For that, Brognola was thankful. He prayed they always would.

Reaching into the front breast pocket of his rumpled suit, he pulled out a chewed stump of a cigar and stuck it between his teeth. He turned toward Barbara Price, Stony Man's mission controller. Price looked back at him, her face expressionless, cool, professional. But Brognola had known the woman too long to let her deadpan face fool him now.

Price might be the consummate pro when it came to coordinating the operations of Stony Man Farm, but she wasn't without emotion. In the eyes behind the woman's captivating face, Brognola saw no fear. The men and women of Stony Man had worked through fear a long time ago. Fear got in the way; it slowed down reaction time and affected the judgment process, and they had learned to control it.

But all of them—the men of Able Team and Phoenix Force, John Kissinger, Leo Turrin, Aaron Kurtzman and his computer crew, even Mack Bolan—they were all human. And those that already knew about the list of research sites that Bolan and Hammersmith had uncovered were concerned about what the sites might mean.

"I'll be in the War Room, Barb," Brognola said.

Price nodded. "I'll send them down as soon as they arrive," she replied, meaning Able Team. "And I'll hook up the rest of the men as soon as the calls come in."

Brognola nodded, opened the door to the Computer Room and started toward the elevator. He passed Akira Tokaido, Carmen Delahunt and Huntington Wethers, all busily at work in front of their respective computer screens. All of Kurtzman's assistants had dropped what they were involved in to take up the electronic search for the biochemical production and dispersion facilities, which brought a thin smile to the Justice man's lips.

Like the field ops, Kurtzman and company had never failed at Stony Man Farm. They had always come though—sometimes by the skin of their teeth—but they had never let him down.

The smile faded as Brognola punched the elevator button. Kurtzman, Tokaido, Wethers and Delahunt were as good with their electronic weapons as Able Team and Phoenix Force were with their guns. But the fact that the computer wizards had never failed could mean one of two things—they wouldn't fail this time, either, or they were long overdue.

The War Room lay directly below the Computer Room. Brognola stepped off the elevator to see that Kurtzman had wheeled up to the long conference table. The Justice man had barely made it to his place at the table's head when the phone next to the inset console rang.

Brognola lifted the receiver. "Go ahead."

"Able Team," Price said. "Coming down. And I've got Striker on line 4. Katz is on screen with Jack."

"Put them both through."

The big Fed tapped a button on the console and a large television screen behind Kurtzman lighted up. The man in the wheelchair whirled to face it as the image of Yakov Katzenelenbogen, leader of Phoenix Force, appeared sitting in the cockpit of the C-17 next to Jack Grimaldi. Brognola could hear the whirl of the wind and the growl of the big bird's engines over the audio portion of the system.

The steel door opposite Kurtzman buzzed. A moment later Carl Lyons, Gadgets Schwarz and Rosario Blancanales entered the War Room and took seats around the table.

Brognola pushed the button for line 4 on the phone and said, "Striker?"

Mack Bolan's voice came over the line from the Czech Republic. "Affirmative, Hal."

"Is your line secure?" Brognola asked.

"Negative," Bolan replied. "But we're at a phone booth we picked at random. I'd say the chances of anybody listening in are at least a thousand to one. But just to be safe, make sure the scrambler is on your end and throw it this way."

Brognola tapped three more buttons and a red light in the console lighted up. He smiled inwardly. Now the scrambler would not only garble the conversation from his end, it would send a microwave signal back across the Atlantic to jumble Bolan's words, as well.

The big Fed dropped the receiver back in the cradle and tapped another button. "Okay, Striker," he said into the speakerphone. "Let's have it."

Bolan cleared his throat. "Bear, I assume you got the stuff we sent you over the modem?"

Kurtzman nodded as if Bolan could see him. "It had almost all gotten here when I left to come down. Akira and Carmen are already working on it. I'm putting Hunt on 'peripherals' for this mission."

"Good. Then everybody knows the situation?"

"Not everybody, Striker," Carl Lyons spoke up. "Able Team has been playing Cowboys and Indians all morning." He paused, then went on. "I'd respectfully like to ask what the hell is going on."

Bolan chuckled. "I'll let Hal give you the details, Ironman. For now, let me just tell you that we've got somebody named Ryba— "

Kurtzman cut in. "I ran him down first, Striker. Joseph Ryba is the Czech Republic's minister of the interior. He's also the leader of the country's Autonomy Party, hard-line right-wingers who'd be wearing sheets and pointy hats if they lived over here." The computer man paused, then added, "There's a militant arm to the party known as the Deliverance Squad, and rumor has it that they're the ones in charge of this revived Biopreparat program. Ryba's got some of them masquerading as hired security guards under the name of Jablonec Security."

"Great," Bolan said. "Anyway, the bottom line is

that Ryba is developing diseases that resist antibiotics. Exactly what he has planned, we don't know. We've got a list of research facilities, and hidden somewhere in the mess of computer stuff we sent over are lists identifying the production and launch sites. We don't know how many there are, but locating those sites are our first priority, and we're going after that priority from three directions. The first is Kurtzman decoding the Intel with his computers.''

Katz spoke for the first time since the screen had come alive. ''We are en route to the U.S. What do you want us to do?''

''Turn around and head my way,'' Bolan replied. ''For what I'm planning, I'm going to need all the help I can get.''

''Just exactly what are you planning, Striker?'' Brognola asked. ''If you go tearing up the research sites, Ryba's going to know someone's on to him. He's undoubtedly got a backup plan to move the sites if that happens.''

''We aren't going to tear anything up, Hal. At least not overtly. But we can't just sit still and wait on the Bear. Hammersmith and I, and Phoenix Force when they get here, are going to start infiltrating more of these lab sites. We might find something of interest. Even if we don't, we can throw a few monkey wrenches in the works and slow the research down.''

Brognola saw Carl Lyons shift in his seat. ''So far I haven't seen where Able Team comes into the picture, Striker,'' he said.

''Besides the research sites in Europe, the Intel Hammersmith already decoded hinted at a storage-

and-launch site in the U.S. At least one and there might be more. Where, we don't know, but it makes sense. With a threat like that, Ryba could hold the U.S. off, keep us from retaliating for what he does over here."

The room fell silent as the mission suddenly took on ramifications closer to home.

Bolan spoke again. "You got the picture now, Ironman?"

Lyons leaned closer to the table. "Any leads to the site mentioned here?"

"Negative. But I'd suggest Hunt do a little research on Ryba. Find out who his friends are, and see if one of them is representing the Czech Republic in some way in the U.S. If one is, my guess is there'll be a connection."

"You got it, Striker."

The room fell into silence again. When Bolan didn't continue, Brognola asked, "Anything else?"

There was a pause on the other end of the line. Finally Bolan said, "I'd wish you all good luck, but I've never believed much in it. But this time we may need it."

"Well, so let's go out and *make* some luck, guys," Brognola growled.

Prague, Czech Republic

THE GLORIOUS SOUNDS of Dvořák's *Four Slavonic Dances* came drifting up from the CD player on the table behind Joseph Ryba's desk. He dropped the pen in his hand to the stack of unsigned documents in front of him, closed his eyes and leaned back in his chair.

There were few of life's issues on which Joseph Ryba didn't hold a definite opinion, but the music of the two most famous Bohemian composers was one of them. Smetana and Dvořák. Dvořák and Smetana. Who did he like better? Which of the two musical geniuses was more talented?

Ryba had no idea.

The indecision brought a smile to his lips. No man was certain of all things in life, Ryba told himself as he opened his eyes. And what a lovely confusion he had been blessed with concerning the two composers. It was a problem he hoped never to solve, as its irresolution necessitated the ongoing review of both men's music.

Ryba turned to the wall, his eyes falling on an original painting by Cranach. He had appropriated the picture from the Sternberk Palace Museum, which also housed many works of Dürer, Brueghel, Rubens, Rembrandt and others. Prague boasted other museums of art—Wallenstein Palace, Zbraslav Castle, the Czechoslovak National Gallery to name only three. These museums seemed the only reminders that Prague had once been the seat of one of the most powerful nations on earth.

The Bohemian Empire.

Ryba's teeth ground together. What had come over his ancient ancestors that they allowed themselves to weaken and be destroyed by Germans, Hungarians— seemingly anyone who decided to invade their bor-

ders? He didn't know. Another puzzle. And another
to which he might never learn the answer.

But one thing Joseph Ryba *did* know. And of that,
he was certain.

He would reestablish the empire.

The Czech minister of the interior closed his eyes
once more. In his mind's eye, he saw the streets of
Prague as they must have been on September 28, 935,
when the Kingdom of Bohemia was still in its infancy
under the benevolent rule of King Wenceslas. He saw
the king leave his palace with a few of his guards on
their way to early-morning mass. Then, suddenly from
the shadows, a swarm of armed warriors appeared.
Swords flashed, their steel blades clanking in the still-
ness. The battle could have only taken seconds, and
at its end, Good King Wenceslas, who would be im-
mortalized in Christmas song for eternity and become
the patron saint of Bohemia, lay dead in the street.

The throne had gone to Wenceslas's brother, Boleslav the Brave. But the beginning of the end had begun.

Ryba opened his eyes once more, the thrill of his
mission in life clear to him. Joseph Ryba. Ryba the
Brave. He would reestablish the Kingdom of Bohemia
for another six hundred years.

The Czech minister glanced over the document in
front of him, then signed his name on the appropriate
line. He chuckled softly as he turned it facedown and
reached for the next text. Read read read. Sign sign
sign. That is all he had done since the fall of communism in Czechoslovakia. Of course it made little
difference what he signed his name to during his ten-

ure with the Czech Republic, for this too was temporary.

As soon as the new Biopreparat program was complete, this government would fall as well. He would take over, creating a new superpower of the twentieth century that would be named for its ancestor of four hundred years earlier. The Kingdom of Bohemia.

Ryba had started to sign his name once more when a soft knock sounded on the door. "Come," he said, and a moment later his secretary stuck her head through the door.

Ryba smiled at what he saw. How Marja had kept her figure after bearing two children was another puzzle in life that pleased him. Today, she wore the short black skirt he had bought her the previous week. It hugged her smooth skin, and the sheer black stockings that clung to her shapely legs beneath the hem accented the muscular limbs. Her hair fell to her shoulders and was as dark as the skirt. Her eyes matched, as well. But her lips were what caught his attention as they blew him a silent kiss before breaking into a secret smile. Bright red. Bloodred. He wished they were on his now.

"Mr. Schoevenec is here," she said, then blew him another kiss.

"Send him in."

The stumpy Slav hadn't yet reached the chair in front of Ryba's desk when the Czech minister said, "What have you learned?"

Schoevenec cleared his throat. "The results of the tests on the .22s are in."

"And?"

"They do not match. There was a second agent present at the lab."

Ryba slammed his fist onto the desk, sending papers flying into the air. Looking up, he said, "Have you located and killed him yet?"

Schoevenec shook his head. "Minister Ryba, it is easier to give that order than to carry it out. We are trying to—"

Ryba felt his blood boil. "Have you put Skrdla on the case?"

"Skrdla is not yet back. I told you yesterday that—"

"And I told *you* yesterday that if he did not return that I wanted you to do the job." Ryba stood behind his chair and pointed toward the door. "Do it. Do it now."

Schoevenec nodded, placed his hands on his knees and stood. "There is little to go on, but I will take the investigation over myself."

"What of the other agent? The one who was killed?"

"He has not been identified."

Ryba felt his eyes narrow as Schoevenec walked to the door. The man wasn't showing the proper respect. He was making it all too obvious that he resented taking orders outside the usual chain of command, which accounted for his dragging his feet. Ryba studied the man. Perhaps Schoevenec didn't fully realize the power that Ryba already had, and how much more he would soon have.

But the man would.

He watched the Slav open the door and disappear.

He closed his eyes again. Boleslav the Brave had gone on to add Pomerania and Danzig to the Kingdom of Bohemia. His dream was a union of all the Slavic nations that would be strong enough to hold Germany at bay. That dream hadn't come true.

But it would.

Ryba sat back down and closed his eyes again. He was about to create a New Kingdom of Bohemia that would not only hold off the Germans, but would conquer them. He would then go after the rest of Europe.

The Czech smiled. And one day, he would even take on the country that had appointed itself to be the "World Watchdog."

The United States.

CHAPTER FOUR

Prague, Czech Republic

Bolan pulled the Fiat to a halt against the curb at the edge of Prague's New Town district. Pulling the keys from the ignition, he turned toward the woman in the passenger's seat.

Jonine Hammersmith looked considerably different than she had previously. Earlier in the day, she had gone shopping while Bolan coordinated the call to Stony Man Farm. Now, instead of her usual jeans and Windbreaker, she wore a black evening gown and matching high heels. A long blond wig hid the British agent's shorter red hair, and she had applied a medium-heavy layer of mascara and other makeup to her face.

Along with the pearls around her neck and the diamonds on her fingers, she looked like any other well-to-do Czech woman on her way to an evening at the theater.

The Executioner exited the tiny Fiat, shifting the FEG Model 7P under the jacket of his tuxedo. Hammersmith had picked up the tux for him that afternoon, as well, and had proved that she was a keen observer. She'd gotten the right size without asking. Unless he bent over, there was no telltale budge from the FEG or the Skorpion.

Bolan circled the Fiat, opened the door and helped Hammersmith out onto the sidewalk. They started along the storefronts toward Number 40, Narodni Trida.

"Ingenious place to hide a lab, when you think of it," Hammersmith said as she took the Executioner's arm. "Must be something big going on, too."

The warrior nodded. The Plzeň lab had been open, only lightly veiled as a site designed to develop antibiotics for the diseases they were actually perfecting. But this lab in nearby Prague was hidden below the world-famous Lanterna Magika—the Magic Lantern Theater. According to the Intel Hammersmith had gained from the computer list, access couldn't be obtained except through the theater itself, which posed a problem.

Lanterna Magika's performances had been sold out for years. Getting a ticket on the evening of the show you wanted to see was about as easy as finding a Super Bowl ticket on game day.

The British woman was evidently thinking along the same lines. "So," she said, squeezing the Executioner's arm, "got any ideas on how we get in?"

The warrior nodded but didn't answer, his mind putting the finishing touches on the plan he'd come up with during the drive up from Plzeň. They turned the corner onto Narodni.

Hammersmith sighed. "You know, Pollock, I like the big dark silent type as much as the next girl," she said. "In fact, in your case, I like it even more. But don't you think it might be a good idea to let me in on things once in a while?"

"I was just wondering if you ever mugged anybody."

Hammersmith's eyebrows lowered in mock seriousness. "Give me a moment...no...I suppose not, really. Always meant to do, but never found the time." She paused, then said, "What in bloody hell are you talking about?"

Bolan smiled. "The only way I can think of to get tickets is to take them away from somebody," he said. "That's not so hard. The trick is to do it without hurting them."

Hammersmith shook her head and the long blond hair twirled around her neck. "There'll be another small problem or two, I should think," she said. "Like do we steal their money, jewelry, all that? It's going to look terribly strange you know, just pilfering the tickets. One might be tempted to mention such an irregularity to the authorities, who might in turn decide the Lanterna Magika was a good place to start looking for crazed theater addicts fitting our description."

Bolan looked down at the woman on his arm. He liked her, was even attracted to her. But he needed to push his personal feelings to the back of his mind. If he didn't, they'd get in the way of the mission. He'd be tempted to start protecting Jonine Hammersmith, which would take his mind off the mission.

Besides, Hammersmith didn't need protection. She was a professional who could take care of herself. A woman well trained, who had known the risks associated with the job when she took it.

"Well?" Hammersmith said. "Do I get my answer?"

Bolan stopped in front of a darkened store window and turned to the woman. "I don't like stealing from innocent people any more than you do. I don't like taking their possessions, and I don't like scaring them. But let me ask you something. If you had to choose between missing a Magic Lantern performance and losing some money and your watch, or risking the death of thousands—maybe millions—of people to biochemical disease, which would you choose?"

Hammersmith's face reddened. "I suppose it goes without saying."

Bolan nodded. "I think this couple ahead of us would probably feel the same way." He pointed toward a plump man and woman dressed in evening clothes who had just passed them on the sidewalk. Taking Hammersmith's arm, he started after them. "Let's make it short," he whispered out of the corner of his mouth, "and as sweet as possible."

As the chubby couple approached an intersecting alley, the Executioner split from Hammersmith and hurried up next to the man. Hammersmith scurried toward the woman.

Both man and woman looked to their sides, surprised.

Bolan drew the FEG from his waistband and shoved it into well-padded ribs. Nodding toward the alley, he shoved the man forward.

Hammersmith was already escorting the whimpering woman off the sidewalk.

Twenty feet into the alley, the Executioner guided the fat man up against the wall, then turned to Hammersmith. "Tell him we want his tickets," he said.

The British agent spoke in Czech.

The man and his wife looked incredulously at the Executioner.

"Tell him we know it's odd, but that's really all we want. Tell them we won't hurt either one of them if they hand the tickets over."

Hammersmith spoke again.

The fat man shrugged, then reached into the inside pocket of his tuxedo and produced a white envelope. Bolan took it, glanced inside and shoved it into his own coat.

"We've got to do something to keep them from reporting this to the police," Hammersmith said. "I assume you've thought of that?"

"I have," Bolan replied. Reaching out, he unbuttoned the fat man's jacket, then ripped the shirt from his chest. The man's suspenders came next, causing his pants to fall downward. The fat man grabbed them with the speed of a cat.

The Executioner herded the couple down the alley to a doorway. "Tell them to get in."

Hammersmith ordered them into the recess.

Bolan positioned them in a sitting position on the concrete steps, facing away from each other. Binding their hands together with the suspenders, the Executioner ripped the shirt in two and fashioned a gag over the man's mouth. He moved to the woman, who looked at Hammersmith, said a few words, then shrugged.

Bolan tied the gag securely over her mouth. "Tell them to stay put for at least an hour. Then they can start trying to free themselves."

"And what if they can't? They'll be here all night."

Bolan shook his head. "No, they won't. They aren't tied that tight."

Hammersmith nodded, spoke a final time, then turned and followed Bolan out of the alley. "Now what?" she asked.

Bolan tapped his pocket where the tickets were. "We go see the show," he said. They left the alley and hurried down the sidewalk. "By the way," he said as they turned the last corner and the theater appeared another block down. "What did the woman say just before I gagged her?"

An impish smile spread across Hammersmith's face. "Loosely translated, she said, 'Enjoy the show.'"

Prague, Czech Republic

YAKOV KATZENELENBOGEN hated the waiting periods that seemed to crop up during missions. He'd rather face bullets than the hour here, the half hour there, during which time he had to wait for something to happen in which he wasn't directly involved.

Katz was doing that now.

He turned sideways, shuffling between the haphazard stacks of used goods that spilled over the shelves and onto the floor of the Store on Main Street. The only privately owned retail outlet of any kind to remain so during Czechoslovakia's Communist regime, the store at Number 3 Tyn Street in Prague's Old Town Square was billed as a secondhand hardware emporium.

It could just as well have been called a junk or antique shop, Katzenelenbogen thought as he lifted a brass candlestick for inspection. So far, in addition to enough tools to outfit a battalion of army engineers, he had seen every other imaginable object. Keys to at least ten thousand forgotten or lost locks had been displayed amid antique household items such as lamps, clocks and other knickknacks. Everything from swords and daggers to picture frames, copper sculptures, and several things Katz couldn't even identify, had met his eye.

He had inspected each object with that careful eye. The other eye he had kept above the shelves and on the front window of the store.

An elderly man with gray hair strolled down the cluttered aisle and stopped next to the Phoenix Force leader. His face beamed with good humor as he spoke in Czech.

Katz shook his head. "English?" he asked.

The man nodded. "I am Hans Capek," he said pleasantly. "My brother Peter and I are the owners. Welcome to our store. Did you know it is the oldest in all of Europe?"

Katz glanced to the front window, then smiled back at the man. "So I've heard." He held up the candlestick. "Can you give me a price?"

Capek lowered his head. "I am sorry, it is not for sale. There is—how do you say in English—sentimental value attached to that item."

Katz gave him an understanding nod and set the candlestick back down. He moved along the aisle, wondering if McCarter had had any luck. The Briton was almost as good a con man as he was a soldier, and if anyone could hustle their way into the lab across the street, it would be McCarter.

Lifting a copper engraving of a man on horseback, Katz said, "This is nice. And the price?"

Capek shook his head. "I am sorry, it belonged to my grandmother's friend. It is for display only."

Katz nodded again, glancing at the window. Gary Manning, Calvin James and Rafael Encizo were in shops along the same street, with Encizo positioned where he could see David McCarter come out of the lab. The little Cuban would then signal the others, who would meet at a small café on the corner.

The Phoenix Force leader moved along the aisle, Capek following like a mother hen. He stopped again in front of an ancient iron reading lamp that sat between two large piles of keys.

Capek followed his gaze. "I am sorry," he said before Katz could speak.

Katz chuckled. "Mr. Capek, is *anything* for sale?"

"About half of what you see," Capek replied, returning the laugh. "Perhaps a little less." He cleared his throat. "Would you consent to signing our guest book?"

"Certainly." Katz followed the man down the aisle past shelves and tables to the front of the store. Hans

Capek lifted a ballpoint pen from the table next to the cash register, handed it to Katz, then pointed to a giant ledger. "If you please."

Katz took the pen, leaned forward, and wrote *Samuel Wilenzick, Haifa, Israel.* "You have had many visitors," he observed as he set the pen back down.

"From every country in the world," Capek said proudly. He pointed overhead to a stack of similar ledgers. "Let me show you something."

As the proprietor pulled another of the guest books from the shelf, Katz saw Encizo suddenly appear at the front window. The little Cuban nodded toward the corner, then walked on.

Katz started toward the door but Capek grabbed him by the arm. "Please, it will only take a moment."

Katz stopped. It wouldn't do to act suspicious at this point. Capek might mention his hurried departure to someone, who would mention it to someone else, who would continue the story. Who knew who might eventually learn the description of the strange man who had waited across from the lab, then hurried out suddenly?

The store owner placed the dusty book on the table. "Years ago, there was a young lad whose father owned a shop nearby," he said. His voice was practiced, as though he had told the story many times. "The boy was shy. He would come look through the window, but never enter the store." Capek began leafing through the pages. "My grandfather finally persuaded him to come in—if only long enough to sign the guest book." Finding the page he wanted, Capek pointed to a signature near the bottom of the book. "There it is. Look."

Katz squinted down at the name. *Franz Kafka.* "The novelist?" he asked.

Capek nodded proudly.

Katz glanced back to the window as Calvin James and Gary Manning walked by. "Thank you, Mr. Capek. It has been a pleasure."

"Please visit us again," Capek said as Katz exited the store.

James and Manning were a block ahead as Katz turned onto the sidewalk and started toward the café. Quickening his pace, he caught up with them. Inside, Encizo had already joined McCarter at a corner booth. A radio behind the counter blared Czech pop music as he and the others found seats around the table.

McCarter wore the face of a salesman who hadn't made his sale, which, Katz knew, was exactly what had to have happened.

McCarter had started to speak when a broad-shouldered waitress ambled over. The woman's hair had been wound into a tight bun and the frayed sleeves of her cotton shirt were rolled above fleshy elbows. She muttered in Czech, obviously bored.

More to get the woman away from the table than because he was hungry, Katz pulled a menu from the wire stand attached to the napkin holder and pointed at the first entrée he saw. He held up five fingers, waved his hand around the table, then added, "Pilsner."

The woman's face was deadpan as she shuffled away.

McCarter leaned forward, lowering his voice. "I got as far as the door," the former British SAS officer reported. "They simply aren't interested in doing business with a discount chemical supply company out of London. Wouldn't even entertain the idea."

"Did you learn *anything?*" Katz asked.

McCarter shrugged. "I suppose. I learned that it'll be bloody near impossible to get in without stirring up a ruckus. Oh, we can kick the door and go in guns blazing, no problem. But all of us infiltrate the place, run recon, and get out without them knowing we were there? There's a better chance of Prince Charles and Lady Di getting back together."

"How about one man?" James asked. "Could one guy get in?"

McCarter shrugged. "That's how it'll have to be, if it can be done at all."

"Well, it has to be done," Katz said. "We can't just sit here waiting for Ryba to blow disease across the world."

The song on the radio changed as the bored waitress came back carrying a tray. She set a dish and beer mug in front of each man, and a basket of crackers in the center of the table. Suddenly the music stopped and the voice of a newscaster came over the airwaves.

The waitress's head shot toward the radio and she hurried away from the table.

"What was that?" James asked.

Encizo shrugged. "I don't speak Czech, Cal." He looked at the soft white blob on the plate in front of him. "The question is, what is this?"

Katz chuckled. "I don't know, but as far as I know the Czechs don't eat monkey brains." He took a sip of beer, then returned to the matter at hand. "Somehow, some way, one of us has to get in there. Any ideas?"

Gary Manning stuck a fork suspiciously into his plate, took a bite and frowned. "Cheese, I think. Yeah, it's cheese…maybe." He looked at Katz as he began to chew. "We'll have to come up with another scam. Something better than the chemical supply thing."

James eyed his food suspiciously, then took a bite. "Tastes kind of like meat." He looked up. "A delivery, maybe? Something they need?"

McCarter lifted his beer and reached for a cracker. Dipping it into his plate, he held it in front of him as he spoke. "My guess is the delivery man wouldn't get any farther past the door than I did."

The waitress returned and spoke in Czech once more.

"No, thank you," Katz said.

The woman frowned. "You are English?" she asked suddenly.

"No, but we speak the language."

"If I had known, *I* would have spoken English," she said. "I asked if you heard the news just now."

"Heard, but didn't understand," Katz replied.

"The store down the street," the woman said. "The oldest store? Four men wearing masks just robbed it. That has never happened before."

Katz looked up from the table as a Czech police

car raced by, its siren blaring through the window into the café. He shook his head. "Terrible."

The woman nodded and turned away.

"Finish eating, gentlemen," the Israeli said. "We may not get another chance for a long time."

The men of Phoenix Force cleared their plates with varying degrees of mistrust.

Katz reached in his pocket and pulled out three rumpled hundred koruna bills. Dropping them next to his plate, he said, "Let's go. I've got an idea." He led the way to the door.

Over his shoulder, he heard Gary Manning say, "Ma'am, what was that we were eating?"

"I do not know the word in English for it," the waitress replied as Katz opened the door.

"Any idea?" Manning asked.

"It is a…small animal, a small, furry animal. With big teeth. I think."

Fredericksburg, Virginia

CARL LYONS SHRUGGED into the shoulder harness, letting the Calico M-950A fall in place under his right arm and covering it with the navy blue blazer. Drawing back the machine pistol's bolt, he let it fall forward again to chamber the first 9 mm round, then flipped the safety.

As the lights of Fredericksburg, Virginia, appeared through the windshield of the van, the Able Team leader rose from the passenger's seat, squeezed past Gadgets Schwarz into the back, and joined Politician

Blancanales next to the footlocker in the rear of the vehicle.

"These things are great," Pol stated, handing Lyons a long cylindrical backup drum with one hand and patting the grip of his Calico submachine gun with the other. "A hundred pops without reloading? Hard to beat."

"Yeah," Schwarz called over the back of the driver's seat as they entered the city limits, "and what's really nice is that they don't jam."

"Weapon malfunctions can definitely put a damper on even the most festive firefights," Blancanales agreed.

Lyons drew the Colt Government Model .45 from his hip holster, checked the chamber and attached the sound suppressor before sliding it back into the leather and fastening the thumb snap. He looked down into the locker at the Colt Python .357 Magnum as the radio in front of Schwarz scratched with static.

No, he'd leave the Python here for now. He didn't need the extra weight. Besides, with the machine pistol, a 50-round drum, 100-round backup and the .45, he had a hundred and fifty-eight rounds at his immediate disposal.

If he couldn't kidnap one elderly, unarmed man with that much firepower, he'd better turn the reins of Able Team over to somebody else.

"Stony Man Base, Able One, come in, One" came over the radio on the van's dashboard.

Schwarz lifted the mike to his lips. "Able Two, here," he said. "One is 10-6 in the back. But he's got his ears on."

"Affirmative," Barbara Price said. "Your mark is staying at the Richard Johnston Inn, a bed and breakfast on Caroline Street, 711. Repeat, 711 Caroline Street. You copy?"

"We copy, Base," Schwarz replied.

"Stay tuned, there's more," Price came back. "If he's not there, try the White Hart Tavern next to the Amtrak train station."

Lyons moved back between the seats, took the mike from Schwarz and glanced to the electronic map on the inset television screen next to the radio. "Base, we pass Amtrak on the way. We'll try it first."

"Affirmative, One. Base, Clear."

Lyons rehooked the mike and sat back in his seat as Schwarz turned onto Caroline Street. A few blocks later, the haunting sound of a train whistle met his ears and then the tracks and trains appeared ahead.

Schwarz slowed as Lyons pulled a black-and-white computer photograph from the pocket of his blazer and stared at it under the streetlights passing overhead. The balding gray pate and thick-lidded eyes of Francis Hunyadi stared back at him.

The man Lyons was about to grab wasn't a Czech, as the Able Team leader had thought he would be. Huntington Wether's computer investigation of Joseph Ryba had turned up no close friends or associates from the new Czech Republic presently in positions of power within the U.S. But Wethers had come across a tie that might prove equally valuable—or better.

Hunyadi, currently the Hungarian ambassador to the United States, had been a classmate of Ryba's at

Prague's Charles University. They had also played on the soccer team together.

It wasn't a great lead, Lyons knew, but it was the best they had. And the ex-LAPD detective had solved cases with far less to go on.

A wooden sign, illuminated by a floodlight on the ground below and bearing the likeness of a snow-white deer, appeared across from the train station. Schwarz pulled off the cobblestone street and into the parking lot.

Lyons swiveled in his seat. "I'll go check. If he's there, I'll come back and we'll put something together as far as snatching him."

Schwarz and Blancanales both nodded.

Taking a final look at the photograph, the Able Team leader stuffed it back into his jacket and exited the van.

The inside of the White Hart had tried hard to resemble an old English pub. It didn't quite make it. Wood and leather had been the building materials of choice when England constructed its famous taverns. In those days, both had been plentiful and cheap. Now, aluminum and Naugahyde were far more cost-effective, and the builders of the White Hart had made use of it without restraint. The wood paneling that covered the walls was the same Lyons had seen in countless discount lumber yards. The plastic, leatherlike substance that covered the booths and chairs had split at the seams.

Behind the plywood bar, mirror-tile had been glued to the wall. Photographs and newspaper clippings hung in cheap black plastic frames around the room.

The White Hart was empty except for the bartender and three men standing in front of the bar, and all turned toward Lyons as he entered. The bartender had long blond hair that fell to his waist, and wore purple eye shadow.

Two of the men in front of the bar wore matching hot-pink pullover shirts, khaki pants and patent-leather loafers.

All three were a good twenty years too young to be Hunyadi.

The third man had dressed in faded black jeans, black knee-high motorcycle boots and a black leather jacket decorated with zippers and chains. Flaming red hair fell to his shoulders, and a matching Fu Manchu mustache and red goatee covered his pockmarked face.

Lyons walked past the bar and heard a snicker from one of the men in pink. He continued past the empty booths to the men's room, checked for feet under the stall doors, then came back out into the bar area.

The leather-clad man looked up from his beer as the Able Team leader headed back for the front door. A moment later, chains clinked and boots tapped across the floor as he moved in front of Lyons.

Lyons stopped in front of him.

"You're new, aren't you?" the man growled, hooking both thumbs over his belt buckle.

The big ex-cop noted the diamond-studded earring in the man's right ear. He nodded, then tried to walk around the hulking figure in front of him.

The man shuffled smoothly to his side, blocking Lyons's path. "Buy you a drink," he said.

Lyons shook his head. "No, thanks." He tried moving around the man in the other direction, but he was blocked again.

The eyes above the red beard took on a vicious, lust-filled glare as the man spoke again. 'Buy you a drink' wasn't a question. It was a statement. "I got my own special way of welcoming new meat to this place."

"Maybe he's just shy, Gordon," one of the men at the bar called.

"That it, New Meat?" The man called Gordon grinned. "You shy? Hell, I'll get you over that fast enough." His hands fell to the crotch of his tight jeans.

Lyons sighed. He'd have preferred to just walk out without trouble, but it didn't look like it was going to go down that way. "Look," the Able Team leader said, "I just came in to use the rest room."

Snickers drifted across the room from the two men at the bar. "We use the rest room sometimes," one of them said slyly.

Gordon licked his lips. "That's right," he said. "Come on. I'll show you a good time."

Lyons quelled the disgust that rose in his throat. He tried once more to walk around the red-haired man. Once more, he was blocked. The man with the beard smiled, then reached out, placing both hands on the Able Team leader's shoulders. "Relax," he soothed, "you're gonna love it."

The Stony Man warrior stared the man in the eyes. He'd wasted enough time trying to keep from hurting the guy, and he had work to do. Forcing a smile, he reached slowly for the man's crotch.

Gordon's red beard and mustache arched up in surprise, then a smile formed on his face. He closed his eyes. "Yeah...."

Lyons fingers circled the man's testicles through the tight jeans, then squeezed hard. The smile on the red-bearded face vanished faster than it had appeared.

The big ex-cop squeezed harder, and Gordon shrieked. He released his grip and the man slumped to the floor.

Lyons walked to the door, left the bar and crossed the parking lot. Pol slid the van door open for him and he crawled in back. "Hunyadi's not there," the Able Team leader stated.

"Damn, Ironman," Blancanales said as Schwarz pulled out of the parking lot toward the Richard Johnston Inn, "you took long enough."

"We were beginning to think you'd found a date," Schwarz cracked from the driver's seat.

"I did," Lyons said dryly. "He just wasn't my type."

Blancanales and Schwarz looked at each other in the rearview mirror, dumbfounded.

Lyons saw no reason to explain.

The restored Richard Johnston Inn, in Fredericksburg's National Historic District, appeared a few minutes later. Schwarz pulled to a halt in front.

"Same plan, different place," Lyons said as he exited the van. "Be ready."

The Able Team leader entered the inn's mammoth front door and stepped onto a gleaming pinewood floor covered with Oriental carpets. He glanced at the rows of elaborately framed portraits of Southern gentry covering the walls as he strode to the front desk.

An elderly woman in eighteenth-century dress stood behind the counter. She smiled as Lyons approached. "May I help you?"

He smiled back. "I'm looking for Francis Hunyadi."

The smile faded slightly. "I'm sorry," she said, "we never give out the room numbers of our guests. I'm sure you can understand—"

Lyons pulled a small credential case from his pocket, flipped it open and held it in front of the woman.

"My goodness," she said, "the Department of Justice?"

Lyons nodded, glanced around the room, then leaned in close. "We have an urgent message for Mr. Hunyadi."

The woman nodded knowingly. Her hand moved toward the phone on the desk. "I'll ring—"

The big ex-cop reached out and gently took her hand. With another glance around the lobby, he said, "Please don't. He might be in danger. It's better if we just get him out of here as quickly as possible."

The woman, unused to such critical events and visits from federal law-enforcement officers, nodded hurriedly. She leaned in closer to Lyons and said, "Around back. There are two suites. The entrances are off the patio."

"Which one?" Lyons asked.

"The one to your left."

He stepped outside and waved to Schwarz and Blancanales. Thirty second later, the three men of Able Team rounded the corner of the Richard Johnston Inn. Opening the gate, they stepped onto the bricked patio. Lyons led the way to the suite on the left, reached out and tried the knob. Locked.

Nodding to his teammates, the Able Team leader stepped back, raised his foot and kicked the door open.

A rustling of bed sheets fluttered from the bed in the center of the room, then a gray head that matched the photo in Lyons's pocket snaked up from the linen.

Lyons wasn't surprised when a moment later, a younger blond head with a matching blond mustache and beard, appeared next to it.

The Able Team leader swung the Calico from under his coat and aimed it at Francis Hunyadi. "Get up and get dressed, Mr. Hunyadi. We're going for a ride."

The blond man next to the Hungarian ambassador stared at Lyons with frightened eyes. "What…what about me?"

Lyons swung the Calico his way. "Go home. Or if you don't want to do that, there's a guy back at the White Hart Pub who's looking for a friend."

CHAPTER FIVE

Prague, Czech Republic

The "magic" of the Lanterna Magika was evident long before Bolan and Hammersmith took their places at the end of the line leading into the theater. Men and women, some in evening dress, others in more casual clothing, chattered excitedly among themselves as they waited for the doors to open.

The Executioner's trained eyes scouted the area. Across the street from the theater, he saw rows of retail shops, their windows darkened for the night. An alley ran between what appeared to be a hardware store and dress shop directly across from the Magic Lantern.

"There's quite a history to this place," Hammersmith told the Executioner as they stopped at the end of the line. "It was started in 1948 by two Czech brothers, and they toured Europe and the U.S. with their shows. Didn't get too popular, though. But the performances have been sold out here since 1977."

Bolan nodded, watching the line ahead of him. The history of Lanterna Magika was probably fascinating. But the Executioner was more interested in the location of the lab, somewhere beneath the theater. And the only way he'd find it was to study the other theatergoers, determine which of them were actually biochemical researchers, and see what they did after they got into the performance.

The wooden door at the front of the line finally opened to a cheer from the crowd. A hand snaked out and inserted a card into a glass holder to the side. As the men and women read the word *Odysseus* on the card, another cheer went up.

A ticket taker took his place and the line began to move slowly forward.

"I've never been before," Hammersmith commented, "but I understand the performances change from show to show. It's potluck what you draw. *Odysseus* is the best they say, but the others are supposed to be good, too."

Ten minutes later, Bolan handed the usher the tickets and followed Hammersmith into the crowded lobby. He noticed two uniformed security men standing near the concession stand.

Both wore Jablonec Security Company shoulder patches, Ryba's cover company for the Deliverance Squad. Was the theater in on the Biopreparat program?

Something told the Executioner it wasn't.

Making their way into the theater proper, Bolan and Hammersmith found their seats midway down an aisle to the left. They sat down amid more excited and expectant chatter from the audience.

Finally the curtain went up to reveal a stage. Then ten film screens fell into view around the theater, and the rattle of five projectors filled the auditorium. They were greeted with more wild applause, whistles and screams from the crowd.

"Never a dull moment at Lanterna Magika." Hammersmith smiled.

A few moments later, the stage was filled with live performers dressed as ancient Greek sailors. Then one of the movie screens lighted up with the image of a ship at sea. The stage actors moved across the deck of the ship, working the sheets and singing along with the music that now blasted Bolan and Hammersmith from all sides. More sailors appeared on screen, conversing with their live stage counterparts in a mixture of reality and illusion. The crowd went wild.

Bolan kept one eye on the stage while the other swept the audience. Before the opening number had ended, one man and a woman had already left the auditorium.

Although all of the actors, stage and screen, spoke in Czech, Bolan had no trouble following the story line of Odysseus, or Ulysses, as he was better known in the West. He watched as stage actors climbed real ropes to reach sails depicted on screen. Gigantic "film" waves spilled over the deck, throwing live crew members about, and the Executioner felt the same impulse to duck that caused many of the watchers to crouch behind the seats in front of them.

Another man left his seat near the front and walked up the aisle and out of the auditorium.

The Executioner watched the scenes change from one hypnotic blend of stage and screen to the next. Then, as an onstage Odysseus drove a red-hot stake into the eye of a Cyclops on screen, he saw a fourth member of the crowd, tall and bald, rise in his chair and hurry toward the lobby.

"Stay here," Bolan told Hammersmith. "I'll be back."

The woman nodded.

Bolan hurried up the aisle in time to enter the lobby and see the bald man enter the men's rest room. The warrior followed, giving the door time to swing shut before he pushed it quietly open again.

The Executioner's shoes moved silently onto the tile of the rest room floor, stopping in front of a row of sinks just inside the door. His eyes scanned the urinals.

The rest room appeared to be empty. The tall bald man had to have entered one of the toilet stalls.

Bolan walked quietly forward to the front of the stalls along the wall. He heard nothing. Dropping to a squatting position, he saw a pair of scuffed brown loafers under the second door. The shoes faced him and the crumpled cuffs of blue trousers had bunched around the ankles.

In the stall at the far end of the row, Bolan saw the heels of a newer pair of black brogans. Facing away from him, the man wearing them had to be standing up. A second later, the toilet flushed within the stall.

And the shoes disappeared.

Bolan frowned. He waited ten seconds to see if they'd reappear, then walked cautiously forward. Peering into the crack between the door and frame, he saw that the stall was empty. Reaching out, he tried the door. It didn't budge.

The warrior turned and started back to get Hammersmith. The setup was simple, as long as you knew it. Something was done inside the stall that opened a hidden door that had to lead to the laboratory. Of course any theater patron might choose that toilet to relieve himself and inadvertently discover the stall's secret. So the door had been purposely jammed.

It could be crawled under, or over, but what man who had to use the bathroom would go to such trouble when there were seven more perfectly good toilets right next to it?

Odysseus was resisting the temptations of the Sirens on screen when Bolan stopped at the end of the aisle and nodded to Hammersmith. The British woman rose and followed him up the aisle.

"You've found it?" she whispered as they entered the lobby.

"In the men's room."

He led the British woman casually through the lobby, keeping one eye on the ushers and Jablonec guards. No one gave them a second look. They waited until the man wearing the scuffed brown shoes and blue trousers came out, then the Executioner opened the door, pushed the woman inside and followed.

"The guy in here earlier flushed the john, then disappeared," he said as they crossed the tile. "There's got to be a secret panel inside the stall."

Hammersmith nodded as she and the Executioner hurried to the far end of the room. "The door's jammed," Bolan whispered.

The British agent reached up, grasped the top of the stall frame and pulled herself up and over.

Bolan followed her a moment later, lowering himself carefully into the tiny space next to the woman. Lifting a foot, he leaned forward and flushed the toilet.

Nothing happened.

The Executioner frowned, quickly scanning the inside of the stall. It looked no different than those of many European countries, and little different than those in America. Hammersmith shifted, moving against the wall to allow him to see the area behind her. As she did, her back scraped the toilet-paper dispenser, and the metal cover fell off, clanging loudly against the tile.

Bolan stared at the uncovered roll of toilet paper. Like the stall itself, it looked no different than hundreds of thousands of other dispensers the world over.

Except for the small red button mounted on the wall behind it.

"Bingo," Hammersmith said, grinning.

"Maybe," Bolan agreed skeptically. Reaching forward, he pushed the button.

Again, nothing happened.

Hammersmith frowned. "Wait a minute." Turning, she lowered herself onto the toilet, then looked at the button. With one hand she reached behind her, gripping the flush handle. With the other, she leaned forward and pushed the button. As the button went in and the toilet flushed, a three-by-three-foot panel opened behind the toilet tank.

The Executioner looked in to see a dark staircase leading down.

Hammersmith reached out and grabbed his arm.

"There could be an alarm attached to this thing, something that alerts them that someone's on their way down."

Bolan nodded. "That's right."

The woman's fingers dug deeper into his flesh. "Do you think there is?"

Bolan shrugged. "I don't know. But I've got a feeling we're about to find out."

Prague, Czech Republic

KATZ LED THE WAY DOWN the sidewalk past Hans Capek's store on the other side of the street. The robbery that had been announced over the radio had taken place less than an hour earlier, and several police cars, lights flashing, stood in front of the building.

With the rest of the men trailing him, the Phoenix Force leader passed the concrete steps leading down from street level to the laboratory where McCarter had been earlier. He took careful note of the steel door, door buzzer to the side, and the surveillance camera mounted above the entryway as they passed.

McCarter had been right—it wouldn't be easy for even *one* man to slip clandestinely into the research lab. For five, it would be impossible. The only way in seemed to be to blast their way through the front door. And it had seemed until now that if they did that, Ryba would get word that they were onto his resurrected Biopreparat program.

"Until now," was the operative phrase.

Katz led the way down the street until he spied a men's apparel store. Turning, he nodded to James,

Encizo, McCarter and Manning, who stopped on the sidewalk.

The former Mossad agent opened the door and went inside. He returned a moment later, carrying a brown paper shopping bag, and stopped at the top just to the side of the steps leading to the lab. Pulling a black stocking cap from the paper sack, he stuffed it into the side pocket of his jacket, then handed it to McCarter who did the same. The bag made the rounds of the men, then the Briton descended the steps again.

Katz stayed to the side of the steps, peeking around the corner, as McCarter rang the buzzer. A minute later, he heard the screech of an unoiled lock as the steel door swung open.

The face of a man wearing horn-rimmed glasses and long sideburns appeared. ''Mr. Blackwelder,'' the man said tiredly, ''we have already told you we are not interest—''

McCarter drew his 9 mm Browning Hi-Power pistol from under his coat, shoved it under the man's chin and pushed him back into the building. Like Bolan, the men of Phoenix Force had chosen to use primarily weapons from the former Eastern Bloc countries. But McCarter had held out, claiming that the Browning could be found the world over.

Katz led the other masked men down the steps three at a time. They pushed past McCarter and the other man into the doorway, stopping in a short entryway that led to another door.

The Phoenix Force leader glanced to the walls. Concrete. Good. They'd need the soundproofing from the police just across the street. Carefully he swung the steel door shut again, making sure the lock caught. Then, turning toward the man who had answered the door, he tore him away from McCarter. Spinning the frightened Czech to face him, Katz demanded, "Where's the safe?"

"Safe? We have no—"

Katz backhanded the man across the face, knocking him into the wall. The black horn-rimmed glasses split at the nose piece and fell to the sides. The Israeli stepped forward. "Take us inside. If we get your money, nobody gets hurt."

"But—"

Another backhand sent the Czech reeling toward the door at the end of the hall. Phoenix Force followed, waiting as the man's shaking hand fished a ring of keys from his pocket. He opened the door.

Manning pushed the man through the door first, then followed. Katz came next, finding himself in the lab proper. He drew the Czech CZ-75 from under his jacket as the surprised heads of men and women working around the tables, test tubes and petri dishes turned to face him. Sliding to the side of the door, he let the rest of the team enter.

Manning shoved the doorman to the floor and fired two shots overhead into the ceiling as McCarter, Encizo and James sprinted to a door across the room and disappeared down a hall.

Screams and cries erupted from the scientists in the room. A man wearing a security uniform went for the gun holstered on his hip.

The Israeli put a round between his eyes, bringing on more screams.

Katz waited for the noise to die down, then shouted, "This is a robbery!" He herded the researchers and two more Jablonec guards to the side of the room and stretched them out facedown on the floor, hands behind their head. "One move," he threatened. "and I kill everyone. Is that understood?"

Enough of the people spoke English to get him a few murmurs of understanding, but he had cautioned them not to move, and none of the heads dared nod.

A moment later, the rest of the men of Phoenix Force herded in several more men and women in lab coats from the other rooms of the facility. One of the men, a man in his late sixties wearing a gray banker's suit, appeared to be in charge.

Katz moved forward and stuck the barrel of the CZ-75 into the man's ample midsection. "Where is the safe?" he demanded.

The man shook his head, muttering in Czech. "No English" were the only words Katz caught.

The Israeli fired two rounds into the wall just over the man's head. "You better learn English, *quick*," he said.

The man in the gray suit did. "We have no safe," he said, his voice trembling. "We…you have made a mistake, come to the wrong place. We are a scientific research—"

Katz fired two more rounds into the ceiling, then turned toward the rest of the ski-masked men as the screams began again. "Tear this place apart until you find it!" he ordered.

Manning, McCarter and James began overturning tables. Glassware smashed to the floor as notebook pages, pens, pencils and other objects sailed through the air.

"Please…" the man in the gray suit pleaded. "We—"

Katz raised the barrel of the CZ to point at the man's head. He turned to James and Encizo. "Watch them," he said, then motioning for McCarter and Manning to follow, he exited the far door and started down the hall.

The first door they came to looked like a bull pen in a detective squad room. Small desks sat within each of the cubicles separated from each other by particleboard. Katz, McCarter and Manning worked their way through the room, overturning the desks and scattering more notebook pages and other documents as they went.

"I feel like a juvenile delinquent," McCarter stated.

At the rear of the room, they came to a bank of five small computers. McCarter shoved a 20-round extended magazine into the grip of his Browning, then fired one carefully placed 9 mm round into the keyboard, disk drive and screen of each unit.

Moving back to the hallway, Katz led the way to another similar office area. It, too, fell to the rounds of the "robbers." A smaller but more elaborately decorated room appeared to serve as the office of the man in the gray suit. Katz took out his personal computer with a trio of CZ-75 rounds while McCarter and Manning wrecked havoc with the furniture and filing cabinets.

The last room in the suite was the research library,

and it contained a long row of bookshelves. Katz saw Manning grin through the mouth hole of his ski mask as the big Canadian threw a rugby block into the first shelf in line, sending books flying as it tumbled into the next and created a domino effect that didn't stop until the last case crashed into the wall on the opposite side of the room.

Katz turned to the two men. "Think that'll do it?" he asked.

"Ought to slow them down a bit," McCarter replied. "It'll take days before they can even sort things out again."

Katz sprinted back down the hall with the other two Phoenix Force warriors at his heels. He found James and Encizo still standing over the prisoners in the lab. Grabbing the man in the gray suit by the lapel, he placed the muzzle of the pistol next to the man's temple and cocked the hammer.

"This is your last chance," he growled. "Where the hell is the safe?"

The chubby little man was almost in tears. "I swear. There isn't any safe. There isn't any money!"

Katz stared into the frightened eyes until they closed in horror. For a moment, he felt pity for the man, then remembered the type of research in which the lab was engaged. They were developing biochemical agents that could kill millions of people. You couldn't exactly call this man an innocent bystander.

"Guess what?" Katz finally said.

"What?" the man whispered, his eyes still clenched tightly.

"I believe you." Katz pulled the CZ-75 from the

man's head, decocked the hammer and shoved the gun into his waistband. "Let's go," he told the men of Phoenix Force as he started for the door leading to the street. "We got the wrong place."

Katz opened the door to the entryway and he and his teammates filed through, dropping their ski masks on the floor as they went.

The men and women on the floor started to rise as Katz turned to leave. Turning back, he said, "One more thing."

The research scientists froze halfway to their feet.

Katz emptied the rest of the magazine from his weapon into the ceiling and the researchers fell back to the floor. The Israeli waited for the echoes to die down, then said, "Don't anybody move for thirty minutes."

The rest of the Stony Man warriors were exiting the building as Katz swung the door shut and followed. They ascended the steps, turned down the sidewalk and walked off.

Stony Man Farm

AARON "BEAR" KURTZMAN subscribed to the theory that you "Never let them see you sweat." He never did, no matter how much pressure he was under.

That didn't mean, however, that Stony Man Farm's top computer wizard didn't occasionally feel a little frustrated. He was only human, after all. But Kurtzman, like Bolan, Lyons, Katz—all the operatives who worked out of the Farm—never let frustration get the better of him.

Kurtzman sat back in his wheelchair and stared at the computer screen in front of him. The assignment to find the codes that would unlock the files and disclose the locations of the storage and launch sites of Joseph Ryba's new Biopreparat diseases should have been relatively simple. But the journey through the magical world of the computer's brain had been wrought with bad luck and obstacles from the onset.

Not the least of those obstacles had been the fact that the entire file was, of course, in Czech. And neither Kurtzman, nor any of the computer staff—or anyone else at the Farm for that matter—spoke the language.

The Bear glanced up briefly at the man standing next to his wheelchair. Louis Tuma's gaze was glued to the screen as tightly as Kurtzman's had been. But the similarities in the two men ended there. Tuma— tall, angular and exhibiting the high cheekbones of the Eastern European Slav—showed *his* frustration. Deep worry lines had etched themselves across his forehead.

"What do you think, Louie?" Kurtzman asked, folding his hands and popping the knuckles.

Tuma shook his head. He continued to stare.

Well, Kurtzman thought, dropping his hands to the rails of his wheelchair. The man had reason to be frustrated. In addition to the code itself, he didn't have the slightest idea of where in the world he was at the moment.

Kurtzman had immediately realized that his first

step in solving the riddle of the codes was to enlist the aid of someone who possessed three qualities: First, the man would have to speak fluent Czech. Second, he'd have to have at least a working knowledge of computer decoding methods, and the more he knew in that area, the better.

And third, whomever Kurtzman got to help him would have to be willing to work under some pretty strange circumstances.

Kurtzman took a deep breath, rubbed his eyes and forced his gaze back to the screen. His first task had been a computer search of all U.S. government employees in law-enforcement computer jobs who spoke Czech. That had narrowed things down considerably. When he added the specification that they be highly trained computer operators, the list had shortened further.

Most of the names had been found on the roles of the CIA and various military intelligence units. But Louis Tuma had been on the list as well, and the name had fairly leapt at Kurtzman as he scanned the list. He had met Tuma several years earlier when they had both been instructors helping with an FBI training seminar for criminal analysts. Tuma, an FBI man himself, had impressed the Bear not only with his knowledge of the magic machines, but with his unorthodox and creative approach. And he was of Bohemian descent on both sides of his family. He'd grown up with Czech as the family language, not even learning English until he'd entered kindergarten.

Which had all gone into Kurtzman's decision that Tuma be brought to the Farm, blindfolded.

Kurtzman leaned forward, his fingers racing across the keyboard as he tried another entry and failed. Together, he and Tuma had put together a systematic approach to the codes, and one by one they were narrowing the field of probability. But the problem was that between the time-consuming program they'd developed, and the fact that Tuma had to translate every step of the way, it might take weeks before the codes were broken and Ryba's death sites located.

The Stony Man computer ace sat back again and rubbed a hand across his chin.

Tuma leaned down. "We'll get it eventually, Aaron," he said. "It might help if you told me more about what the hell is going on."

Kurtzman shook his head. "Can't do it, Louie. You know that."

Tuma stiffened slightly. "Yes, the blindfold was my first clue," he said with a trace of sarcasm. "In spite of that, I agreed to do everything I could, based on the *one* time I met you when you were apparently with the Justice Department." His point made, Tuma's voice softened. "And I'll keep my word, regardless of whatever this operation is. Because I can know we're on the same side." His eyes turned back to the screen and he shrugged. "I just thought it might give me a broader perspective if I knew more about what was going on."

Kurtzman frowned in concentration. The man had a point. A good one. Kurtzman knew he might be the computer expert of Stony Man Farm, but Tuma had proved to be damn good himself. And two heads were almost always better than one.

On the other hand, Kurtzman had taken an oath not to reveal any of the details of the Farm or its missions when he'd signed on. In fact, he'd sworn not to reveal even the existence of the place.

"I mean, Aaron," Tuma said, "we're fighting for the same thing here, aren't we? *Svobadu?*"

Kurtzman looked up curiously. "Svo…what?"

The deep lines in Tuma's face relaxed momentarily. He chuckled. "Sorry. I've been translating so much I forgot what language I was in for a minute." He cleared his throat, the smile vanished and the wrinkles returned. "*Svobadu! Svobadu!* was the slogan of the resistance fighters during the days of communism in Czechoslovakia. *Svobadu* means freedom. It's what they were fighting for then, and what we're both fighting for now. Right?"

Kurtzman didn't answer. Lifting the phone to his side, he buzzed Barbara Price. "Get the director on the line, will you, Barb?" he asked.

Fredericksburg, Virginia

A CLEAR THREE-QUARTER moon fell over the wooded area ten miles south of Fredericksburg as Schwarz pulled the van off the highway onto the dirt road.

Lyons glanced into the rearview mirror attached to the sun visor in front of the passenger's seat. The mirror had come as a stock item when the van arrived at Stony Man Farm, long before the Farm's mechanics had added the aftermarket "extras" that didn't come even on special order. No, special high-frequency band radios, computerized map screens and gun ports weren't on the list of GM's options. But the mirror had been standard equipment.

Lyons had planned to take it out while they were outfitting the van. It was intended for use by women who wanted to freshen their makeup while their husbands drove, and try as he might, the Able Team leader couldn't remember the last time he'd seen either Gadgets Schwarz or Pol Blancanales in lipstick. But he'd forgotten all about the mirror and not remembered it until they'd been en route somewhere one afternoon and he'd pulled the visor down to shield his eyes.

And realized it gave him a clear view of the back of the van.

Lyons had pulled the visor down again as soon as he'd taken the seat after herding Francis Hunyadi into the back. He'd used it to watch Blancanales handcuff the Hungarian diplomat to the armrest of the captain's chair in which Hunyadi now sat, and he'd continued to use it to clandestinely watch Pol whisper to the man almost continuously as they'd left Fredericksburg.

Though he couldn't hear what was being said, Lyons could see the expression on Hunyadi's face as Blancanales whispered on. He knew that Pol was using his near-perfect South African accent, as well as making use of all he'd learned over the years in his relentless pursuit of the art of psychological warfare.

And whatever Pol was saying, he could tell by Hunyadi's nervous twitching, fearful face and telltale body language that it was having an effect.

Lyons leaned toward Schwarz behind the wheel of the van. "How much farther?" he whispered.

"Mile, maybe mile and a half," Schwarz replied quietly. Neither man wanted Hunyadi to hear their voices. Their South African accents were nonexistent, and the success of this mission might well depend on the Hungarian believing they actually were what they claimed to be—agents of the South African government intent on developing their own biochemical warfare project.

Gadgets slowed the van as they bumped over a washboard road, then curved around a small pond. In the moonlight, Lyons could see a dozen or so Jersey cows standing next to a trough. A barbed-wire fence ran along the road, separating it from the pond.

South Africa hadn't been picked to be their "cover country" randomly. Lyons knew they needed to present the illusion that they represented a nation that had the capability, and the desire, to create weapons of mass destruction. And word of what had happened would get back to Ryba just as soon as they finished with Hunyadi and let him go. So that same cover nation needed to be one that wasn't likely to be aligned with the U.S. or Western Europe.

South Africa fit the bill perfectly.

Schwarz pulled to a halt in front of a cattle guard that led to a gate. Lyons got out and walked forward, seeing several large padlocks linked together within the sturdy chain that circled the posts. Whoever owned the land sold fishing permits, and each permit holder added his own lock to the chain.

The former L.A. cop pulled a Lockaid gun from his pocket, inserted needles into the largest of the padlocks and adjusted the tension wrench. He pulled the trigger and heard the crunch as the tumblers lined up. Pulling the lock from the chain, he walked the gate in away from the van.

A second later, Schwarz drove through.

Blancanales was speaking louder in his South African accent by the time Lyons returned to the van. "So you see, Mr. Hunyadi, we have no desire to harm you. But make no mistake. We will if it becomes necessary."

Schwarz took a narrow road that led around the pond, then turned off away from the water into a stand of trees.

"What...where...are we going?" Hunyadi asked in a high, nervous voice.

"All in good time," Blancanales replied. "But keep in mind what I have told you. This will not be a long interrogation. You will either tell us what we need to know, or you will not leave these trees."

In the visor mirror, Lyons saw Hunyadi shrink back into his seat.

Schwarz pulled to a halt in a small clearing. Lyons glanced into the side-view mirror. Behind them, the waters of the pond sparkled brightly under the moon. He opened the door, got out, then slid the rear door open amid a concert of chirping crickets. Pol stepped down, handed Lyons his Calico, then pulled Hunyadi out of the van.

Lyons heard a rustling in the trees behind him as he handed the submachine gun back to Blancanales. He saw Hunyadi look into the trees, turned and saw the silhouette of a deer flash before his eyes before disappearing deeper into the forest.

The Able Team leader fought a grin. Contrast had been the psychological ploy Blancanales had chosen after studying Wethers's computer profile of Francis Hunyadi. Show the Hungarian the things he loved most in life, then threaten to take them away for all of eternity.

Francis Hunyadi had been born in the clement hills of western Hungary, near the Danube River separating his country from Czechoslovakia. As a boy he had lived in the village of Tata, which might have been only forty-five miles from Budapest on the map, but was light-years away from the Hungarian capital in pace. Known as an outdoor nature center since the Middle Ages, Blancanales had felt certain that the area had to have ingrained itself deeply into the psyche of the man.

Well, Lyons thought, as he stepped back up into the van and pulled out the shovel. This pond was no river, and the deer might not be exactly the same breed as that found in the woods near Tata. But it was the best they could come up with on the spur of the moment. And with Able Team's ace headshrinker behind the controls of the plan, Lyons had no doubt it would be effective.

Blancanales and Schwarz prodded Hunyadi to the center of the clearing with their submachine guns. The Hungarian's eyes darted back and forth, a whimper issuing forth from his lips with each step he took.

Lyons handed him the shovel.

"Dig," Blancanales said simply.

"But…" Hunyadi said, his chest heaving now in sobs. "Please—"

"I will ask you questions as you dig," Pol said. "You will answer. If we like what we hear, you will be returned safely to Fredericksburg. If we do not, the hole you dig yourself will become your final resting place."

Hunyadi started to speak. Blancanales's hand rose as if to strike him. The Hungarian leaned forward and stuck the shovel into the soft earth.

"As I told you during our drive," Pol went on, "we know you are involved with Joseph Ryba in the new Biopreparat program. We intend to develop our own similar program. And we intend to do that by learning all we can from you."

A choking sound issued forth from Hunyadi's throat as he overturned a shovelful of dirt. "I do not know—"

Blancanales sighed dramatically. "Then dig, Francis Hunyadi. It will be a peaceful place where you will spend eternity."

Hunyadi shivered as he dug the shovel blade back into the ground. He threw three more loads of dirt to the side, then said, "Please, you must believe me. Ryba and I knew each other at university. But we were not close friends."

"You played soccer together," Blancanales pointed out.

"Yes, but we never saw each other off the playing field. We were not close. I had…a different sort of friends."

Pol smiled. "Yes, so we saw back at the inn. We know that Ryba does not share your sexual tastes. But we know you are involved with his program here in the United States." The smile faded. "So, you are lying when you say that you know nothing. And I hope you change your mind and speak the truth." He stepped forward, grabbed the shovel handle and pointed through the trees toward the glistening water. "Because if not, you will never see the beauty of nature again."

Hunyadi dug on, sniffling as the hole grew larger. When it was three feet deep, Blancanales suddenly changed tactics. Lunging forward, he shoved the Hungarian into the grave.

Hunyadi landed on his side with a grunt, the shovel still clutched tightly in his hands. He rose to his knees, using the tool for support.

Blancanales moved to the edge of the grave and jammed the muzzle of the Calico M-960A into the man's temple. The click of the fire selector coming off safety echoed hollowly against the trees in the still night.

"You have convinced me," Blancanales said. "You know nothing." He paused for effect, then added, "So, I suppose, we must kill you."

"No!" Hunyadi screamed, falling forward onto his face. "I do know something!"

Blancanales clicked the weapon back onto safe. "Speak quickly, Francis Hunyadi," he said, sounding for all the world to Lyons as if he had been born and raised in the heart of the Transvaal, "and pray that it is enough to keep you alive."

"I know of a storage site in the U.S," Hunyadi moaned, closing his eyes. "There might be more. But I know the location of only one."

"Tell us," Blancanales ordered.

Francis Hunyadi did.

CHAPTER SIX

Prague, Czech Republic

Bolan led the way through the opening at the back of the toilet stall, turned and held out his hand. Hammersmith took it and stepped onto the small platform at the top of the dark steps.

The Executioner paused, letting his eyes grow accustomed to the darkness. Hammersmith could very well be right—it wasn't only possible, it seemed quite likely that there would be some warning system attached to the sliding door. Joseph Ryba and the Deliverance Squad arm of the Autonomy Party had gone to a lot of trouble to hide this particular research lab, far more than he had at the one in Plzeň.

Why?

Bolan continued to stare into the dim light. He couldn't be sure, but it seemed likely that Ryba was hedging his bets. Because of time, money or perhaps a lack of manpower, the leader of the newly revived Biopreparat project probably couldn't afford to isolate all of his research labs to this extent. But he could some of them.

Therefore, if easily located sites like the one in

Plzeň were found, the heavily concealed labs like this one hidden below the Lanterna Magika would remain operational.

Bolan turned back toward the door as his eyes adjusted. The secret to closing the sliding panel was far less complex than opening it. A dull gray metal lever extended from the wall next to the entrance, and he reached forward and pulled down. The panel closed.

Hammersmith's hand squeezed the Executioner's. "Do you think the Magic Lantern people are in on this?" she whispered.

Bolan shrugged. "I doubt it. This place has been a theater for years, and my guess is that the Jablonec men really do provide security services, which helps keep the cover intact. Before it became a theater, the building looks like it used to be a warehouse. Probably had a basement floor that they blocked off, then forgot about. With the Jablonec men legitimately in place upstairs, they could have slipped people in after hours and set things up." He paused. "You ready?"

Hammersmith nodded. She opened her clutch purse and produced the silenced .22 Beretta.

The Executioner shook his head. "Use your cannon," he said. "If we have to fire, it'll mean they're firing at us, and they won't have suppressed weapons. Besides—" he pointed back toward the theater "—I'm counting on the noise on stage and from the audience to mask our sounds."

Hammersmith dropped the .22 back into her purse and pulled out the H&K P-7 as Bolan drew the Skorpion machine pistol from beneath his jacket.

He stepped down on the first step, the creak of the ancient wood sounding thunderous in the silence.

Slowly, methodically, the Executioner made his way down the steps, doing the best he could to keep the creaks to a minimum. He felt Hammersmith's breath on the back of his neck as he came to another small landing before the steps bent to the right. Turning, he saw a door at the bottom of the next flight. A small diamond-shaped window was inset in the top, and fluorescent light glowed through the opening.

Bolan made his way down the steps, halting in front of the door. He inched an eye around the edge of the glass and saw a laboratory similar to the one he and Hammersmith had infiltrated in Plzeň. The walls, however, were bare brick, leading him to believe that his assumption that the subterranean lab had once been a storage area for the warehouse was correct.

Lab tables littered with the normal test-tube holders, beakers, and petri dishes filled the room. A dark brown curtain hung over the far wall, covering what he guessed to be another test chamber.

Moving to the side, the Executioner let Hammersmith take a look. She turned to him and frowned. "Where is everybody?" she whispered.

"That's what I'd like to know."

"I don't get the feeling it's tea," Hammersmith ventured, then took a deep breath. "They know we're here."

Bolan nodded, taking a moment to consider the situation. At this point, they might still be able to sneak out, regroup and form another plan to infiltrate the lab. But if they did that, word would get to Ryba that the West had discovered the lab.

No, it was time to hit, and hit hard, then cut their losses as best they could. Somehow, they'd have to cover the attack.

Bolan started to open the door when he heard the sound of the sliding panel open above. Light from the men's rest room shot through the opening.

"This is known as being between the devil and the deep blue sea," Hammersmith whispered. "What do we do?"

"You take care of whoever's on the stairs—quietly—in case someone else is in the rest room," Bolan said as the door above slid closed again. "I'm going to meet the devil."

Hammersmith pulled the silenced .22 back out and transferred the P-7 to her left hand.

Years of training and experience, but more importantly instinct, told Bolan what would happen even before he pushed open the door to the lab. The Executioner saw the eight-point cap of a uniformed Jablonec guard rise from behind the lab table closest to him. A face joined the hat, and then an arm and hand as the man continued to rise.

The hand held a stainless-steel revolver. The gun fell to the floor of the lab as four rounds from the Skorpion hammered into the guard's chest.

More men, some in uniforms, others wearing lab coats, rose from hiding around the lab. Regardless of what they wore, all held weapons.

In the split second it took for Bolan to swing the

Skorpion onto a mustached man in lab wear, he heard two soft *pffffts* come from behind him.

Then the sound of a body tumbling down the steps met his ears before he squeezed the trigger of the Skorpion again, splitting the mustache in two equal parts. The surprised researcher fell forward over the table that had hidden him, sending a stand of test tubes crashing to the floor.

Suddenly the small lab area became a battleground.

Bolan dived forward onto his belly as a hailstorm of lead exploded over his head and ricocheted off the brick walls. He rolled under the nearest table as the gunners corrected their aim, firing down into the floor where he'd been a split second earlier. Coming to a halt against a leg of one of the tables, he felt the cold metal against his back. Two feet away, he saw a pair of black shoes.

The Executioner pushed the muzzle of the Skorpion into the nearest ankle and pulled the trigger. A 3-round burst shattered bone.

A sharp yell of surprise was followed by a squeal of agony as the wounded man fell to the floor. The warrior's next burst caught the man under the chin, three rounds flying up into his brain and exiting the top of his head in a spray of blood.

Bolan rolled away from the table leg as bullets pounded down through the thin top, singing against the steel. One of the rounds skimmed across his thigh, ripping the material of his tux pants and singeing the skin. Climbing to his hands and knees, the Executioner scrambled forward, his gaze traveling across the floor as he moved away from the onslaught of fire that followed his every step.

He counted six sets of legs still standing.

Bolan came to the end of the table, stopped and fired two rounds upward through the barrier at a forty-five-degree angle. He heard a dull grunt, then saw a Jablonec cap fall to the concrete floor. A gray-templed head followed the hat as the man sank to the ground open-eyed next to it.

Five.

A whoosh of air blew past the Executioner as the door to the stairs suddenly opened. Beneath the table, he saw two black high-heeled pumps in nylon-clad feet appear in the doorway.

The distinct roar of a 9 mm H&K P-7 sounded from that direction, and a set of legs to the Executioner's right fell to the floor.

Four.

Bolan rolled out from under cover, firing up as his back met the concrete. A Jablonec guard holding a CZ-75 caught a trio of rounds in the chest.

Three.

The warrior turned onto his belly, facing the other direction and sending another triple-tap into the face of a lab tech wielding an Uzi. The man's neck snapped back as the subgun fell forward.

Rolling onto his back again, the Executioner saw the CZ-75 tumble from the uniformed man's dead hands. The guard slumped to his knees, then fell forward onto his face, his forehead striking the concrete with a hollow thump.

Two.

Scrabbling under the next table, Bolan saw the door to the stairs close again as Hammersmith dived away from an assault of automatic fire that came from one of the last men standing. The Executioner could see only a pair of brown shoes at the end of a cuffed pair of light gray slacks.

Slamming a fresh magazine into the Skorpion, he swung the weapon that way and ripped a burst of full-auto fire through the slacks into the calves.

A scream echoed against the walls of the lab. Two hands dropped to the wounds.

The Executioner added another burst into the hands and arms, then finished the researcher off with a lone round to the head as it dropped below table level. Rolling on, he emerged on the other side of the table, turned and rose to face the door.

A lone Jablonec guard stood dumbfounded near the center of the room, the Uzi in his hands weaving back and forth uncertainly.

Bolan trained the Skorpion on the man's chest as the stairway door opened once more. As he pulled the trigger, Jonine Hammersmith's black-gowned form stepped back into the lab.

The 9 mm Parabellum and 7.65 mm rounds teamed up to fill the last guard's chest with blood-soaked cavities.

Once more, silence fell over the lab.

The warrior turned quickly to Hammersmith. "Get back upstairs," he ordered. "Find out if anybody heard anything."

When the woman nodded and hurried back through the door, Bolan sprinted toward the only other door from the lab. The Skorpion led the way as he raced down a short hallway to an office area. A steel door was set in the far wall.

The Executioner's mind raced back to the building's layout. The steel door had to lead to the alley. But why didn't they just use *that* means of entry into the lab?

Because curious eyes might see someone entering. So did they keep it locked? He moved forward and twisted the knob.

It turned easily.

Well, maybe some of the guards and researchers *did* come and go that way. More likely, it served as an emergency exit should their rest-room door be discovered. Or there could be some other reason he didn't know about.

At the moment, it didn't matter. The important thing now was to ascertain whether the theatergoers upstairs had heard the gunfire. If they hadn't, he had an idea on how to cover the assault, at least temporarily, from Ryba.

Bolan spotted another door just behind the office desk and walked hurriedly forward. A supply closet. It had to be—he'd seen no other storage facilities on the grounds, and the researchers had to store their provisions somewhere.

The Executioner swung the door open and stepped inside. The closet was almost as large as the office, with shelves extending around the walls from floor to ceiling. His gaze flew across the stacked cans and boxes, then stopped on several large metal containers.

The gallon cans brought a smile to the Executioner's lips.

Footsteps were pounding down the steps by the time Bolan returned to the lab area. He dropped to one knee behind the nearest table, leveling the Skorpion at the door.

Hammersmith stepped back into the lab.

Bolan lowered the weapon, noting that a thin line of sweat ran down the woman's forehead. Other than that, she looked no different than if she'd just left the theater to powder her nose.

"Business as usual upstairs," the British agent said, closing the door behind her. "If the crowd heard anything at all, they thought it was part of the show."

Bolan nodded, dropping the Skorpion onto the table as he rose to his feet. "We still have a problem here."

"You Yanks have an expression I find quite useful at times," Hammersmith said. "'No shit.'" She walked forward, shaking her head. "We're going to have the devil's own time keeping this one from Ryba. Any ideas?"

Bolan nodded. "We torch the place."

"What! The people upstairs—"

"You'll get them out first."

Hammersmith frowned. "Then the question becomes, what happens to the chemicals in this place when the glass containers break during the fire? Anything superexplosive?"

Bolan shook his head. "They're creating disease, not bombs."

Hammersmith nodded, then stopped abruptly. "But

what's to prevent the biochemical agents from getting loose in the fire?''

''That shouldn't happen, either. Remember, one of the things they're experimenting with are ways to disperse this stuff. If it was easy, they wouldn't have to worry about it. Assuming that there *are* diseases already concocted here—'' He stopped suddenly, walked to the curtain against the wall and drew it open.

Just as he'd suspected, the curtain hid another of the test cubicles. But unlike the one in Plzeň, no animals or humans had been tethered to the floor. The concrete on the other side of the glass was clean, neat.

This chamber, if it had been used at all, hadn't been used for some time.

Bolan moved back to the British agent. ''I don't think they've gotten that far,'' he said. ''But even if they have, it'll be small amounts. It'll be destroyed by the fire.'' He reached out, rested his hands on the woman's shoulders and looked into her eyes. ''Listen carefully. Here's what we do.''

Five minutes later, Bolan and Hammersmith had rounded up all the spent brass casings from the floor. The bodies had been dragged to the door by the staircase leading up to the toilet stall and dropped back to the floor. Returning to the storage room, the warrior pulled two of the metal containers he had seen earlier from the shelf and looked down at the labels. They had been printed in English. Ethyl Alcohol.

The Executioner jogged back down the hall, through the lab, to the stairway. Hammersmith was already on the landing by the time he returned. Twisting one of the caps from the can, he looked up as he began pouring the alcohol up and down the steps. "Give me five minutes, then run through the theater screaming the truth."

"Fire?"

"Fire."

Hammersmith frowned. "The idea is to make it look like the stairs burned before anybody could get out, right?"

Bolan emptied the rest of the first can on the body of the man Hammersmith had dropped coming down the steps. He twisted the cap on the second. "Right."

"Tell me this, then. What was to keep them from going out the door to the alley you mentioned?"

The Executioner poured more ethyl alcohol onto the rotting wood. "Same thing. They were trapped between the two exits. I'll get that fire going just before I back out."

"Won't arson examiners be able to tell what really happened?"

The Executioner finished emptying the second can, saturating the wood. "Sure. We're buying time," he said, "hoping that when Ryba learns the truth it'll be too late anyway."

Hammersmith nodded, the long strands of her blond wig bobbing over her face. She wiped the hair away from her eyes with her hand and said, "Five minutes?"

"Five minutes."

Bolan heard her footsteps as she mounted the rest of the stairs. Hurrying back to the storage room, he grabbed more cans of ethyl alcohol and began soaking the rest of the lab. He poured more over the bodies, concentrating on the bullet wound areas.

Like Hammersmith had said, short of complete consumption by fire, there was no way to hide the truth from the discerning eye of a trained arson investigator or the pathologist during the autopsies that were sure to follow. And the Executioner had been around too many fires to think it likely that the bodies would burn totally, in spite of his efforts.

But that wouldn't be necessary. All they needed to do was hide the bullet holes and other evidence of attack for a little while. If he could just keep the truth from Ryba for a few more days, it wouldn't make any difference.

The Executioner returned to the storage area, found a hammer amid a pile of tools on one of the shelves and used the claw end to puncture a hole in one of the remaining cans of ethyl alcohol. The combustible liquid dripped from the shelf to the floor, forming a pool. He moved several more of the cans to the floor on top of it, then carried the punctured can with him, backing out of the storage area into the office and leaving a wet trail behind him.

He stopped at the door to the alley and pulled a book of matches from his pocket. The trail would act as a fuse, burning across the carpet to the explosive cans in the closet. The explosion would blow the flames into the office area.

Hurrying back through the lab to the steps, the Executioner struck a match and dropped it next to the steps. The ancient wood caught fire, the flames growing slowly as he hurried back to the office.

Bolan stopped, his back to the alley door, and struck another match. Above, he could hear the pounding of running footsteps. Hammersmith had done her job. The people upstairs would easily be out of the building before the flames reached that floor, and by then fire fighters would be on the scene anyway.

The warrior bent and dropped the match into the wet trail of alcohol that led to the storage area. He turned, grasped the knob of the door to the alley and opened the door.

The Executioner stopped in his tracks.

Before him, behind the door that should have led to the alley, and at one time had, he saw a solid brick wall.

JOSEPH RYBA SHIFTED uncomfortably in his seat at the Tyl Theater, Prague's oldest and most distinguished opera house. He shifted again as the score of Mozart's *Don Giovanni* filled his ears. He had tried valiantly to shut out the noise, but had been unable to do so as successfully as he had with the libretto.

Joseph Ryba hated Mozart and *Don Giovanni,* because he hated Germans and Italians, and damn near anyone else who wasn't a purebred Czech.

But tonight, most of all, he hated the fact that his wife had dragged him to this performance when he could have spent a quiet evening in Marja's apartment with her.

The thought brought a smile to Ryba's lips. Well, perhaps it would not have been all *that* quiet.

Ryba stared ahead, watching his wife out of the

corner of his eye. The woman fairly swooned with the music, her eyes half-closed. Ryba frowned. His wife looked in some strange way much like Marja after she'd climaxed, during that magical period of enchanted afterglow. Perhaps Mozart was his wife's way of having sex, Ryba thought, her way of achieving orgasm.

If so, more power to her. She had certainly held no interest in conventional sex during the past decade, and her preoccupation with Mozart had at least kept her out of his hair much of the time.

Ryba shifted again, intent on making the best of the rest of the opera. His thoughts drifted to Marja again, and in his mind's eye he began slowly undressing his lover. The soft white cotton blouse she had worn at the office that day came slipping over her even softer, whiter shoulders. The navy skirt rose over the tops of her stockings, exposing the bare skin of her thighs and garters.

Behind him, coming down the aisle, Ryba vaguely heard the footsteps.

In his mind's eye, Marja breathed deeply as she reached behind her, unfastening the hooks of her brassiere and letting her breasts fall free. She smiled at him, then slowly sank to her knees. Ryba felt his erection begin to grow.

Then hot breath in his ear ripped him from his fantasy. "Mr. Ryba, please come with me," the usher whispered. "There is an urgent message."

Ryba's head jerked up as the words jolted him back to reality. He felt a certain gratefulness overtake him at the interruption. Perhaps he could take care of whatever the problem was, then use it as an excuse to slip off from this damnable German opera.

The usher dropped to a squat in the aisle as a series of disgusted sighs came from the theater patrons directly behind him. Ryba turned to his wife, who gave him a look of far more disgust, then nodded.

"I will return as soon as possible...*if* it is possible," Ryba told the woman, feigning regret. He rose, straightened his jacket and suddenly remembered his erection. He felt his face redden.

How would it look for the minister of the interior to leave the Tyl with a hard-on jutting from his trousers? By morning the story would have made it all over Prague. Readjusting his jacket to cover himself, he stepped into the aisle.

Ryba felt himself shrink as he followed the usher to the lobby. He found the theater manager standing next to the two burly Deliverance Squad men he had brought along tonight as bodyguards. The manager held a cellular phone in one hand as his other gripped Ryba's.

"You had a call from a Mr. Schoevenec, Mr. Ryba," the manager said, smiling. "I am sorry to have bothered you, but he sounded urgent. You can reach him at this number if you choose. If not, please excuse me for disturbing you. And please...use my office." He pointed toward a door off the lobby.

The Deliverance Squad men flanked Ryba as he crossed the lobby to the office. One of them—Ryba couldn't remember his name, as they both looked like blocky bookends to him—opened the door and stuck his head inside. Nodding the room's safety, he held the door for Ryba, then stepped back into the lobby.

Ryba dialed Schoevenec's office, let it ring, then hung up. He tried the man's home and got an answer.

"What did you want?" he asked Schoevenec. "Have you learned the identity of the second agent?"

There was a long pause on the other end of the phone. "No. But Skrdla has returned. I thought you would want to know."

Ryba felt a mixture of emotions flood his system. Skrdla was a strange man, but he was good, the best the new Czech Republic had to offer, and perhaps the best at what he did in the world. If the job could be done, Skrdla was the man who could get it done. That knowledge excited him.

But Joseph Ryba also felt anger run in his veins. Schoevenec's own excitement was all too evident in his voice, which meant the director of state security was thrilled that he could now pass his assignment on to someone else, and rid himself of Ryba.

That attitude didn't fit into the program of loyalty that Ryba would soon be instituting.

"I will be at my office in fifteen minutes," Ryba said into the phone.

"I will send Skrdla to meet you."

"I want you there, too."

Another long pause was followed by a soft sigh. "I will see you then," Schoevenec said and hung up.

Ryba left the phone on the desk in the office and stepped back out to the lobby. Addressing the Deliverance Squad man who had opened the door, he said,

"I must leave. Please see that Mrs. Ryba returns home safely."

The man bowed slightly, then turned to stand at the door leading to the theater.

Ryba nodded toward the front door. "Come," he told the other burly bodyguard.

Ten minutes later, Ryba sat behind his desk contemplating the fate of the man who now headed the Czech police. Schoevenec had proved incompetent. He was a Slav, another holdover from the Communist system. He would be relieved of his command as soon as Ryba took power.

A smile crossed his face as he turned toward the coffeemaker behind him. Why wait? he thought. Why not relieve the Slav of his command immediately? The revived Biopreparat project wasn't yet complete, but already he had some launch sites supplied with a strain of anthrax that would resist all drugs the Western world presently had. With the sites that were ready in Europe, he could threaten everything between the Baltic and Adriatic seas. That same threat would stretch east and west from Stuttgart to Kiev.

And with the site hidden in the United States, he could put a muzzle on the World Police Dog, holding them at bay indefinitely.

Yes, Ryba thought, he didn't want to, but if worse came to worst, he could act immediately.

Ryba rose and opened the cabinet door above the coffeemaker, pulling down a large tin box. He found the paper filters next to the can and fitted one into the machine.

Opening the can, Ryba stuck a spoon inside and

shoveled out several mounds of the leafy substance he found inside. The American-made appliance had been designed to make coffee, but he had found it worked equally well with tea. He returned the can to the shelf, then pulled down a small cardboard box. Several spoonfuls of the substance inside went on top of the tea.

Placing the glass carafe on the burner, Ryba flipped the switch, sat down in his chair and spun back to his desk as he heard the door in the outer office open. A moment later, the bookend bodyguard stuck his head in. "They are here," he announced.

"Send them in."

Ryba sat back as the tea began to brew. Schoevenec entered the office first, wearing a dark blue suit and an expression of tired disgust. He took a seat in front of Ryba's desk.

The tall hulking figure seemed to come from nowhere, filling the doorway and blocking the light from the outer office.

Heavy eyebrows fell over Skrdla's eyes. The rest of his face seemed devoid of any distinguishing features. He wore a dark gray suit, scuffed black shoes, and held a battered gray fedora in thick fingers.

Ryba's eyes fell from the face to a series of bumps just below the collar of the man's shirt. He had noticed the bumps before, wondering what they were. Strange.

The Czech minister of the interior's mind flashed over what he knew about the man who had just returned from assignment. There was documentation that Skrdla had grown up in a Communist orphanage

in the Moravian area of the country. He had entered
the Czechoslovakian army upon reaching the proper
age, where he had first served with a secret regiment
sent to help the Soviets in Afghanistan.

Skrdla had grown famous within the ranks for his
ability to use the same tactics as the Afghan opposi-
tion. In spite of his size and imposing appearance, he
possessed an uncanny ability to blend into any sur-
roundings in which he found himself. Many an Afghan freedom fighter, thinking the group was well
concealed in the mountains, had gone to sleep at night
only to awaken the next morning and find the throats
of the men on each side of him slit.

Skrdla had also great talents in interrogation, showing an extraordinary ability to keep his victims alive
under the most strenuous torture. When it came to
tracking, he could follow the most battle-proved enemy through the hardest of terrain. He was like a hungry lion on the trail of a wildebeest—he never let up
once the scent of blood filled his nostrils.

Ryba sat back in his chair and clasped his hands
behind his head as Skrdla took the seat next to
Schoevenec. He knew the man had gone from the
armed service into the clandestine service, and like
Ryba himself, been one of the survivors when communism fell in Czechoslovakia.

Talent and brains. They were the key to survival.
And although his talent lay in a different area than
Skrdla's, he felt a certain kinship with the man.

Ryba stood, shook Schoevenec's hand, then looked
to the hulking figure who still stood by the door.
''Gentlemen, would you care for some tea? I have just

brewed it.'' He added the last sentence to ensure that a bureaucrat like Schoevenec would accept the offer.

''Yes,'' Schoevenec said.

Skrdla shook his head, his face emotionless.

The Czech minister turned, poured tea into two plastic cups and handed one to Schoevenec. He sat back down in his chair and rested his cup on the desk.

''What do you have in mind?'' Ryba asked.

Schoevenec crossed his legs and rested his teacup on his knee, steadying it with his hand. ''To turn the investigation over to Mr. Skrdla…as was your wish from the beginning.'' He glanced down at the tea, a slight frown marring his face for less than a second.

Ryba refused to let the smile in his heart break onto his face. The big-headed Slav suspected something. Good. It would test his theory that communism had instilled a new order of importance in the bureaucrats it had bred. Had conformity really taken a higher place on the scale than survival? He would see.

''Have you briefed Skrdla on what has been done so far?'' Ryba asked offhandedly.

Schoevenec shifted uncomfortably in his seat.

Ryba's attitude changed. ''If so, the briefing should not have taken long,'' he said sarcastically. ''We will turn this problem over to Skrdla, Mr. Schoevenec, and you can return to your other important duties. I will have no more need of your services in this matter after this evening.'' Finally allowing himself to smile, he added, ''Please, drink your tea.''

Ryba raised his own cup in salute, then touched the outer edge to his lips as he watched Schoevenec drink.

A moment later, the cup fell from the Slav's hand,

hit his knee, then bounced to the floor, spilling the remainder of the tea. Schoevenec's hands shot to his throat, then fell away in wild abandon as the poison rushed through his bloodstream.

Eyes wide in shock, he slumped in his chair.

His face devoid of any emotion other than curiosity, Skrdla turned slightly, leaned toward Schoevenec's open mouth and sniffed. His gaze traveled to the cup on the floor, then he looked up past Ryba to the cabinet. "Sodium fluoride?" he asked softly.

Ryba shrugged. "If that is what rat poison contains."

A thin smile flashed onto Skrdla's face, then vanished as quickly as it had come. "It does."

The Czech minister was impressed. "How did you know so quickly?"

"It is my business to know such things," Skrdla droned in his monotone voice. "The immediate symptoms, and the fact that the plastic cup from which he drank was not affected, but if you will look behind you—" Ryba followed the suggestion "—you will see that the glass carafe is about to—"

The glass suddenly cracked and sent sodium-fluoride-spiked tea spilling down over the coffeemaker.

"—break," Skrdla finished. He stood, walked to the window and opened it. "It is a good way to kill a man." He stuck his head out the opening and took a deep breath. "But I suggest you let me school you in the proper administration of such chemical agents before you attempt to do something like this again." He paused, moved to another window and opened it.

"You see, Mr. Ryba, the fumes created by the brewing process might well have killed you and me, as well."

Ryba felt a chill come over him. Yes, he had been playing in someone else's ballpark.

The minister watched silently as the mysterious man calmly opened the rest of the windows along the wall. He had found a man who was at home in that ballpark, and he intended to use that man to his fullest extent.

CHAPTER SEVEN

Above Turkey

The C-17's engines hummed peacefully, lulling the men of Phoenix Force into a much-needed doze in the iron bunks bolted to the floor of the cargo area. As Jack Grimaldi guided the aircraft south toward Turkey, only Gary Manning didn't seem tired.

"Istanbul was Constantinople," he sang softly under his breath. "Now it's Istanbul, not Constantinople, it was Istanbul, now it's—"

David McCarter opened one eye. "I think I can speak for the rest of the team when I say that if you don't cease singing immediately, if singing it is, we'll have no choice but to shoot you."

Katz, James and Encizo nodded.

Manning chuckled. "Sorry, guys. But don't you remember that song? It was catchy."

"It was when it was sung by someone who could carry a tune," James grumbled.

"It doesn't hurt to know the right lyrics, either," Encizo added.

"Okay, okay, okay," Manning said. "I think I got the message."

Grimaldi's voice came back from the cabin. "Wake up, guys," the pilot said. "You got ninety seconds."

The men of Phoenix Force had already donned their jump gear, and now pulled their tired limbs to standing positions and moved toward the door. Manning led the way.

The next stop was a research lab located in Istanbul. It had been on the list that Bolan and Hammersmith had come up with in Plzeň. The "gate to the East" for centuries, Istanbul also seemed like an obvious choice as a launch site for the dangerous diseases that Ryba was cooking up. That meant the middle step in the plan—manufacturing the deadly plagues—might be located nearby as well.

It was one of the reasons that Katz had decided to leave the closer sites on the list for later.

Manning stopped at the door, waiting further instruction from Grimaldi. The other reason they had left the Czech Republic was that too many suspicious things were happening at the Biopreparat labs in that area. Ryba was no fool, and even a fool would put two and two together if enough "twos" came along.

The big Canadian pulled the oxygen mask over his face, took a deep breath and slid open the door. The cool air rushed in. He looked behind him to Katz.

The Phoenix Force leader nodded behind his own mask.

Manning jumped, plummeting earthward, taking pleasure as he always did in the feeling of flight. The cool air and adrenaline that always accompanied a free-fall cleared his mind and senses.

Looking below, the explosives expert saw the dark

spot he knew to be Istanbul. To its sides, the waters of both the Black Sea and the Sea of Marmara were visible. Istanbul lay on the Bosporus Strait, separating Europe and Asia, and was truly one of the crossroads of the world.

Manning looked up and saw the rest of Phoenix Force fanning out across the sky as Grimaldi flew on. As Katz and the others shrank to become little more than specks, the big Canadian pulled his rip cord.

The chute opened, jerking him momentarily upward. Descending slower now, Manning checked his compass, then glided toward the prearranged coordinates where he knew he'd find a small wooded area just off the highway.

Katz had contacted Stony Man Farm during their flight, learning that Bolan and Hammersmith had located another of the research labs hidden below some theater in Prague. The last contact Price had had with Striker, they'd been prepared to infiltrate the place and sabotage. With the site Bolan and Hammersmith had already hit, and the one Phoenix Force had just ''robbed,'' that made three of the labs that had fallen victim to strange circumstances during the past twenty-four hours.

The coincidences were piling up, so Phoenix Force was taking no chances. They were entering Turkey separately, and they'd take a totally different approach to slowing things down at the lab in Istanbul.

In fact, Manning thought as he soared through the sky, they didn't even plan to get near the lab.

The Canadian saw the woods ahead and adjusted the lines, falling faster now as the trees flew closer.

The wind was strong, and he held tightly, ready to pull loose and drop to the ground at the last second if necessary to avoid crashing headlong into one of the sturdy trunks.

His grip and the wind both held, and the explosives expert's boots hit the ground running, ten feet from the edge of the woods. Thirty seconds later, he had hauled in his chute and stepped into the cover of the trees.

Manning hid the chute and unzipped his jumpsuit to reveal a pair of khaki cargo jeans and matching bush jacket. With a last check of the weapons hidden beneath his jacket, he stepped back out of the woods and walked swiftly toward the highway.

The fourth car that passed answered his thumb, and the big Canadian slid into the back seat of a Nissan Maxima bearing Belgian plates. The car was driven by a man, contained a toddler on his mother's lap in the front seat, and a girl of perhaps nineteen in the back.

"Thanks," Manning said to the driver as he turned from the wheel. "English?"

"*Oui,*" the man said, then laughed. "I mean, yes." He pulled away and started toward Istanbul.

Manning glanced at the girl next to him. Jet black hair fell in thick ringlets over her shoulders as her dark brown eyes flashed a seductive smile his way. She uncrossed her legs, let her short leather skirt creep up her thighs, stared into the Canadian's eyes and smiled.

He returned the smile instinctively, then glanced up in time to catch the father's concerned frown in the rearview mirror. With no little effort, he tore his eyes from the girl and faced the front. He had more important things to think about right now, and by the looks of things, Papa had enough problems with his little girl without one of Stony Man's finest adding to them.

The big Canadian chatted with the father as they drove, putting out a story about his own car breaking down near the Bulgarian border and being forced to hitch on to Istanbul for an important business meeting. He learned that the family was on holiday.

A few miles later, they topped a crest in the road, and the ancient city that had at various times in history belonged to the Romans, the Byzantines, the Ottomans and the Turks appeared. Atop the tallest hill on the skyline, Manning saw the spiraled towers of the Suleymaniye Mosque. As they entered the city, the strange blend of East and West that made up Istanbul entered the vehicle in sight, sound and scent.

"Where would you like us to drop you?" the Belgian driver asked.

Manning sat forward, speaking over the seat. "Do you know the Istanbul Hilton?"

"Ah, yes," the man replied. "Perhaps the finest Hilton in the world."

"Is it out of your way?"

"No. We must pass right by it."

"There, then." Manning sat back again. The Maxima left the highway and began navigating a combination of modern thoroughfares and narrow streets, passing through some areas of Istanbul that appeared no different than those found in busy American cities.

Other sections of town looked to Manning as if Aladdin might fly past any moment on a magic carpet.

When they pulled up in front of the Hilton, Manning got out, then turned back to speak through the window. "Thanks," he told the driver, then glanced one last time at the girl in the back seat and winked.

Manning entered the lobby. A clerk dressed in a blue European-cut suit looked up from a stack of papers as he stopped in front of the desk. "Mr. Samuel Wilenzick," the big Canadian said. "I'm supposed to meet him."

The clerk consulted a register book beneath the desk, then lifted the phone. He spoke quietly into the receiver, then hung up and said, "Mr. Wilenzick asked that you come up. Suite 15. Take the second elevator." His gaze dropped back to the papers.

Manning crossed the lobby to the elevators, studying the walls and furnishings as he walked. The decor, like the city of Istanbul itself, seemed an interesting blend of modern and ancient. The carpet on which he walked was as modern as you got, a plush stain-resistant beige that might survive as many as three or four years on the heavily traveled route from desk to elevator. But the furniture—love seats, couches, end tables and lamps—all appeared to have come from the treasures in the cave of Ali Baba's forty thieves.

A moment later, Manning was knocking at the door of suite 15. He saw the light in the peephole disappear momentarily, then the lock was thrown back and the door opened.

The big Canadian stepped past Calvin James to find that the rest of Phoenix Force had already assembled.

Most had changed into battle fatigues and gun belts and sat waiting to hide them with raincoats stacked haphazardly on the couch against the wall.

Manning began to change. "You got the name yet?" he asked Katz, who sat in the desk chair next to the phone.

"The name, yes," the Israeli replied. "We are waiting for Aaron to come up with more information." Katz sighed. He drew his CZ-75, gripped it with his prosthetic hand, and pulled the slide to check the chamber. "I want this to go down as far away from the lab itself as possible."

The phone rang. Katz lifted the receiver and pressed it to his ear, nodded to the other men of Phoenix Force, then said, "Yes, Hunt?"

The Israeli lifted a pen from the desk and scribbled on a piece of paper. "Kilyos? You have an address?"

Manning and the others pulled the raincoats over their shoulders, hiding their weapons, as Katz stood and said, "Hunt has located his house. Let's go."

Ozark, Missouri

THE GREEN HILLS and valleys of southern Missouri unrolled beneath the Beechcraft Baron as Carl Lyons watched through the windshield. He glanced to his side.

Behind the control column, wearing his trademark mirrored aviator glasses and baseball cap, Charlie Mott grinned. Stony Man Farm's number-two pilot guided the plane into its final descent toward Ozark, Missouri.

Lyons unhooked the radio mike from the clip on the panel in front of him, keyed it with his thumb and spoke. "Justice 941 to Christian County Sheriff's Department. Come in Christian County." He released the button.

A harsh, snappy voice came back over the airwaves. "You got Sheriff Coats his own self here, 941. I'm waitin' down to the runway. Come on down."

"We'll be there in a second, Sheriff," Lyons said. He released the button and shook his head.

Most of the small-town peace officers Lyons had known over the years disproved the dim-witted, tobacco-spitting, "good ol' boy" stereotype encouraged by movies and television. Most were intelligent, professional, dedicated and on a par with their big-city counterparts.

But there were exceptions to every rule, and Carl Lyons's gut instinct—not to mention the briefing from Huntington Wethers of the Stony Man computer team concerning the sheriff—told him he was about to deal with one of those exceptions.

Blancanales, in the seat directly behind the Able Team leader, voiced Lyons's thoughts for him. "Coats, right? Sheriff Coats? You suppose his name is something like Billy Bob?"

"My guess is Bubba," Schwarz cut in. "Bubba Bob."

"Or Cooter," Blancanales added.

"Or Scooter."

"Okay, okay," Lyons said as the wheels hit the grass runway. "Let's show a little respect for the office, if nothing else.'' He turned and threw an arm over the back of his seat.

All three men of Able Team were dressed similarly. They wore neatly cut conservative gray suits, white button-down-collar shirts, and black wraparound sunglasses. The front breast pockets of their jackets bulged with black leather credential cases, compliments of Hal Brognola. The credentials ID'd them as agents of the Justice Department.

The Able Team leader turned back to the front. They had injected Francis Hunyadi with enough Valium to ensure that the man slept the rest of the night, then left him in a motel room back in Virginia. He'd wake up wondering at first if it had all been just a bad dream.

But as soon as he realized what had really happened, Hunyadi would play an important role by providing valuable disinformation to Joseph Ryba. South Africa was involved in their own Biopreparat program. With any luck, the boys from Pretoria would be blamed for any other suspicions that Ryba had concerning the coincidences going on at the labs in Europe.

The Beechcraft's wheels hit the grass landing strip and Mott slowed the plane to a crawl, turning toward a row of small sheet-metal hangars. Parked in front of the structures, Lyons saw a brown-and-white sedan with "Sheriff" printed on the door.

Standing next to the car, a tall spindly man with wild wavy hair and black horn-rimmed glasses leaned against the open door. He held a radio mike in one hand, the corkscrewed cord stretching back through the window into the vehicle.

Mott chuckled as he pulled the plane to a halt. "Welcome to Hootersville, gentlemen," he said. "Next stop, Mayberry RFD."

Lyons opened the door, dropped to the ground and led Schwarz and Blancanales to the car, reaching into his pocket for his credentials as he walked. He stopped in front of the sheriff and flashed them up to the man's face. "Sheriff, I'm Special Agent Marsh. These men are Special Agents Gilmour and Aguilar. Thanks for meeting us."

"Sheriff Coats," the skinny man replied. "But everybody round these parts just calls me Willy Dean."

Lyons saw Schwarz and Blancanales glance at each other, deadpan.

Coats shook Lyons's hand with a callused paw that felt as if it were more used to holding a plow than a gun. He wore a light blue uniform, black Sam Browne belt, burgundy cowboy boots with scuffed moccasin toes and what appeared to be a fifty-five gallon cowboy hat.

Lyons cleared his throat. "Sheriff Coats—"

Coats pushed himself off the side of the car, standing swaybacked in the sun. "Willy Dean, damn it."

"Willy Dean, I understand you have some information on the location we're interested in."

"Damn right. Had ol' Frank—that's my chief deputy, you understand—start puttin' a file together back at the office soon as that fella from Washington called. It's on the new computer." He beamed with pride. "Hop in."

Lyons suppressed a frown. All they needed was the exact location of the site Hunyadi had told them about, and they didn't need a computer to tell them that. But they *did* need to keep the charade going. It was vital that when word got back to Joseph Ryba that the storage site had been discovered, he believed that it had been the chance strike of local law enforcement rather than part of an organized international operation.

Which meant Lyons, Schwarz and Blancanales would have to humor Willy Dean Coats. At least to a certain extent.

"Only saw this feller once," Coats said, sliding behind the wheel of his car as Lyons got in the front and the other two Able Team warriors took the back. "He was over to the Goodyear store, gettin' a set of white walls for his car from Ace Brody. But I could hear him. And your man in Washington was right—foreigner. He sure talks funny."

Lyons nodded as the sheriff cut across the landing strip to the road and turned toward town. Hunyadi had known only that the storage site was at an isolated farmhouse in the northern part of Christian County. But the Hungarian had known one other fact that had proved vital.

The man in charge was Franz Smrka, a native of Brno, Czechoslovakia.

Brognola had made contact with the sheriff's department, sure that the comings and goings of a man with a foreign accent would have drawn attention in the small community. He hadn't been wrong.

The drive into Ozark took less than five minutes,

and Lyons, Schwarz and Blancanales found themselves following the sheriff up four floors of the winding steps inside an ancient WPA courthouse. Coats led the way into a small reception area.

An immensely obese woman with dyed hair the color of burned coal sat perched on a stool behind the counter. She stared blankly at the bare wall.

"Angeline, where's Frank?" Coats demanded, tapping the plastic top.

Angeline shrugged, barely moving her body.

Coats led them into an even smaller room and cautiously took a seat in a chair in front of a computer.

"Okeydoke," he said as the men of Able Team crowded into the office. "Don't understand these things real good myself, but we'll see…" He reached out tentatively and pushed the On button.

Tolerance for incompetency—in fact patience of any sort—had never come naturally to Carl Lyons, and he felt the hair on the back of his neck rise as he listened to Coats drum his fingers against the desk as the computer warmed up. A yellow menu finally appeared on the screen.

Coats sat back in his chair and crossed his arms behind his head. "Frank, that's my chief deputy—but I already tol' you that—he runs this thing usually. And damn it all if I can remember exactly what he told me to do next."

Schwarz leaned over the sheriff's shoulder, pushed Enter, then called up the file list for the hard drive.

"Well…*yeah,*" Coats said. The black glasses slid down his nose as he squinted at the monitor. His lips moved silently as he read down the list.

Finally, Coats tapped several keys and a document entitled "Cabin" appeared. The sheriff cackled excitedly at his success, then frowned again as he studied the monitor. "Well...hell," he mumbled under his breath. "This must be it," he said. "Place is sort of like a cabin out there."

Schwarz stepped forward, "Sheriff," he said, "'Cabin' is one of the training programs that comes with the computer you're using. Maybe we could—"

Coats held up a hand. "Just a minute there, fella. You're breakin' my chain of thought."

Schwarz looked at Blancanales, who raised his eyebrows.

The sheriff's lips moved again as he began to read the document designed to teach students to write business letters. Finally he said, "This must be some other case Frank's working on."

Lyons had had enough. As Coats stared at the screen, he hooked his foot under the cord linking the computer to the electrical plug and jerked it from the wall.

The screen went blank. The disk drive ground to a halt.

"Now what in tarnation?" Coats said.

Schwarz stepped in quickly. "Can't trust this modern technology," he said, shaking his head. "Breaks down too easy."

Lyons maneuvered between him and the sheriff. "Let's forget the computer, Willy Dean," he said. "We're all just simple peace officers. What do you say we take a little ride out to this place and look it over for ourselves. The old-fashioned way.''

Coats stood up. "Good enough for me.''

Prague, Czech Republic

THE EXECUTIONER WASTED no time staring at the brick wall.

Pivoting on the balls of his feet, he sprinted toward the door leading to the hallway as the liquid fuse of ethyl alcohol burned toward the fire bomb waiting in the closet.

He was halfway through the opening when the office erupted in flame.

The concussion blew the warrior into the air, hurling him down the hall toward the lab. Slamming into a wall, he fell to his side, rolled onto his belly, then scrambled back to his feet.

The heat of a thousand branding irons blazed across his back as the Executioner raced into the lab. Flames leapt from his tuxedo jacket as smoke filled his nostrils. Ripping the smoking coat from his shoulders, he ran on.

Waist-high fire jumped up the wooden steps by the time Bolan reached the stairs. The flames along the wall of the stairwell shot to the ceiling. Angry black smoke billowed from the rotten wood steps into the lab, and the heat from the small area blew back into the Executioner's face.

Bolan dropped to one knee, coughing, as he tore the lab coat from one of the bodies on the floor. He had only minutes before the flames engulfed him, perhaps seconds before the smoke destroyed his lungs, and the only way out was blocked by a wall of fire.

Rising to a squat, the Executioner duck-walked to a metal sink along the wall, twisted the knob and stuffed the coat under the spout assembly.

Fire shot suddenly into the lab from the hallway as a secondary explosion went up from the storage closet. Bolan ducked a tidal wave of flame as he waited for the lab coat to soak.

He finally ripped the drenched lab coat from the sink and hurried back to the steps. The flames were as high as his face as he threw the lab coat over his head, took a deep breath and started to run.

He had reached the landing before the pain of the fire had time to travel through his central nervous system to his brain. But when it hit, it was a three-hundred pound defensive tackle blindsiding a running back, slamming him into the wall with an intensity he had never before felt. Still, he forced himself up the second flight of steps, his legs leaden as red and yellow flames danced on his trousers.

Bolan dived from the fiery steps against the sliding door to the men's room. The wallboard panel split into pieces as he crashed through to the floor. His vision blurred. He hit the cold tile, cast the fiery coat aside and began to roll.

As if from far away, he heard the choking sound that escaped his lips, then an icy spray covered his face, arms and legs. He rolled to his back, the tile feeling like ice. As his vision cleared, he looked up to see Jonnie Hammersmith standing over him, a fire extinguisher in her hands.

The British woman shot a final burst from the extinguisher at the Executioner's feet, then let the tank fall to the floor and dropped to her knees. Bolan watched as her eyes traveled intently up and down his body, determining his condition. Seemingly satisfied that he would live, she looped an arm around his neck and struggled to help him to his feet.

"Did the others get out?" Bolan asked.

Hammersmith nodded. A tear rolled down her face as she looked up into his eyes. "Can you walk?"

"I'd better be able to *run*," he said, and started toward the door. "I don't care to explain all this to the cops."

Hammersmith walked next to him, holding his arm. They hurried out of the men's room, through the lobby and out the front door into the crowd of excited people. The Executioner heard several gasps as they came down the front steps of the building.

All of the other theater patrons had escaped unharmed, thanks to Hammersmith's warning. His singed clothes and body were the rarity. "Let's get out of here," Bolan said. "Nobody else is hurt. I'm attracting too much attention."

"You need attention. Medical attention. There should be ambulances—"

"No," Bolan said forcefully. "Get me out of here."

"But—"

The Executioner pushed his way past the astounded faces in the throng of people outside the theater as the first of three fire trucks screeched to a halt on the street. He and Hammersmith walked calmly through the parting crowd as men in fire helmets leapt from the vehicles carrying hoses and other equipment.

An ambulance was arriving as they crossed the street toward the alley. Bolan heard someone scream and turned back.

A young man pointed at him as a Czech police car braked to a halt. Two uniformed officers exited the vehicle, staring at Bolan and Hammersmith. The one who had driven raised a whistle to his lips and blew.

But by the time the shrill sound reached the Executioner's ears, he and Hammersmith were halfway down the alley between the dress shop and hardware store.

CHAPTER EIGHT

Istanbul, Turkey

"The man we have to neutralize is Boris Stavropek," Yakov Katzenelenbogen said from his seat between Manning and Encizo in the back of the rented Plymouth. "And he was one of the top researchers in the old Soviet Biopreparat program."

"He's running the show here, right?" Calvin James asked from the front seat.

"He's the man in charge of the local human sacrifices in the test chamber in Plzeň." Katz nodded.

"That's enough for me," David McCarter said from behind the wheel.

Next to him, Katz saw Manning and Encizo nod silently.

McCarter pulled out of the car-rental parking lot and onto the streets of Istanbul. "How do you suppose he got hooked up with Ryba?"

Katz shrugged. "Wethers didn't go looking for the details. But I expect that after the fall of the Soviet Union, he found himself looking for a job."

"And found Ryba," Encizo concluded. "Or Ryba found him."

"Blokes like that do have a way of finding each other," McCarter agreed. "I'd bet the queen's bodice he's not the only former Russkie on Ryba's payroll." He pulled onto a busy four-lane and the Plymouth mingled in with the traffic.

Katz watched through the windows as they passed in and out of the lanes, between vintage cars from the golden era of American automobiles. Nearly every vehicle sported tail fins, or a chrome-plated grille that looked like the gaping teeth of a great white shark. Katz remembered reading somewhere that Istanbul was one of the world's premier centers for automobile collecting.

McCarter drove on. The Stony Man warriors fell silent as the architectural time line of Istanbul's eras paraded past. Modern buildings of concrete and steel stood next to Byzantine ruins. Here and there, a wooden structure from the Ottoman epoch had weathered the hardships of the centuries.

The Plymouth drove through a middle-income residential area with carefully tended flower beds and gardens. The houses couldn't have been more than ten years old, but Katz saw that the yards had been decorated with ancient Roman-cut stones and bricks.

Traffic thinned as they left the city proper, and McCarter guided them along a highway paralleling the sea. Soft white waves broke against the coastline. Sea gulls glided overhead. Everything about the Turkish coastline seemed to imply tranquillity, a tranquillity the men from Stony Man Farm knew they were about to disrupt.

Manning finally broke the silence. "You decided on a battle plan yet, Katz?"

The Israeli shook his head. "We'll have to play it by ear."

"I brought plenty of firecrackers," Manning said, tapping his raincoat.

The Phoenix Force leader shook his head. "It has to look like an accident."

The occupants of the car lapsed back into silence as they neared the resort village of Kilyos. Newly constructed seaside hotels and condominiums began to pop up with increasing frequency. The heads of men, women and children bobbed in the incoming waves. Umbrellas, chairs and towels dotted the beach in a multitude of colors.

Katz sat back against the seat as he watched a man in a horse-drawn wagon stop next to a hotel and begin selling soda pop and other refreshments. He knew that Phoenix Force—and Able Team and Mack Bolan, for that matter—were beginning to press their luck. How many "coincidences" would it take before Joseph Ryba twigged to the fact that somebody was onto him? Not many more. They were pushing it to the hilt already.

So what was the answer? Katz wondered. The answer was that there wasn't a good answer. They couldn't just sit back and wait, doing nothing, while Kurtzman continued to try to break codes that might never get broken. So the next best thing was to change their plan of attack, continue to slow down the Biopreparat research.

But do it in a different way.

"How about here?" McCarter asked. He nodded toward a small gas station at the first intersection in the village. Next to the station was a coin-operated car wash. "Stavropek will have to come this way."

Katz nodded. "He'll be in a '64 white Chevrolet Corvette convertible. It appears he's caught the car-collecting fever along with the natives."

"How'd the computer bugs get that?" Encizo asked in amazement. "The car info?"

Katz shrugged. "Turkey is bound to have something along the lines of a Department of Motor Vehicles," he said. "I imagine our computer people hooked into it."

McCarter pulled into the station and circled into one of the car-wash stalls, pointing the Plymouth back toward the road.

"Let's make it look good in case somebody's watching," Katz said.

Manning got out, dropped a coin into the machine, then pulled the wand out and began to spray the car with water.

McCarter tapped the windshield to get the big Canadian's attention. He pointed to a spot on the glass and grinned.

Manning raised his hand, extending his middle finger.

Katz chuckled. There was always tension before a mission. A little good-natured humor was often the best way to deal with it.

Five minutes later, the Plymouth sparkled in cleanliness. McCarter pulled out of the stall, and Manning began to dry the vehicle with paper towels.

Katz kept one eye on his watch, the other on the intersection. Unless Stavropek had stayed late at the lab, or been detained, he should arrive at the intersection soon.

The car was almost dry when the Corvette pulled up to the corner, its left-turn signal blinking. The top was down, and Katz could see a heavy man with thinning hair and a drooping set of jowls.

Manning dropped the paper towels into a trash can and hurried back into the car. McCarter pulled out and cut across the lot, pulling in behind a panel truck as the Corvette made the turn.

"Keep the truck between us and him," Katz said. "No sense taking a chance on him spotting us."

The Corvette led them along a winding road that left the waterfront, entered a commercial area, then returned to the sea farther down the beach.

Stavropek hit his turn signal again, then pulled into one of the crowded parking lots and stopped. McCarter drove past, circling into another lot before pointing the Plymouth back toward the Russian.

Katz watched Stavropek roll the top back over his car, lock the door and disappear into the closest building. He had considered simply running the Russian researcher off the road, but there had been too many innocents around. Besides, there was no way to make sure a wreck took the man out for good.

So, how were they going to deal with Boris Stavropek? For all they knew, the man might well go into his apartment and not come back out until morning. Katz glanced out at the sea, and a plan suddenly hit him. It would take time, but not as much time as waiting until morning. And it would virtually assure that when Ryba got the news of Stavropek's death, he would believe it to be an accident.

"So," Calvin James said, "any ideas?"

Katz turned to the former Navy Seal. "Sometimes we overlook the obvious, gentlemen. It's right there in front of you, yet you can't see it."

"As in 'Can't see the forest for the trees'?" McCarter asked.

Katz turned back to the incoming tide. "Precisely," he said. "But this time, it was the sea I couldn't see for the water."

Ozark, Missouri

LYONS'S PATIENCE had been stretched to the limit. He turned toward the window of the patrol car, away from Sheriff Coats, as the man raised a foam coffee cup to his lips and spit a sharp stream of chewing tobacco into the receptacle.

The car continued slowly up Main Street toward the north edge of Ozark. Coats began to hum under his breath, and a trickle of brown juice ran down his chin onto his shirt.

Lyons, Schwarz and Blancanales had tried to ditch the man on the way out of the courthouse by asking for directions and telling the sheriff they knew he had other work to do.

It hadn't worked. It was an election year in Christian County, and Willy Dean Coats might not have known a .38 Special from a writ of habeas corpus, but he could smell free publicity when it wafted his way. He had stuck to the men of Able Team like glue on the sole of a combat boot.

The squad car passed a park and picnic area before rounding a curve in the road and creeping up the access ramp to the highway leading north. "What did you fellers say the search warrant was for?" Coats asked. "Drugs?"

"Right," Lyons lied.

Coats looked at him blankly. He continued to hum as they drove on.

A green-and-white sign announcing the south edge of Springfield appeared eight miles later. Coats changed lanes, pulled off, then followed another sign that promised they would soon be in Nixa.

The men of Able Team rode silently as the sheriff drove them through the southern outskirts of Springfield. As they reached another rural area, Coats asked, "You ol' boys bring me a copy of that warrant?"

Lyons saw Schwarz and Blancanales glance at each other in the back seat. Not knowing they'd be facing Missouri's answer to Barney Fife, the Able Team leader's decision to use the "drug search" story had come on the spur of the moment. If they'd concocted it earlier, Brognola could have provided them a warrant, and enough supporting paperwork to convince Willy Dean Coats that they were special agents from the planet Jupiter, if necessary.

But now it was too late. They'd have to come up with something on their own.

Schwarz leaned forward and put a hand on the seat between Coats and Lyons. "You know, Willy Dean," he said, "I just realized I left your copy of the warrant back on the plane. We'll get it when the pilot comes back for us.''

Coats seemed satisfied. ''No problem,'' he said as he spit more brown tobacco juice into the cup.

The small city of Nixa appeared ahead on the two-lane highway. They passed a variety of liquor stores, service stations, curio stores selling crafts of the Ozarks, and other small businesses. Coats waved at every car they met.

Most of the drivers waved back.

Coats grinned from ear to ear. Turning to Lyons again, he said simply, ''Election year, you know.''

Lyons nodded. ''Yeah, you told us.''

Passing through Nixa, they entered the countryside again and drove by small farms and pastureland with a maddening slowness. Barbed-wire fence lined the roadway, waving up and down the gentle slope of the hills.

Coats came to a dirt road that led off the blacktop and into a thickly forested area. He pulled across a cattle guard. ''Now, I might better tell you fellers ahead of time,'' he said. ''This place sits on top of a little hill about a half mile on down. They're gonna be able to see us coming a long time before we get there.''

Lyons's arm shot across the car to the steering wheel. ''Stop the car,'' he ordered, as the final straw fell on the camel's back. Coats should have told them something that important long before now. That was one of the reasons he had chosen to tell the sheriff it was drug dealers they were about to arrest.

It didn't take much police training to know that the

drug dealers were usually armed, and that the ones in the house would have time to react if they saw a patrol car coming. All it took was common sense. Of course, the Able Team leader told himself, by now he should have known that common sense was a commodity of which Willy Dean Coats was in short supply.

Lyons looked over the seat. "Pol," he said, "go check it out. We'll wait here."

Coats looked over to Lyons as he pulled the emergency brake. "I was wonderin' what his first name was. Sure can't pronounce his last one." He hooked a thumb toward Blancanales. "Maybe I should go with Paul since I know the area."

Lyons forced a smile. He shook his head as Blancanales got out. "No, Sheriff. We need you with us."

Lyons and Gadgets listened to a disjointed lecture on the history of Christian County while they waited on Blancanales's recon. When the history lesson ended, Coats filled his mouth with a new plug of tobacco and began a discourse on his childhood in the hills.

After what seemed like an eternity to Lyons, Blancanales appeared again. He walked to the car and bent to speak through the window.

"Sentries?" Lyons asked.

"Sentries?" Coats echoed incredulously.

"Er, guards," Blancanales said.

"They got guards?" Coats repeated dumbly. "Guards guarding their dope?" A quick flash of fear crossed his face as he realized he was in deeper than he'd thought.

Lyons turned to the man. It was time to get this

show on the road, and maybe the fear he had just seen, combined with the fact that it was an election year for Coats, could be used to Able Team's advantage. "Sheriff," he said, "this could be more serious than we thought. We're obviously going to need more men. How many deputies do you have?"

"Just ol' Frank and another. But I can call out the reserve posse if you want."

"Good idea," Lyons said. He opened the door and got out. "Call out the posse, Willy Dean," he said through the open door. "Go back and call *all* of them out. We'll stay here and watch things."

Coats frowned. His hand moved toward the radio mike.

"No, Sheriff," Lyons said. "These are big-time dope dealers."

"Big-time?"

"From, uh, from New York," Schwarz said.

"*New York!*" Coats almost shouted.

"They might, no, they *will* have radio scanners inside," Blancanales said. "Better go back and use the phone."

Lyons and Schwarz opened their doors and joined Blancanales outside the car.

"Take your time, too, Willy Dean," Schwarz said. "A job worth doing is a job worth doing well, and all that." He glanced toward Blancanales. "Right, Paul?"

"Right."

The sheriff started to protest, but Lyons leaned back in the window and cut him off. "I can see the headlines now, can't you?'' he said. '''Christian County Sheriff Busts Drug Ring.'''

"From New York," Schwarz reminded him.

"New York," Coats echoed again.

"Why, the newspaper might as well just say, 'Everybody vote for Willy Dean Coats,''' Blancanales finished.

Sheriff Coats grinned, backed off the cattle guard and turned toward Ozark.

Lyons, Blancanales and Schwarz shook their heads as he drove away.

"Damn, Ironman," Schwarz said, "why didn't you think of that earlier?"

Prague, Czech Republic

THE COP IN FRONT of the Lanterna Magika blew his whistle a second time as the Executioner grabbed Hammersmith's hand and hurried into the alley. Bolan fought both exhaustion and shock from the burns as his mind willed his footsteps over the cobblestone. Ahead, he saw an intersecting alley between the blocks.

The whistle sounded again, closer this time, from the end of the alley where they'd entered. The shrill sound was followed by harsh orders barked in Czech.

The Executioner didn't understand the words. But he knew their meaning—"stop!" or "halt!"

He had no intention of doing either.

Bolan and Hammersmith neared the corner behind the hardware store, hearing running footsteps behind them. The Executioner took quick inventory of his burns. They didn't appear as bad as he'd first feared, but it was hard to tell this early. Burns could fool you, often being far worse than they first appeared.

The warrior rounded the corner, spotting the overturned trash can a split second before his foot hit it. He leapt instinctively into the air, vaulting the obstacle.

Hammersmith was a second too slow. Her foot hit the top of the rounded hurdle, and she went spinning out of Bolan's grasp onto the cobblestone. She sprawled in a heap at his feet as a moan escaped her lips and her hand flew to her ankle.

The Executioner sprinted forward as the footsteps behind them grew louder. Grabbing the British woman around the waist, he hauled her to her feet and drew her back against the rear door of the hardware store.

There was no way they were going to outrun the cops now. Not with his weakened condition and what appeared to be a sprained ankle on Hammersmith's part. Bolan's hand fell to the FEG. He had abandoned the Skorpion back at the lab. Other things, such as avoiding being burned to death, had taken precedence. It would be mistaken for one of the Jablonec Security weapons, anyway.

Not that it mattered what gun he had now. The movement to the weapon had been instinctive, and he removed his hand just as quickly. The man known as the Executioner had fought his war for more years than he cared remember. The bodies had stacked up into piles that could never be counted. But never in the entire war had he been responsible for the death of an honest cop or soldier doing his job. And he didn't intend to change that code now.

"Can you run?" Bolan whispered as the footsteps pounded closer.

Hammersmith's chest heaved. She shook her head. "Go…on…" she breathed.

Bolan didn't answer. He didn't have time.

The first Czech cop rounded the corner full speed, the whistle still clamped between his teeth. Bolan reached out, circling an arm around the man's neck and stepping behind him at the same time. With a swift back kick against the calf, the Executioner swept the man from his feet to the cobblestone.

The back of the cop's head struck the ground with a sickening thump. Bolan bent to check his pulse, but as he did, a second flash of blue appeared at the corner.

The second cop ran into the Executioner's lowered head, knocking Bolan two steps back. A whoosh burst from the uniformed man's mouth as the air was driven from his lungs.

Bolan caught his balance, stepped back in and threw a right cross from the hip. His fist caught the second cop on the jaw, and the man dropped like a felled oak.

The Executioner heard more sirens as he knelt and pressed an index finger into the necks of the two men. The screech of brakes sounded at the mouth of the alley as he felt the pulse.

Both cops were out cold, but they breathed steadily. They'd recover.

Rising, Bolan turned to Hammersmith as the

woman limped toward him painfully. His eyes fell to her ankle. It had already swollen to twice the normal size.

The Executioner's eyes scanned the alley. Trash cans, doorways and bare brick walls met his eyes. The doors offered their only hope.

Turning back to the rear door to the hardware store, Bolan studied the knob, a simple snap lock. His eyes skimmed the doorframe, then the bricks on both sides. A small window sat in the wall to the right. The venetian blinds inside had been closed. There appeared to be no alarm. If there was one, it was sophisticated enough to be hidden. In any case, they'd have to chance it.

Loud voices sounded at the end of the alley. More running footsteps started their way.

Dropping in front of the nearest cop, the Executioner rifled his pockets, coming up with a billfold. He found a laminated police commission card, rose and wedged the stiff plastic between the door and wooden frame.

Hammersmith limped toward him as the lock snapped open. Bolan shoved her past the entryway, rushed in and closed the door behind him.

A second later, he heard a gasp on the other side of the wood. Excited voices spoke in Czech as the new arrivals discovered their unconscious comrades. As his eyes adjusted to the darkness, the Executioner moved cautiously to the window. Kneeling at the corner, he peered through the cracks in the blinds.

At least a dozen uniformed police officers now crowded the alley, pistols and walkie-talkies in their hands. A man in plain clothes snarled orders. The men broke into two groups, racing down the alley in both directions.

The plainclothes officer was joined by another man in uniform. They knelt next to the cops on the ground.

Behind him, Bolan could hear Hammersmith's labored breathing. She started to whisper, but he spun her way, holding a finger to her lips.

The Executioner was still watching when the stretchers arrived ten minutes later. Both of the cops he had knocked out had regained consciousness. They protested, indicating that they could both walk out of the alley.

Several harsh words from the plainclothesman in charge sent them climbing on board the stretchers.

Bolan waited until the alley was clear again before moving back to where Hammersmith stood painfully on one leg. "How bad is it?" he asked.

"It's not broken," she whispered. "I feel so bloody silly. You're the one who's hurt."

Bolan turned away from the door. The small entryway led into the main showroom of the hardware store. Another door, which stood open, revealed a rest room in the dim light. Ushering Hammersmith inside, he closed the door, pulled a Brinkman Micro-Mag flashlight from his pocket and twisted on the beam.

The rest-room walls were painted a dull olive green. Dirt and oil stained the sink and toilet. A mirrored medicine cabinet had been bolted to the wall above the sink, and a storage door opened beneath it. None of which particularly interested the Executioner. What did catch his attention, and bring a faint smile to his lips, was the fact that the walls were of solid concrete.

No windows led out of the rest room to let telltale light creep out into the alley. He switched on the overhead light, then opened the medicine cabinet, digging through a maze of half-used prescription bottles. He found a bottle of shampoo, several different colors of nail polish and a toothbrush, but no first-aid supplies.

Hammersmith guessed his intentions. "Try the cabinet below," she whispered.

The Executioner knelt and opened the door beneath the sink. The small metal first-aid box lay next to the drainage pipe.

The Executioner opened the box. Inside, he found a crystallized cold-compress envelope, slammed it against the sink to activate the crystals and handed it to Hammersmith.

"For bloody sake, Pollock," the woman whispered, "it's a sprained ankle." She limped forward and knelt next to him. "Let's treat your burns."

Bolan took a seat on the floor, finally allowing himself to relax after the ordeal on the fiery stairs and the chase that followed. He felt fatigue drift over him like a dark cloud, and fought against the eyelids that threatened to close. He saw Hammersmith wrap the compress fasteners around her ankle, then begin rummaging through the first-aid kit.

The Executioner's eyelids fell shut. They opened again as what felt like ice hit his left arm. He looked up to see Jonnie Hammersmith staring into his eyes as she carefully rubbed his arm with ointment.

"The majority of burns are just first-degree," the

British agent whispered. "But there are a few blisters."

Bolan looked down at his arm. Most of his forearm had turned a bright pink, and the color extended past the elbow. But in the middle of that joint, angry red bubbles had risen from the skin.

Hammersmith moved carefully around the second-degree burns, avoiding the blisters. She applied ointment to his other arm, then returned to the first-aid kit.

Bolan gritted his teeth.

The MI-6 agent found a roll of sterile dressing and began to bandage the Executioner's arms. Again, Bolan's jaw clamped shut as the fire shot through him. Then the pain subsided and the drowsiness returned, and his mind switched to fighting it once again.

He had to stay awake. They had to get out of there before the police search revealed that they hadn't left the area, but had hidden someplace.

Hammersmith finished wrapping his arms, then stood and walked to the sink. Bolan stared straight ahead. His mind grew fuzzy. Time passed; maybe ten seconds, maybe ten minutes. He couldn't tell.

The next thing he knew, Hammersmith was kneeling before him again. "Here," she said, pressing a paper cup to his lips. "I found some salt and baking soda. It'll help with fluid loss." She motioned for him to open his mouth, then popped something inside before letting him drink.

"What is it?" Bolan asked before swallowing.

"Antibiotic," she said, sounding suddenly like a weary mother talking to her sick child. "They were in the kit. Those deeper burns are subject to infection. Now take it.''

Bolan swallowed the antibiotic, then drank the rest of the mixture. He leaned back, resting against the cabinet. ''We've got to get...'' he said, then his eyelids finally closed for good.

SOME TIME LATER the Executioner awakened. He felt the pain sear through his arms as he forced himself forward, away from the sink. He looked down at the bandages.

He felt better. There would be a lot of pain for the next few days, but he'd get over it. Turning toward Hammersmith, he saw the British agent asleep in the corner of the rest room.

He had risen to his feet when he heard the key in the lock. The door to the alley opened.

Bolan pulled Hammersmith to her feet. It was too late to close the rest-room door. Whoever came in— whether it be the owner of the hardware store, an employee or a brigade of the Czech cops now canvasing the neighborhood for the suspicious couple seen leaving the Lanterna Magika—was about to see them.

The Executioner drew the FEG and turned to face the door.

Istanbul, Turkey

CALVIN JAMES LED the way up the steps inside the condominium building, turned the corner at the top and started down the hall toward Boris Stavropek's apartment. The former U.S. Navy Seal felt a little silly in his purple print swimsuit and matching jacket. He felt even sillier carrying the six-pack of beer and walking with a carefully practiced drunken sway.

But he had only to look at Katz and Manning dressed in similar garb, with Katz carrying a wine bottle and Manning toting a fifth of Canadian Club, to feel company in his absurdity.

Blending in with the tourists had been part of the Phoenix Force leader's plan, and had necessitated McCarter and Encizo watching the condo while the other three left to buy suitable clothes and equipment. The equipment had been necessarily odd for Phoenix Force, as well.

A volleyball net, stand and ball.

Encizo had continued to watch the front of Stavropek's building as the team had set up the net on the beach. James and McCarter had then proceeded to beat Katz and Manning six games running while they kept an eye on the back entrance.

James turned a corner and started toward the end of the hall. The plan was simple. He slowed his pace as he neared the door. Yeah, the plan was simple. And if it went right, there wouldn't even be a fight.

He continued down the hall, leading the way past an open doorway. Inside, he saw candy, soft drink and ice machines. He looked at Manning and Katz. Both men nodded. Katz took a swig out of his open bottle of Roederer Cristal champagne.

The former Seal stopped in front of Stavropek's door, reached out and knocked. The rapping sound echoed down the hallway.

James waited, then knocked again.

Katz turned, waving them back down the hall. They ducked into the room housing the vending machines.

"You suppose he went out?" James asked.

The Israeli shook his head. "I don't see how. Pescado's been watching the front. We were on the beach. Those are the only two exits."

"Maybe he's asleep," Manning offered.

Katz shrugged. "Could be. We'll try again. Louder. But just in case…" He reached into the pocket of his paisley swim jacket and pulled out the wraparound walkie-talkie headset. Holding the microphone to his lips, he whispered, "Phoenix One to Three."

"Come in, One."

"David, go to the car and bring us the picks," Katz ordered. "Gary will meet you at the door."

Manning turned and disappeared into the hallway as Katz shoved the radio back into his jacket.

James set the six-pack on a shelf, shoved several coins into a pop machine and punched the Coca-Cola button. The can fell, and he pulled it from the machine. He held another coin up to Katz, but the Israeli shook his head.

James popped the top and took a drink. Stavropek hadn't left the condo. Not unless he'd tunneled down through three floors and halfway down the block before surfacing. No, he was inside. But for some reason, he wasn't answering the door.

Manning returned, patted the side pocket of his Hawaiian-style beach shirt to indicate he had the lock picks, and they started back down the hall. James knocked again, then again, louder.

Katz nodded his head. Manning knelt before the

door and inserted two of the picks. Thirty seconds later, the lock clicked.

James reached inside the paper sack that held the six-pack and drew the CZ-75 from the top of the beer cans. Slowly he twisted the knob, opened the door and stuck his nose inside.

The condo was silent, except for a soft snoring from down the hall.

James stepped inside, followed by Manning, then Katz. Both men held weapons identical to his own. Katz motioned for Manning to stay with him, then waved James down the hall. The former Seal set the sack on a table near the door, then crept cautiously through the living room, using the moonlight drifting through the open window for illumination.

The snoring got louder as he neared the open door. It was soft, light, feminine.

James knew why Stavropek hadn't heard the knock even before he stuck his head around the corner and saw the nude woman sleeping next to the Russian.

The Phoenix Force warrior took quick inventory of the room. Clothes were strewed about the floor. Two empty magnum bottles of a cheap local wine rested on a nightstand, both empty.

The reason Stavropek hadn't heard the knocking was obvious. The Russian had gotten drunk after getting lucky. Or who knew? James thought. Maybe he'd gotten drunk before getting lucky.

Not that it mattered. The luck of the man in charge of the Istanbul Biopreparat project was about to run out.

Creeping back to the living room, James advised

the other two men. "We can't kill her," he whispered. "We don't even know if she's associated with Ryba." He paused. "But if we don't, and she is hooked in, Ryba will know—"

Katz held up his hand. "We'll try to get Stavropek out without waking her," he whispered back. "If we can't, we take her with us." He set his champagne bottle on the table next to the beer. Manning's bottle of Canadian Club went next to it.

James led the two men back down the hall and into the bedroom. He and Katz walked around the bed to where Stavropek lay sleeping on his back.

Manning stopped above the woman as she snored on.

James leaned forward, pressing the CZ into the hollow under Boris Stavropek's nose. His other hand cupped the Russian's mouth.

Stavropek opened his eyes. His blurry vision told James he was trying to decide if what he saw was real or some alcohol-induced nightmare.

Then the man's eyes cleared. He swatted the CZ-75 to the side, rolled his mouth away from James's hand and screamed.

The woman sat bolt upright in bed as if she'd been shot from a cannon. A scream erupted from her lips before Manning's huge hand shot out and covered her mouth.

James raised the CZ and brought the barrel down on the crown of Stavropek's head. The Russian moaned, falling back on the sheets.

Manning twisted the woman around on the bed, pressed one wrist into her throat and slid his other forearm across the back of her neck in the time-honored "sleeper" hold.

As Katz stepped in and placed the muzzle of his pistol against Stavropek's temple, the woman closed her eyes. Her head fell forward to her breasts.

James leaned in, his lips almost against Stavropek's ear. "Don't move," he whispered. "Do exactly as we tell you."

Stavropek nodded, his eyes filled with drunken fear.

Katz pulled his gun from the Russian's temple, and James pressed his own into Stavropek's neck. The Israeli turned to Manning. "Get her dressed," he told the Canadian.

Manning looked at him quizzically.

James glanced at the woman in the big Canadian's arms. She wasn't bad. Probably a local hooker. "Just do what comes naturally, Gary," he whispered to Manning, grinning. "But in reverse."

Manning placed the unconscious woman back on the bed and reached for a crumpled pair of stockings on the floor.

Katz disappeared down the hall, returning a moment later with the champagne bottle. He glanced at the label, shaking his head. "Such a waste," he said, then forced the wine into Stavropek's mouth.

The Russian took several gulps.

Katz pulled the bottle away and poured champagne over the man's shoulders. The room began to reek even more than it had. "Where's your swimsuit?" he asked Stavropek.

The Russian pointed to a chest of drawers. "Top," he mumbled.

Katz found the suit, threw it to Stavropek and said, "Put it on."

The confused Russian sat up in bed. "We are going... swimming?"

James thought of the millions of people who might die because of this man's work, leaned forward, and gave the man a shake. "Just put it on," he growled.

Stavropek struggled into the suit.

As soon as Manning had finished dressing the unconscious woman, he hoisted her over one shoulder and led the way into the living room. The men of Phoenix Force retrieved the beer and whiskey, then Katz pulled the radio from his jacket again. "All clear?" he asked McCarter.

"For now," the Briton said from the beach. "But there's an occasional couple walking hand in hand along here. Be careful. Be a shame to ruin a romance."

James pulled the six-pack of beer from the sack and shoved the CZ-75 inside, his hand still on the grip. He jammed the sack into Stavropek's rib cage and said, "In case we come across anybody, Boris, we're all out having one hell of a party. The lady had too much to drink. You got that?"

Stavropek nodded.

The sack-covered pistol in one hand, the six-pack in the other, James pushed the man to the door. Katz led the way down the hall toward the stairs.

Ascending footsteps met their ears as they neared the steps. James moved closer to Stavropek, the barrel of the 9 mm still in the man's ribs.

Suddenly a bright flash of steel stepped up from the

staircase. James's eyes zeroed in on the badge, then the uniform.

The bearded security officer hadn't expected to encounter anyone. He jumped in surprise, his hand dropping to the 9 mm pistol on his belt.

Katz's foot hit an imaginary bump in the carpet. The Israeli went sprawling across the floor of the hall. James and Manning burst into drunken laughter as Katz struggled to his knees, joining in the merriment.

The security guard's face relaxed. His hand moved away from his holster. He spoke in Turkish. Katz answered in Hebrew. The guard switched to Arabic. They settled on French.

"What are you doing?" the guard demanded.

"Celebrating," Katz replied through a face full of laughing tears. "My friend—"

The guard cut him off. "What is wrong with her?" he asked, pointing to the woman on Manning's back.

The big Canadian slapped the woman across the rear and held up the whiskey bottle. They all laughed again.

The guard didn't see the humor in it. "Get her home," he ordered. "All of you go home. There are residents trying to sleep."

Katz nodded, and the men of Phoenix Force lowered their laughter to chuckles as they passed the guard, descended the stairs and left the building.

McCarter stepped from behind a beach umbrella as they neared the water. They heard running footsteps behind them, and turned to see Encizo cutting across the sand.

Katz stepped up to Stavropek and handed him the champagne bottle.

The Russian stared drunkenly at it, then took it.

"Finish it," Katz said.

"I—"

"No, really. Be my guest."

Stavropek guzzled what remained in the bottle, then handed it back to Katz.

"Do you know what you've been doing?" Katz asked. "The research project? Do you know what you've been creating? Death."

"You're going to kill me, aren't you?" Stavropek asked drunkenly before launching himself at the Isreali.

The Phoenix Force leader stepped aside, then grabbed the Russian by the neck and applied just enough force until he blacked out and dropped to the wet sand.

James and Manning dragged the body to the edge of the water. As James began towing the Biopreparat researcher out to sea, Katz led the rest of Phoenix Force and the sleeping woman back toward the car.

CHAPTER NINE

Nixa, Missouri

"I didn't think we'd ever get rid of him," Schwarz commented as Sheriff Coats's patrol car disappeared down the road.

"Okay," Lyons said. "Let's get going. I'd like to get this over and get out of here before the posse shows up with a hangman's noose." He glanced at the thick trees that led to the house, then looked back to both of his men.

Humoring Coats had left Able Team at a tactical disadvantage, to say the least. They all still wore the gray "Justice Department" suits in which they'd come to Christian County, hardly ideal assault attire. But the real problem was that Schwarz and Blancanales had been forced to leave their primary firepower on the plane.

Lyons still had his Calico machine pistol beneath his jacket, but the larger M-960A subguns had been too big to hide. And they were definitely not Justice Department issue.

A useless precaution, Lyons realized now. After meeting Coats, it was obvious the man wouldn't have known what was, and was not, JD issue. In fact it had become painfully obvious that the sheriff didn't know much of anything.

"Any idea how many men we'll be facing?" Lyons asked Blancanales.

He shrugged. "Hard to say. No sentries. I only saw two vehicles parked outside, but there's a barn where more could be hidden."

"Inventory," Lyons ordered. He swung the machine pistol to the end of his shoulder rig. "Got a 50-round mag, 100-round backup. Plus my Government Model and two extra loads."

Schwarz patted his left armpit. "Beretta 92," he said, "and two more mags. Forty-six rounds, plus my backup." He drew a Colt Officer's Model .45 from the small of his back. "Add seven, which makes fifty-three."

Blancanales nodded. "The same with the Beretta," he said. "And this." He drew an American Derringer Double from the side pocket of his coat. "One .410 shotgun shell, one .45 Colt, no extras. Forty-eight."

Lyons turned back to the trees. It was time for a judgment call. Together, Able Team had a little more than two hundred fifty rounds. It sounded like a lot. But they had no idea how many men they'd be facing. To add to the problem, nearly three-fourths of their rounds rode with Lyons in the Calico and his .45. Bad distribution of firepower.

On the other hand, this deal needed to go down now if they didn't want to do it with Coats and the Christian County Sheriff's Department reserve posse. And Lyons definitely didn't.

"Let's do it, get it over with and get on to something else," Lyons said. "The day Able Team can't take out a bunch of laboratory rats barehanded is the day we need to turn this job over to Pinkerton's."

"Which would still be better than turning it over to Willy Dean," Schwarz said. He turned to Blancanales and pointed toward the trees. "Lead on, *Paul*," he said.

Blancanales pulled a branch out of the way and stepped into the forest. Lyons followed, stepping across a soft bed of pine needles. Behind him, he could hear Schwarz's quiet footsteps as Able Team's electronics expert brought up the rear.

They came to a muddy creek bank, crossing on a homemade bridge of stones and discarded scrap wood that looked like it had been built by kids.

Pol turned and held up a hand on the other side of the stream. "About thirty more yards," he whispered.

Lyons motioned Schwarz to the left, knowing the Able Team warrior would understand that he was to circle the house. Blancanales went right.

The former LAPD cop continued through the thick trees until a flash of white caught his eye between the branches. He dropped to his hands and knees, crawling on, until the bright paint of the farmhouse became clear. As he neared the edge of the trees, he fell to his belly, crawling through the twigs and pine needles until he came to the end of the trees.

Lyons rolled to one side, unsnapping the barrel of the Calico from his belt and swinging it out to the end of the sling. Rolling to his other side, he pulled the headset from his coat, wrapped it over his ears, then studied the house.

The wooden siding was in the process of being painted. Half-empty cans of paint, brushes, rollers and trays had been scattered around the sides of the house. An aging blue Datsun minitruck and a newer Ford Bronco had been parked near the front door of the one-story dwelling.

The house itself was small, appearing to contain no more than two bedrooms. Lyons breathed a cautious sigh of relief.

The place didn't look like it could hold many men.

He turned to the barn, about thirty yards to the left of the back of the house. It was a different story. A typical two-story structure with bales of hay visible through the open door to the loft, it might hide any number of the enemy. On the other hand, it didn't look like it had been put to use for some time. The main door below was closed, and wooden shutters covered the windows.

Behind the barn, a seemingly endless cow pasture stretched to the north.

Lyons spoke quietly into the headset. "Able One to Two and Three. Everybody in position?"

He got two "affirmatives" in reply.

"Gadgets," he whispered, "you're closest to the barn. Maneuver on in. Tell us if you see anything. We'll cover you."

"That's a 10-4, Able One."

Far to the left, Lyons saw a slight movement in the trees. Then Schwarz sprinted from cover, the Beretta 92 in his hand. The electronics specialist raced to the barn, threw his back against the wall, then bent low and began to move toward the nearest window. He moved the shutter slightly and looked in.

"Nothing," Schwarz whispered into the radio. "I don't think they're even using it."

Lyons was sighing again when he heard the front door of the house open. Three men wearing paint-spotted overalls walked out, dropped down from the porch and turned the corner to the side of the house. Each carried a gallon can of paint.

Schwarz dropped to a squatting position beneath the barn window and froze. For the moment, at least, it appeared the men hadn't spotted him.

Lyons pulled a set of compact IR binoculars from his jacket, quickly focusing the nitrogen-filled lenses on the lead painter. There was always a chance that Ryba's men had contracted the paint job, and he had no intention of starting a firefight with innocents. But as the lenses focused on the lead man's overalls, Lyons caught a glimpse of the grips of an automatic pistol sticking out from the side of the man's bib.

Swinging the binoculars to the second man, Lyons saw that another gun pushed his pin-striped bib outward.

The third painter hadn't even tried to conceal his weapon. He'd wrapped a thick leather belt and holster around his overalls and wore his 9 mm Makarov pistol openly.

As Lyons shoved the binoculars back in his jacket, he heard a distant thump, followed by what could only have been some Czech curse. Looking back to the house, the Able Team leader saw the man with the Makarov bend to retrieve the dropped can of paint.

In doing so, he turned toward the barn and saw Schwarz squatting beneath the barn window. The can of paint suddenly forgotten, the painter cursed again and whipped the Makarov from his holster.

As Lyons rose to his feet, swinging the Calico in front of him, he saw Schwarz raise the Beretta. Two 9 mm hollowpoints hammered from the pistol, drilling through the painter's bib and echoing through the clearing. For a moment, there was silence.

Then all hell broke loose.

A fourth man, clad in green military fatigue pants and bare-chested, burst from the door where the painters had emerged. An M-16 sputtered in his hands, peppering the wall of the barn above Schwarz's head.

Lyons stepped from the clearing and trained the sights of the Calico just above the green fatigue pants. A full-auto burst of 9 mm rounds flew from the machine pistol, leaving tiny red dots on the man's chest as he fell forward.

The Able Team leader swung the Calico back to the painters, as the nearest man drew his pistol from the bib of his overalls. Another burst of fire caught the painter in the upper chest and throat, sending him sprawling onto the grass.

The third painter, momentarily stunned by the lightning-fast strike, now recovered. Dropping the paint can in his hand, he reached inside his overalls for his weapon.

Lyons squeezed the Calico's trigger, and a third autoburst cut the painter's legs from under him. As he fell to the ground, the Able Team leader drilled a quick trio of 9 mm rounds into the man's head.

More hardmen suddenly poured from the front door, each carrying automatic rifles or submachine guns.

A pair of rounds roared from the trees to Lyons's right, where Blancanales had set up. The two men in the lead fell to the ground.

Another duo, following them, tripped over the corpses and sprawled in the dirt.

Schwarz fired a single round that took out the man nearest him. Lyons got off a burst that felled the other man.

A man wearing jeans and a T-shirt, another in overalls, and a third in slacks emerged from the rear of the house. All three carried Uzis, firing from the hip as they joined the battle.

Lyons held the Calico's trigger back, spraying the trio with a steady stream of Parabellum rounds. They fell to the earth in a jumble of arms and legs, only to be replaced by four more gunners.

The screen door on the front of the house banged against the wall as another half-dozen armed enemy emerged.

"Gadgets, take cover!" Lyons shouted into the radio. He backpedaled toward the trees, firing into the mob of men who had materialized at the front. Two of the six went down immediately. A third was driven back into the doorway, temporarily blocking the flow from the house.

As he ducked back into the forest, the Able Team leader saw Schwarz skirt around the corner of the barn, rounds flying past him to chip the paint and splinter the wood at his side. He glanced to his right. Blancanales had disappeared again into the woods.

Dropping to one knee, Lyons steadied the machine pistol on the side of a tree, feeling the concussion reverberate down his arms each time an enemy round struck the trunk. Glancing down to the top of the Calico, he saw brass gleaming through the plastic-covered aperture next to the "9." The next indicator hole, marked "23," was empty.

Lyons leaned around the tree trunk, raising the machine pistol to his eyes. Sighting down the top of the drum mag, he dropped the front sight on an Uzi-bearing man in black Levi's jeans and a white shirt. He tapped lightly on the trigger and several rounds drilled into the enemy, turning the shirt a bright crimson.

The Able Team leader switched to a denim jacketed gunner firing a Government Model .45 from the porch. As he emptied the machine pistol into the man, more gunners streamed out of the house past the dancing body.

Letting up on the trigger as the bolt locked open, Lyons clawed under his jacket for the 100-round backup drum. How could the house hold so many men? It looked like clowns exiting a Volkswagen at the circus—they just kept coming.

Lyons unclamped the 50-round drum, let it fall to the ground and slammed the 100-rounder on top of the weapon. A split second later, the machine pistol was firing again, spraying blue-tipped Nyclad 9 mm hollowpoints into a brace of gunners trying to make their way toward the barn, and Schwarz.

The new drum was longer, and the Able Team leader adjusted his hold. Tapping the trigger once more, he sent a long burst into the porch, dropping four men.

The remaining gunmen took cover behind the pile of bodies, firing over the top. Lyons pumped full-auto rounds into the wall of human flesh, praying the Nyclads would penetrate.

A faint scream sounded from behind the bodies as his prayer was answered by at least one of the gunmen.

The Able Team leader let up on the trigger. It was the wrong plan of attack. They were running low on ammo, and random sprays, even with the Calico, might mean their doom.

As if Blancanales had read his mind, Lyons suddenly heard the Politician's voice in his ear. ''I'm down to one Beretta mag, Ironman. Just that and the derringer.''

Steady fire continued from the direction of the barn as Lyons snapped a round into the head of a gunner who foolishly rose from behind the bodies. Then Schwarz spoke over the radio. ''Mag and a half, Ironman. That's all for me.'' His words were punctuated by rounds from the Beretta. ''Then I'm down to the Officer's Model.''

Lyons fired again, the hollowpoints drilling into the men around the porch. He heard the sound of shattering glass, then saw a rifle barrel poke out of the window next to the door.

The Able Team leader swung the Calico that way, firing a short burst into the opening. An AK-47 fell out onto the porch.

"Pol, stay where you are!" Lyons shouted into the mike. He rose from behind the tree, took two steps deeper into the woods, then turned, angling toward where Blancanales had to be. Dodging tree trunks and low-hanging limbs, he fired through the branches as the men rushing from the house began to make their way across the yard toward Blancanales.

Pol's tattered gray suit and white shirt finally appeared through the green trees ahead. Blancanales had taken refuge behind the thick trunk of a fir tree, firing around the bark with careful, aimed rounds.

As he raced forward, Lyons saw a group of eight men nearing the trees.

Pol fired two rounds and dropped two of the men.

Out of the corner of his eye, Lyons saw Blancanales's Beretta lock open, empty. Then a flurry of automatic fire forced the Able Team warrior to the ground.

Lyons turned the Calico toward the clearing as he ran, firing a full-auto burst from the hip. Two of the rounds made it through the branches, dropping a gunner with a wild handlebar mustache. The rest of the Nyclads lodged harmlessly in the thick trunks and branches between the Able Team leader and the oncoming men.

Blancanales leaned around the tree, the derringer in his fist. An ear-piercing crack bounded off the tree trunks as a .45 Long Colt blasted from the short barrel and lodged in a chest.

Lyons reached behind him, drawing the .45 from

his inside-the-pants holster with his left hand. "Pol!" he yelled into the headset. "Three o'clock!"

Blancanales fired the derringer again, his hand bouncing high with the heavy recoil. The oncoming man who now held the lead blew back in his tracks, his face peppered with .410 shot that looked like someone had stabbed him repeatedly with an ice pick.

"Pol!" Lyons yelled again. "Three o'clock!"

Blancanales turned his way.

The Able Team leader flipped the .45 underhand, sending the weapon end over end toward Blancanales. Pol's left hand stretched out. He caught the gun by the barrel and transferred it to his right in time to turn and pump a round into the belly of the first man to break into the trees.

Lyons ground to a halt, shoulder to shoulder with Blancanales. Raising the Calico to eye level, he tapped three 9 mm rounds into a man wearing a St. Louis Cardinals baseball cap. The gunner fell back into the last member of the assault.

The man at the rear backpedaled away from his friend. Suddenly realizing he was alone, he turned to retreat.

He was too late. Lyons stitched a row of rounds up his spine from tailbone to neck.

Fire still rained toward them from the house and more rounds could be heard popping around the barn.

Lyons turned his back to Blancanales and lifted the tail of his jacket. "The extra mags, Pol," he said. "Take them." He felt the .45 magazines pull free of their carrier.

"Ironman! Pol!" Schwarz said suddenly over the headsets. "I'm down to my backup!"

"We're on our way!" Lyons yelled. He turned to Blancanales and nodded toward the ground. Blancanales bent and snatched up a fallen Uzi. He pulled back the bolt, then dropped the weapon in disgust. "Empty," he snarled.

Lyons looked down to his drum mag again. He'd expended well over half of the hundred loads inside. He scooped up another of the subguns from the fallen men. It was dry as well, and there was no time to keep checking the fallen weapons. "We'll have to make do," he said.

Starting back through the trees, Lyons and Blancanales angled toward the barn. Pol's pounding feet echoed in the Able Team leader's ears as they broke cover and sprinted into the clearing.

Then, as they raced across the yard in front of the house, dodging the bullets that still flew from the porch and windows, the words Carl Lyons had dreaded hearing ever since he'd made the decision to go ahead with the attack suddenly pounded in his ears.

"Ironman! Pol!" Schwarz called over an explosion of autofire in the background. "I'm out of ammo!"

Prague, Czech Republic

BOLAN SLID SILENTLY across the concrete floor to the rest-room door, the burned flesh beneath his bandages screaming to his brain as he moved. He held the FEG before him, aiming at the ceiling as he stopped.

From the entryway, the sound of the back door

clicking shut behind whoever had entered the building echoed down the hallway. Behind him, the faint sound of Hammersmith's purse opening met his ears.

The Executioner peered around the doorframe. In the semidarkness, he saw a small, slender figure. Man or woman? Friend or foe? It was too dark to tell.

The figure turned back from the door. A ray of light from the front of the building flashed across his face.

Male. Late sixties. Gray hair poked from the sides of the navy driving cap that covered his hair, and a neatly trimmed pencil mustache paralleled his upper lip. In his sharply pressed sapphire suit, carefully knotted necktie and patent-leather shoes, the little man looked for all the world like an aging peacock.

The old man started forward, then stopped in his tracks. Horror filled his eyes as the Executioner stepped from the rest room. His mouth opened to scream.

Bolan leapt forward, pushing the old man back against the door and pressing a big hand over the quivering mouth. The little man froze like a statue.

Holding the FEG up into the light, the Executioner whispered, "Do you see this?"

The man understood English. He nodded.

"Do you know what it is?"

Another nod.

"Don't make me use it."

The little head shook back and forth.

Bolan glanced to the wall and saw the light switch. Flipping it on with the heel of his gun hand, he turned back to the man. "If I take my hand away, will you scream?"

The head shook even more vigorously this time.

Bolan removed his hand. "Who are you?" he demanded.

Fear continued to radiate from the man's eyes. "Anton Ku-Kutna," he stammered. "This is m-my store." He paused, then forced himself on. "Please...take the money. There is not much, but—"

"Relax, Anton," Bolan said as Hammersmith appeared at his side holding the Beretta. "We don't want your money."

The old man stared up into the Executioner's eyes. The fear on his face faded slightly, as if something he saw there reassured him. He straightened his jacket, adjusted his tie and spoke in a quaking voice, "Then may I ask who you are and what you want?"

"I can't tell you who we are, but believe it or not, we're wearing white hats."

Kutna's eyebrows lowered curiously.

Hammersmith spoke in Czech.

The old man nodded. "Ah, you are the good guys," he said with a thick accent. "I do not know how I can be certain." He glanced back at the door through which he'd come in. "Is it you that the police are looking for?"

Bolan nodded. "Are they still out there?"

A loud pounding at the front of the store answered his question. A voice called through the door in Czech.

"It appears that they are," Hammersmith said. "They're calling for Mr. Kutna. By name."

Bolan moved down the hall to the entrance to the showroom. "Don't answer," he said. "You haven't arrived at work yet.''

Kutna shook his head. ''Several officers were in the alley. They watched me come in the back door.''

Bolan hesitated. Was the little man lying? There was no way to know. He studied Kutna's face for a clue. ''Answer it,'' he finally said. He took the man's arm and led him into the showroom, up an aisle and to the door. ''Tell them you're alone.'' He stepped to one side of the door. Hammersmith took the other.

Kutna threw back the bolt and swung the door open. He spoke briefly through the doorway.

Bolan waited, wondering what he and Hammersmith would do if Kutna suddenly screamed and bolted through the door. There was a good chance that might be exactly what happened. The Executioner wasn't sure what course of action he'd take in that event—if Czech police suddenly flooded the room. Break and run for it, he supposed. But he didn't shoot cops and he didn't shoot innocent old men, which had left him with no other alternative than to take a calculated risk with Anton Kutna.

Kutna spoke again, his voice sounding irritated. He shook his head, then shut the door and turned to Bolan. ''I told them I was alone,'' he whispered. ''They wanted to check for themselves, but I said I was busy.''

The yellow caution light in the Executioner's brain flashed brightly. The cops might be satisfied, they might not. In any case, the sooner he and Hammersmith were out of the hardware store, the better.

Hammersmith moved in front of Kutna. "Why didn't you tell them we were here?" she asked.

A twinkle appeared in the old man's eyes. The pencil-thin mustache turned upward at the corners. "My brain told me I should," he said, eyeing Hammersmith head to toe, "but my heart said no. And I have always been a man who followed his heart." He paused. "Especially where beautiful women are concerned."

Hammersmith chuckled. "Why, Anton, you old flirt."

Kutna beamed. With a dramatic bow, he said, "What else do you want from me?"

Bolan stepped back from the man, shoving the gun into his belt as Hammersmith returned the .22 to her purse. "We've got to get out of here before the cops come back," he said. "We need other clothes, Anton. Do you have anything?"

The old man grinned. "My clothes?" he said. "You expect them to fit you?"

"No," Bolan answered. "But surely you've got something for her." He turned to Hammersmith who still wore the formal black gown and blond wig. "A woman works here. There were female items in the rest room."

"Yes, well, we will see what we can find." He pushed past the Executioner and led them back to the hallway, to a closet next to the rest room. Opening the door, he stepped back and waved a hand inside.

Bolan looked in to see a pair of khaki pants, several small shirts and a variety of other work clothes—

clothing the man had to have worn when he cleaned and did maintenance around the hardware store.

Reaching in, the Executioner pulled the khakis and a shirt down and handed them to Hammersmith. "Any shoes that would fit her?" he asked as the British woman grabbed a battered felt hat off the top of a cardboard box.

Kutna stuck his head inside the closet and pulled a worn pair of work shoes from the box. He handed them to Hammersmith himself, then looked her up and down again. "What a shame," he said. "A beautiful woman like you wearing such things."

Hammersmith laughed and took the shoes. "Keep talking, Anton," she said. "You might just get to watch me put them on."

Kutna grinned.

The old man turned to Bolan. "I have something for you," he said. He stuck his head back into the closet, rummaged through another box and came out with a pair of paint-spotted navy double-knit slacks. "My other employee's," the old man said. "He is not as large as you, but he is much bigger than me." Digging further, he found a plaid shirt.

Bolan was already shrugging out of his shirt and tux pants.

The pants' cuffs rode well above the warrior's ankles and the shirtsleeves had to be rolled up, but these clothes were all he had. They'd have to do. "When does the store open?" he asked Kutna.

The old man looked at his watch. "Ten minutes."

"We'll wait until a few customers have come in,

then slip out,'' the Executioner said. He glanced at Hammersmith and tapped his head.

The British woman looked momentarily puzzled, then realization cleared her eyes. She pulled the blond wig from her head.

Kutna gasped. "How sad," he said, as her short red hair appeared.

Bolan moved to the window next to the door. Parting the shade, he saw the city coming to life. Men and women hurried along the cobblestone walking street. Farther in the distance, he could hear the sounds of traffic.

Across the street the Executioner saw two uniformed police officers. They stared at the hardware store. Reaching behind him, Bolan pulled Kutna to the window. "Are those the two who came to the door?"

Kutna pressed his face to the shade, then nodded.

As Bolan watched, another cop wearing sergeant's stripes joined the two. One of the men spoke and pointed across the street. The sergeant turned toward the store.

"Scratch plan A," Bolan said, drawing the FEG.

"What's plan B?" Hammersmith asked as the sergeant and one of the uniformed men started across the street.

A hard smile crossed the Executioner's face as the three cops neared the door. Plan B would be risky. It might work, and it might not. But like the clothes Anton Kutna had found in the closet, it was the best they had.

"Plan B," the Executioner replied as the loud

knock sounded on the door, "is that we open the door and let them in."

Plzeň, Czech Republic

SKRDLA PARKED HIS CAR next to the Plzeň Biopreparat lab, got out and locked the door. His hand rose to his neck as he walked slowly toward the concrete steps leading down into the building. His fingers traced lightly over the bumps just below the collar of his shirt.

As he neared the steps he felt the thrill of adrenaline rush through his body like a drug. It always did when the hunt began. And as also always happened at the onset of the hunt, his mind traveled back to his childhood—to the moment in time when he had realized his calling, and been taught the philosophy that had molded his life.

The scuffed black shoes started down the steps to the lab, but the mind in the body above them was suddenly back at the orphanage in Moravia. Skrdla was ten years old, and he and the other boys had just been given an IQ test by their Communist instructors.

Skrdla had failed miserably, scoring well below average, and had been told he might even be "borderline retarded." The memory of the event hurt almost as much now as it had twenty years before.

He had left the examination room full of despair, taking to the woods surrounding the orphanage as he always did when he needed a moment of privacy. He had walked and cried, finally collapsing onto a fallen tree in despair.

But the gray wolf had heard, and he had come.

Only ten feet away, at the edge of the clearing, the huge animal had stared at him, its fur glistening almost silver in the sunlight. Their eyes met, and Skrdla knew instinctively that the wolf was trying to speak. Then a fluttering movement twenty yards deeper in the woods caused them both to look that way.

Skrdla had seen a white-tailed deer prance deeper into the forest.

The wolf turned back to him as if to say "follow me," then turned to stalk the deer. Skrdla had ignored the request, letting his face fall back into his hands in desperation once more. Then, perhaps twenty minutes later, he had heard movement from the other side of the clearing. Fearing that the wolf had given up on the fleet-footed deer and come back for him, he hurried into the trees.

A moment later, the huge gray animal entered the clearing and stretched out beneath the dead tree.

The deer entered the clearing cautiously, sniffing the air for the hunter's sent. But he had been upwind of the wolf. Skrdla saw what appeared to be a smile on the wolf's face as the deer started toward the tree.

As the deer leapt over the tree, the wolf rose quietly, catching a rear leg in his bared teeth. Skrdla heard a snapping sound as the bone broke. The deer screamed, falling to the ground. It tried to drag itself away.

The wolf was on it in a heartbeat, snarling and snapping the other rear leg, then taking a front hoof in its mouth. Then, as the whitetail lay helpless on the ground, the wolf had turned once again to Skrdla as if to say, "See? See how easy it is? It does not take great intelligence—only great cunning."

Then the wolf had ripped the deer's throat from its neck and began devouring the animal's flesh.

Skrdla had realized at that moment that cunning was far more important than measurable intelligence. That the true mark of wisdom was to wait for your opportunity, then seize it, overlooking nothing while you waited.

Skrdla stopped at the steel door, pulled his identification card from the breast pocket of his gray suit and pushed the buzzer. He grinned, not unlike the wolf, as his hand continued to trace the claws suspended on the leather thong around his neck.

He had worn the claws ever since that day, when the wolf had taught him his lesson, and he had put the new knowledge to use immediately.

Creeping from the woods while the wolf feasted, the ten-year-old Skrdla had crushed the animal's head with a stone.

The door opened and Skrdla saw the frightened eyes of a slender man in a lab coat. He held up his card and said simply, "Skrdla."

The man swallowed hard. He had heard the name. "Y-yes," he stammered. "We were told you were coming. Please...follow me." He led the way down the concrete hall.

Skrdla's footsteps fell to silence on the concrete.

The man in the white coat opened the door to the lab and stood back as Skrdla entered. Several other men and women stopped what they were doing around the tables and looked up. Skrdla saw the same fear on their faces.

The man in the lab coat swallowed once more, then started to speak. "I will—"

"Leave," Skrdla said. "You will all leave. All of you, stay out of my way."

The room emptied quickly.

Skrdla started on the left-hand side of the lab, his mind sectioning the floor into tiny quadrants as his eyes took in every detail of each section before moving on to the next. He saw a dead fly lying near the baseboard at the bottom of the wall. A paper clip had been kicked by an unknowing shoe. It rested over the fly's hind legs.

He moved around the lab where the gun battle had taken place, his eyes missing nothing. He wished momentarily that he had been here before the first investigation had taken place, then pushed the unproductive thoughts from his mind. The wolf, he imagined, might have wished that the deer's legs were broken before he encountered the animal, too.

Skrdla saw nothing of interest until he had circled the room and returned to the door behind him. Then his eyes fell to a large red blotch on the concrete wall next to the door.

He stepped forward, his nose a millimeter away from the spot, and sniffed.

Blood. Yes, blood. But something else, as well.

He sniffed again.

Lipstick?

Skrdla grinned widely. There *had* been at least one

more agent in the lab that night. They had learned that from the ballistic report.

But they had not learned that the agent was a woman.

Skrdla opened the door, walked down the hall and exited the building.

CHAPTER TEN

Stony Man Farm

Louis Tuma loosened his tie, thought about it, then unknotted it and pulled it off. The dress code here at—wherever the hell here was—appeared to be a lot more relaxed than at the Federal Bureau of Investigation.

Tuma glanced down at Aaron Kurtzman. The man's fingers flew across the computer keyboard with the nimbleness of a concert pianist and the stamina of a triathlon athlete. Tuma had met the man nicknamed "Bear" only once before, at the law-enforcement training session. He had been led to believe that Kurtzman worked for the Justice Department.

That no longer appeared to be the truth. At least not the whole truth.

Tuma continued to divide his gaze between the keyboard and the screen as he recalled the training seminar. It hadn't taken long for him to realize that Kurtzman was light-years ahead of his time. The man combined science with art, and seemed able to make the computer dance, sing or fly to the moon when he chose.

Who was Kurtzman? What was this place? Some top-secret CIA installation? Somehow, Tuma didn't think so. Somehow, he knew that wherever he was, even though he'd been brought here wearing a blindfold, he now knew more about this place than any CIA operative had ever learned.

Kurtzman stopped tapping the keys, sat back, folded his hands behind his head and waited.

ACCESS DATA INCOMPLETE flashed on the screen in Czech.

The FBI man didn't bother to translate. By now, Kurtzman recognized the foreign letters himself.

"Surprise, surprise," Kurtzman said in disgust.

Tuma turned to glance around the room. In some ways, it looked very similar to the computer room he ran at FBI headquarters. A little bigger, perhaps, with even more state-of-the-art electronics than they had at the Bureau, but very similar.

It was the personnel that was drastically different. In the room he headed, men wore business suits, white shirts, ties, and carried on the tradition of attorneylike professionalism that J. Edgar Hoover had begun. Hoover would have approved.

What Tuma saw before him here would make J. Edgar roll over in his grave.

Tuma's eyes drifted down the ramp to the black man on the far side of the room. Hunt? Wasn't that what Kurtzman had called him? Mr. Hunt was in charge of what Kurtzman had called 'peripherals,' meaning he was handling the odds and ends of the mission that came up while the others concentrated on breaking the code. Mr. Hunt wore a white shirt and

tie all right, but he had topped things off with a pale
yellow cardigan sweater. Combine that with the un-
lighted pipe clenched between his teeth, and Hunt
looked more like some college liberal-arts professor
than a government agent.

The FBI man's eyes moved to the middle-aged
woman seated next to Hunt. With her shoulder-length
red hair and bright red dress, she could have been the
mother of three children hurrying to get her oldest son
to a baseball game, drop the daughter off at dancing
class, take the younger boy to the baby-sitter, and still
make it to the PTA meeting on time.

And the Japanese youth next to her? He defied description for a government employee. A top-knot
ponytail and cutoff jean jacket? The headphones stuck
in his ears?

J. Edgar Hoover wouldn't just roll, he'd climb right
out of the grave and go after the kid.

Yet as Tuma watched Kurtzman's three assistants
type furiously on their keyboards, with precision almost as impressive as that of the boss himself, he
realized intuitively that, in spite of their looks, they
were even more professional than their counterparts
at the FBI.

Tuma looked back at the screen as Kurtzman tried
another access code with the same disappointing results. So far, the FBI man had been kept pretty much
out in the cold. His duties had been limited to translating Czech into English. But Kurtzman had tried to
call someone earlier, and Tuma guessed he'd been
seeking permission to reveal the details of the operation.

It made sense. Louis Tuma knew he wasn't in Kurtzman's class when it came to computer wizardry. But he *was* good, and he *was* another brain, another viewpoint. The result of two minds working together was still more than the sum of the individual parts, and Kurtzman was too sharp not to know that.

The phone rang shrilly as if reading Tuma's mind. The FBI man stepped back as Kurtzman ripped the receiver from the cradle. "Yeah?"

Kurtzman spoke in hushed tones, then raised his voice to say, "Right...okay...got you," before hanging up and turning to Tuma. "I've been cleared to fill you in on all details of the mission. Except those that might jeopardize the confidentiality of...this place," he said. "You understand?"

Tuma nodded.

The man in the wheelchair cleared his throat. "I've got to swear you to secrecy."

"You've got it."

"That includes your bosses at the FBI."

Tuma hesitated. "They're gonna ask questions, Aaron," he finally said. "Like why I didn't show up at work today."

Kurtzman waved a hand in front of his face as if swatting a mosquito. "That can be taken care of." He looked Tuma squarely in the eye. "Then I've got your word that you'll keep all this to yourself?"

Tuma nodded again.

Kurtzman smiled. "Well, let me tell you what's going on, and then we'll get back to work."

Prague, Czech Republic

JOSEPH RYBA FILLED the bowl of the pipe with tobacco, packed it down and stuck it in his mouth. He flipped the wheel of his gold lighter, held it over the pipe, then stopped.

He'd been smoking too much the past two days. He'd been letting the tension get to him. The time was drawing close when the new Biopreparat program would be complete. His scientists would have perfected the anthrax and other diseases, and the launching system would include both rockets and aerial bomblets. He would have over thirty launch sites scattered throughout Europe, and five in the United States. He would be able to call the shots, and if anyone stood in his way, millions would pay the price.

Ryba returned the flame to the pipe, lighted the tobacco and sucked hard. Until then, he was limited to the aerial bombs at three sites here, and one in the U.S. And the bomblets dropped from small private aircraft were his only means of dispensing the anthrax, which had been the first of the diseases to be perfected.

He pulled the pipe from his mouth and studied the glowing embers in the bowl. But was that so bad? He could still threaten the world with hundreds of thousands of deaths if he had to put his plan into operation, even now.

The Czech minister set the pipe on his desk, leaned back and clasped his arms behind his head. He should look relaxed, at least. Skrdla was on his way up, and it wouldn't do to appear worried in front of the man. Not that he didn't have reason—good reason—to be somewhat alarmed.

Strange things were happening at the lab sites.

First, there had been the break-in at the Plzeň lab by the British agents. That meant that the West had at least some suspicion that something was going on. Ryba felt his blood pressure rise. Next had come the fire at the site below the Magic Lantern. The cause was still unknown.

Arson?

Then, another of the research sites, right here in Prague, had fallen victim to what appeared to be a botched robbery attempt by the same masked thieves who had struck the Store on Main Street nearby. They had come back to hit the lab two hours later, probably confusing it with one of the cash businesses along the street.

Probably?

In the meantime, two more mysterious things had happened. Boris Stavropek, his chief researcher at the Istanbul lab, had washed ashore in front of his condominium, apparently drowned during a drunken swim.

Apparently?

In the U.S., his old friend Francis Hunyadi, in charge of overseeing the program there, had gone missing. Perhaps the old queen had simply found some attractive young man and was holed up in a motel somewhere.

Perhaps?

And last, when Ryba tried calling the storage site in Missouri, he had gotten a dead line.

By themselves, none of these "coincidences"

seemed like much. But when you added them together...

Relax, Ryba told himself. If the worst scenario was
true, he was already in a position to act.

Ryba heard the knock on the door. "Enter," he
called out.

The door opened, and the hulking gray figure filled
the doorway.

Ryba rose from behind his desk. There was something about Skrdla—some primeval, animallike violence—that demanded respect. "Please," he said cor-
dially, indicating the chair in front of him with a hand.
"Make yourself comfortable."

Skrdla moved silently across the carpet with the
grace of an eagle swooping down on its prey. He lowered himself into the chair and set his battered hat in
his lap. "Your suspicion that there was more the one
agent in the Plzeň lab was correct," he said without
preamble. "At least one. A woman."

Ryba felt his heart leap to his throat. "Are you
sure?" he asked.

"Yes," Skrdla said simply.

"What did you find?"

"More blood on the wall. Mixed with lipstick."

"Were samples taken?"

"I called the appropriate laboratory personnel,"
Skrdla replied. "I assume they came and did so. But
they will only confirm what I know."

Ryba sat back down in his chair and crossed his
arms on the desk. "The blood—could it have come
from the agent who was killed? Or one of the guards
who was shot?"

"No."

"How do you know that the lipstick is not that of one of the female employees at the lab?"

Skrdla's voice sounded monotone. "I do not know how I know, but I know. The other agent was a woman. Approximately five feet, three inches tall. Probably with red hair." He paused, took a breath, then added, "And she was accompanied by a third person."

"Red hair? How can you know that?"

"I did not say I knew that. I said probably." Skrdla stared Ryba in the eye with an intensity that made the minister glance down. "The shade of lipstick on the wall is called Coral Reef. It is manufactured by Princess Sylvie, a British company, and most commonly used by redheaded women."

"How do you know all this?"

Skrdla shrugged his massive shoulders. "I smelled it."

Ryba nodded. The man was good. "A third person? How do you—"

"It is simple. It seems to me that to strike the wall with her face under the circumstances suggests that she bumped into someone during the escape."

"Yes!" Ryba said excitedly. "Yes! And the third person—"

"Would be a leak within your organization," Skrdla droned. "Someone with a key. They gained access to the laboratory without forcible entry."

Ryba fell back into his chair. He realized suddenly that what Skrdla said had to be true, and kicked himself for not realizing it earlier. Lifting the phone to his ear, he said, "I will assign my top computer analysts to you. You can scan the intelligence files. We will find this British woman and the leak—"

Skrdla held up a hand. "Have your computer people check if they like," he said, rising to his feet and donning his hat. "I have my own ways of working." He started toward the door.

Ryba recradled the telephone. He had barely lifted his hand when it rang. "Please wait," he told Skrdla.

The man in the gray suit turned around.

Ryba pressed the phone to his ear. "Yes."

For the next three minutes, he listened to the near hysterical ravings of Francis Hunyadi.

Hanging up, Ryba looked back at Skrdla. "My man in the U.S. was kidnapped by South African agents," he said breathlessly. "Now we know who is behind this. South Africa is starting their own biochemical program. They must have masqueraded as British agents…" His voice trailed off as he saw Skrdla's face change.

Skrdla's heavy eyebrows lowered in concentration, and Ryba could almost see the wheels moving in the man's head. "With all due respect, Mr. Ryba," the hulking man said. "That is nonsense."

"But—"

"The body found in the lab was a British MI-6 agent. You have confirmed that fact. The South Africans and British are not on good working terms. Therefore it is the British, undoubtedly aided by the Americans, who are causing you trouble. South Africa? A mere red herring thrown in to confuse things.

Like the Beretta .22 that is usually used by the Mossad." He turned toward the door again.

Ryba cleared his throat. He was both impressed with Skrdla's quick analysis, and embarrassed by his willingness to believe the deception. "When you find the woman, and the informant, bring them to my house for interrogation," he said.

Skrdla stopped, his hand on the doorknob. He turned back slowly. There was something frighteningly primitive about the face now, like some prehistoric predator. "Mr. Ryba," Skrdla said, his grin widening to terrifying proportions, "I believe it is better for me to conduct the interrogations privately. Especially the one of the woman."

He turned back to the door and opened it. "I do not believe my interrogations are a sight that a man like yourself would like to see."

Skrdla closed the door and was gone.

Ryba felt the blood in his veins run cold with the man's final words. He wondered exactly what the agent had meant. Then, pushing the curiosity to the side, he lifted the phone.

It was time to prepare the launch sites and be ready to go with what he already had, if necessary.

Just in case.

Nixa, Missouri

THE GUNFIRE FROM the house still came in sporadic streams as Lyons and Schwarz sprinted across the yard toward the barn.

Lyons twisted as he ran, sending a precious few

cover rounds from the dwindling 9 mm stores within the Calico. He heard two loud roars behind him as Blancanales fired the Able Team leader's .45.

Harsh orders inside the house drifted out, and the gunfire from within suddenly stopped.

Lyons made it to the front of the barn, pressing his back against the splintered wood and sliding quickly along the surface. When he reached the corner, he dropped to one knee, peering around the corner.

Six men were moving cautiously along the side of the barn toward the back. Toward where Schwarz waited defenselessly.

The Able Team leader waved a hand over his shoulder, motioning Blancanales forward. The two Stony Man warriors stepped around the side of the building.

Lyons opened fire with the Calico, stitching a 3-round burst up the spine of the man at the rear of the column. To the side, his .45 boomed in Blancanales's hand and the second man went down. Raising the hot barrel of the subgun slightly, the big ex-cop fired past the two men in the middle, concentrating on the two closest to the corner as they tried to duck around to the rear of the barn.

He got one.

The other, wielding a sawed-off double-barreled shotgun, disappeared around the corner toward Schwarz.

A near-sonic boom blasted from the back of the barn as Lyons opened fire once more with the Calico, dropping one of the men remaining near the side of the barn. Blancanales emptied the last of the .45s in his magazine into the other, sending another of the gunners to the ground on top of his Uzi.

Carl Lyons's heart sank to the bottom of his stomach as he moved over the bodies toward the corner. He had heard no sound since both barrels of the shotgun exploded. Behind him, metal scratched metal as Pol slid one of the final mags into the Government Model.

Reaching the corner, Lyons took a deep breath, mentally preparing himself for what he might see behind the barn. He, Pol and Gadgets had been together longer than he cared to remember. They had been bonded in combat, baptized with fire. They were joined together in spirit like some metaphysical set of Siamese triplets.

Anger filled the Able Team leader's soul as he dropped again to one knee. He glanced down to the windows atop the Calico's hexagonal drum. Less than nine rounds remained in the weapon.

And most of them would go into the man who had killed Hermann "Gadgets" Schwarz.

Suppressing the urge to leap into action, quelling the growl that threatened to roar from his throat, Lyons leaned around the corner, the Calico's muzzle leading the way.

A look of disbelief replaced the grimace on his face as the front sights fell on Schwarz.

Able Team's electronics genius squatted over the body of the man still gripping the shotgun. He twisted the leaf-shaped blade of a Cold Steel push dagger twice in the man's throat, then ripped the weapon out and stood.

Schwarz looked up at Lyons and grinned. "You planning to shoot me, or what?" he asked.

Lyons dropped the gun barrel to the ground and walked forward. "What happened?"

Schwarz shrugged. "He missed."

"Not by much," Blancanales said behind Lyons.

The Able Team leader glanced at Blancanales as the man moved in next to him. Pol wore a grin as wide as Schwarz's. "I'd find a new barber is I was you, Gadg."

Lyons turned back to Schwarz, for the first time focusing completely on the man. Ninety percent of the hair on the right side of the Able Team warrior's head had been blown away by the double 12-gauge blast. The strands that remained had been singed, and now curled uncontrollably over his ear. A tiny drop of blood, where a pellet had nicked the earlobe, was the only injury.

Schwarz stuck a finger in his ear. "It's going to be a little hard to hear out of this thing for a while," he commented.

"Get a hearing aid," Blancanales said. "It'll be a lot easier than getting a date."

Lyons turned away from Schwarz, moving back around the corner where he could see the house. The gunfire from inside the structure, which had gradually built, then dwindled, had stopped completely after the abrupt voice had given orders as they crossed the yard. The Able Team leader's eyes dropped to the bodies scattered around the farmhouse and barn. At least twenty-five, maybe thirty men lay dead on the grass and gravel. More had been in the house when the firing ceased.

Far too many for the one-bedroom shack to hold.

Blancanales read Lyon's mind. "A tunnel," he said.

"Has to be," Schwarz agreed. "They didn't get out the front, and we'd have seen them leaving the back." He pointed toward the open field behind the house.

Lyons stooped and lifted four Uzi mags from the back pockets of one of the downed men. He began to strip the 9 mm rounds and feed them into the Calico. "Grab some firepower," he told his two companions. Both men lifted Uzis and spare loads from the dead men.

Lyons turned back toward the house as he twisted the winder at the rear of the Calico's drum. "I'm ninety-nine percent sure they've all left," he said. "But let's watch out for that one percent."

With the Calico leading the way, Lyons bent low and sprinted toward the front door of the house. Schwarz and Blancanales fanned out, finally merging back with him as he vaulted onto the porch.

The Able Team leader ripped the shredded screen door open and stepped inside.

The house was quiet.

Blancanales and Schwarz hurried past Lyons, quickly checking the rest of the house. "Clear," Gadgets reported, returning to the living room from the kitchen.

"Clear," Pol repeated as he stepped out of the small bedroom.

Lyons scanned the living room floor systematically, searching for signs of a trapdoor. He saw nothing.

Schwarz called out from the kitchen. "It's in here. Under the sink." The Able Team leader had started that way when he heard the sirens on the road. Looking through the front window, he saw the flashing red and blue lights streaking up the dirt road.

Lyons shook his head in disgust. Another dose of Willy Dean Coats was exactly what he didn't need right now. "Stay here," he ordered Gadgets and Pol. "I've got an idea." Hurrying out of the house, he made it to the middle of the yard as the sheriff's patrol car skidded to a halt on the gravel.

Coats's face was livid as he leapt from the car. "What the hell's going on?" he screamed. "I...dead citizens...election...election..."

"Settle down, Willy Dean," Lyons said softly as two more cars and a half-dozen pickups skidded in behind the sheriff's. Three men in uniform and two dozen more in jeans and overalls leapt out carrying shotguns and hunting rifles.

"Settle down!" Coats screamed. "Settle down? You've killed darn near half my county! How's that gonna look?"

Lyons smiled. "It's going to look great, Willy Dean, because none of these guys are from this county. In fact, they aren't even from this country."

Coats's mouth dropped open. "New York?" he asked, then stared stupidly at the Able Team leader.

Lyons draped an arm around Coats's shoulders and guided him away from the others, who had taken formation behind the sheriff. "Willy Dean," he whispered, ''it's time I came clean with you. These guys aren't drug dealers, and we aren't with the Justice Department.''

The sheriff's expression didn't change.

''Spies,'' Lyons said, glancing around furtively. ''They're spies, Willy Dean.''

''Spies?'' Coats repeated. ''Then, if you ain't with the Justice Department, you gotta be—''

''Can't tell you, Willy Dean.''

Coats's face changed to an expression of deep, complete comprehension. He squinted up at Lyons, nodding. ''CIA,'' he whispered.

Lyons winked. ''I never said so.''

Coats grinned.

''We've got to disappear,'' the Able Team leader stated. ''We weren't even here. But I won't leave you hanging. Somebody—really from the Justice Department this time—will have search-and-arrest warrants for you within three hours. And *you* get credit for all this. Think of the election.''

The smile widened. ''Then, uh, me and my men did all this shootin'? It was us shot the spies?''

''No, they'll be drug dealers again. Just like we said.'' He saw Coats's face return to the familiar mask of bewilderment. ''Don't worry. The Justice Department will help you if you forget. Now…we have to disappear.''

Coats shifted nervously on one leg, then the other. ''Want one of my men to take you back to town?''

''No, Willy Dean. Like I said, we're just going to disappear.''

The sheriff's mouth fell open again. "You can really do that?"

"Remember who we are."

Lyons turned and started back to the house. As he opened the screen door again, he heard Coats's voice speak excitedly into the radio. "Angeline, get me Stella over to the *Ozarkian*. And get Channel 4 up to Springfield on the line."

The big ex-cop found the other two warriors in the kitchen. The cabinet under the sink was open, and he could see a dark crawl space leading downward. "Everybody loaded and ready?" he asked.

Schwarz and Blancanales nodded.

"Then let's disappear."

"Yeah, we heard all that through the window," Gadgets said. "You ought to be ashamed of yourself, Ironman."

Lyons dropped to all fours and stuck his head into the crawl space. "Why's that?" he asked over his shoulder.

Schwarz chuckled. "With all the publicity he's going to get, and with Brognola covering his butt to protect Stony Man, you've just stuck the good people of Christian County with Willy Dean Coats for another four years."

Romania

THE SQUELCH on Yakov Katzenelenbogen's radio squealed with an irritatingly high pitch. The Phoenix Force leader adjusted the control in time to hear Manning's voice come over the airwaves.

"I can't believe this place," the big Canadian said. "It's like something out of a Dracula movie."

McCarter came on the air with his dry English humor. "You don't suppose that's because this is where Bram Stoker set the novel, now do you, Gary?"

A moment later, Manning and McCarter both stepped out of the woods on different sides of the clearing to join Katz, James and Encizo.

The men of Phoenix Force had left Istanbul only a few hours earlier, on board the C-17 once more with Jack Grimaldi. Their next strike—far enough from Turkey that they hoped it wouldn't be associated with the hit on Boris Stavropek—lay in Romania, seventeen miles south of Brasov, in the Transylvanian region of the country. They had flown low enough over Brasov to see the mysterious spiral architecture, and even the peasants in pointed "Robin Hood" hats, as Manning had called them. Horse-drawn carts had clomped down the cobblestone streets no differently than they had centuries earlier, and all this had lent itself to the dark, somber mood of the mission.

Indeed, Katz felt almost as if he were going after Vlad Tepes, better known as Vlad the Impaler, and even better known as Count Dracula. But there were two major differences.

The diseases being developed in the old castle in the mountains near Bran would suck the life out of far more people than any vampire ever could. And the biochemical agents were real.

Katz pulled his backpack around to the front, fishing through the gear for the titanium compass. Phoenix Force had resupplied on board the plane as soon as Grimaldi had picked them up and were well armed and outfitted for the next stage of the mission. With one possible exception.

The Israeli looked at the weapon slung over his shoulder with mild disgust as his hand found the compass—a Chinese AK-47, 7.62 X 39 mm, 30-round magazines, filled with metal-cased softpoints. A good weapon, usually.

The exception was that Katz's AK—like those carried by the other four men of Phoenix Force—was only semiautomatic.

The former Mossad agent pulled the compass out, took a reading and dropped it into the side pocket of his BDU pants. Huntington Wethers had noted that a shipment of the Chinese Kalashnikov rifles bound for the Western civilian market had been hijacked a week earlier. Several had already shown up in the hands of a radical group in Peru.

Stony Man Farm had felt that the AKs were the perfect cover, and while Katz and the other men of Phoenix Force had to agree, they didn't have to like the reduction in firepower.

"Everybody ready?" Katz asked.

Manning held up his AK. "Got my repeater and trusty six-gun," he said. "Hey, you suppose we'll get a chance to use bows and arrows someday?"

Katz gave him a dirty look. "We use what's available, and what's appropriate to the mission," the Israeli said sternly. "And this is what's appropriate under the circumstances."

Manning nodded. "Right. Sorry."

The Israeli led the way out of the clearing into the

forest. Manning, McCarter and James followed, with Encizo bringing up the rear as they threaded their way through the dense trees. Fifteen minutes later, they came to a larger clearing. Katz dropped to one knee, still inside the woods. Through the branches, he could see the village of Bran, and in its center, the infamous Castle Bran.

James dropped down next to him, pulling a set of minibinoculars from his pack. The black Phoenix Force warrior held them to his forehead and whistled. He turned to Katz. "Manning was right. That was the real Dracula's castle?"

"So they say."

James stood. "Hope we brought enough garlic." He grinned.

Katz smiled. "Let's move on. The castle *we* are looking for is over there." He pointed past the village, to the face of the mountain in the background, then turned to lead the way through the forest once more. The men of Phoenix Force remained silent as they circled the clearing inside the tree line, staying deep enough to be hidden behind the trees.

Thirty minutes later, they had circumnavigated the village and stood face-to-face with the mountain. A narrow road led up into the rocks, barely wide enough for the horse-drawn carts.

Darkness began to fall as Katz started up the path, his nylon combat boots moving smoothly up the steep grade. He shifted the pack frequently, feeling the straps bite into his shoulders.

The Israeli let himself drift into a brief moment of sentimentality as the sun dropped below the mountains. How many times had he led men into battle during his long career with the Israeli army, Mossad, and now Stony Man Farm? He couldn't remember. But as he moved on, willing his aging muscles and bones up the mountain, he could read the history of his vocation in the aches and pains that accompanied every step.

With the day in near-total darkness now, Katz stopped on a ridge. He held up a hand and the others halted behind him. Reaching into his pack once more, his fingers located the long tubular Cyalume light stick. He bent it slightly, shook it and the area suddenly glowed with a cool green light.

Katz checked his compass for the last time, then dropped it in his pack. He turned toward the men. ''We're near.''

Four heads nodded in the green light. Then Manning and Encizo moved off to the left along the ridge, disappearing around the mountain. James and McCarter took the right.

Katz moved on up the trail, cautiously now, the AK-47 held in front of him. Ahead, at the edge of the light, he could see the trail top another ridge and descend on the other side. If Intel was correct, there should be one more rise before the castle came into view. The Israeli moved on.

Katz didn't hear the movement in the rocks above him. He didn't see, feel or smell the man preparing to drop from the top of the boulder to his side. But somehow he sensed the presence of the enemy, even if that perception came a split second too late.

Katzenelenbogen looked up and saw the shadowy outline of a man and what looked like a rifle against the dark sky. A moment later, he felt as if the entire planet had fallen on top of his head.

CHAPTER ELEVEN

Prague, Czech Republic

Anton Kutna turned toward the Executioner, his face uncertain. "You want me to let them in?"

Bolan nodded. Grabbing Hammersmith by the arm, he pulled her behind the door. "Let them in, then step to the side—away from us—and close the door."

Kutna shrugged. He pushed his face to the window again. His face hardened. "The sergeant," he said, as the two men crossed the street. "I recognize him. His name is Hromas. He is…" He paused, searched for the word in English, then gave up and said something in Czech.

Hammersmith turned to Bolan. "An extortionist," she whispered. "What you Yanks call a 'shakedown artist.'"

Heavy knuckles rapped on the wood.

Kutna looked at Bolan one last time, then shrugged again. He opened the door.

Bolan watched through the crack between the door and frame as Sergeant Hromas spoke harshly in Czech. Hammersmith pushed her lips up to Bolan's ear. "They are demanding to come inside and look for themselves."

"Get ready," Bolan whispered back.

Kutna stepped away from them and bowed dramatically, sweeping the cops in with an arm. The two men stepped in and the little shopkeeper swung the door shut.

As soon as the door was out of the way, Bolan slid forward. The hard right cross shot straight from his shoulder, striking the sergeant in the back of the skull and causing the fat hanging on his neck to shimmy as he fell to the ground.

The younger policeman turned toward the Executioner, his hand groping for the pistol on his belt. The flap holster slowed him, and Hammersmith stepped in and shoved the little .22 under his nose.

The young man's eyes opened wide in surprise, but they didn't stay open long.

Bolan looped a left hook around Hammersmith's Beretta and sent the cop tumbling to the floor to sleep on top of the sergeant. Dropping to the concrete, the Executioner pulled the younger man to the side. A quick search of Hromas's uniform turned up a thick roll of bills in a money clip. "How much has he shaken you down for?" the Executioner asked Kutna.

"Over the years? There is no way of telling."

Bolan flipped the money clips through the air to Kutna. "Here's part of it," he said.

Two minutes later, Bolan wore the rank of a Czech police sergeant. The pants, like the ones he'd found in Kutna's closet, were too short. The tunic not only crowded his shoulders, it gaped at the waist. And the wool scratched the burns on his arms like the claws of a cat. But the uniforms were a better disguise than the clothes they'd found in Kutna's closet, and once again, it was the best they had and would have to do.

Hammersmith finished buttoning the patrolman's tunic, rolled the cuffs under at the ankles and placed the eight-point cap over her red hair. "Well, Sergeant Pollock," she said, "what now?"

"We slip out the back, put as much ground between us and the cops as fast as we can, then move on with the mission." He led the British agent down the hall toward the rear of the building.

Kutna's feet pattered across the concrete floor behind them. The Executioner felt a hand reach out and grab his arm. He turned.

"Please," Kutna said, looking back at the cops on the floor. "you must hit me."

Bolan saw what he meant. Unless it looked like the little shopkeeper had been a hostage, Kutna would have more explaining than he could handle when the two men woke up.

The Executioner drew back his fist.

Kutna clasped his hands together under his chin as if in prayer. His eyes closed tightly, like a child feigning sleep.

Bolan dropped his hand and shook his head. He couldn't hit the old man. At least not hard enough to knock him out—it might kill him. With the front knuckles of his fist, he rapped Kutna smartly on the forehead.

"Ouch!" the little man said, his eyes popping open.

An angry red welt began to rise on his forehead.

"Now go lie down and keep quiet," Bolan ordered.

Kutna nodded, turned and hurried back into the showroom.

Bolan and Hammersmith headed on to the back door, cracking it open. The alley looked clear. Closing the door carefully behind them, they stepped into the morning sunshine. "Look natural," the warrior said as they started toward the end of the alley. "As soon as we're out of the area, we'll—"

His jaw clamped shut as a trio of uniformed men crossed the alley on the adjacent sidewalk.

Bolan slowed, hoping they'd pass without looking down the alley. They didn't.

The Executioner resumed pace as the three cops turned their way and stopped. He glanced casually over his shoulder. The other end of the alley was clear. But if they turned now, it would look too suspicious.

Hammersmith kept stride to his side. "Any ideas?" she asked out of the side of her mouth.

"Not a one."

The Executioner wasn't lying. The cops had appeared too quick to formulate a plan. But it wasn't the first time Bolan had been in such situations over his long career.

The cop closest to the alley frowned, then called out.

Bolan and Hammersmith walked forward to meet the Czech police.

Nixa, Missouri

SCHWARZ WATCHED Lyons kneel on the kitchen floor, squeeze his six-foot-plus frame into the cabinet under the sink, then drop into the hole beneath the plumbing.

Blancanales followed, having an easier time of it than the big Able Team leader. Schwarz brought up the rear.

Dust fell through the narrow dirt passageway as Lyons switched on his miniflashlight. The Able Team warriors found themselves in a narrow crawl space leading under the open field behind the house.

Lyons glanced overhead, then killed the light. He spoke in the darkness that engulfed them, whispering, "Be careful, guys. This place looks like it was dug pretty quick. There's no reinforcement."

Schwarz didn't need to be told. Although the tunnel was now blacker than the inside of a tomb, he could feel the dust drifting from the top into his hair and sinuses. Who knew how many men had just scrambled down this path, banging the sides and ceiling and loosening the earth?

He sensed Lyons's and Blancanales's movement in front of him, and suppressing a sneeze, crawled forward. During the brief second that Lyons had risked the light, he had seen that the tunnel stretched far into the distance. They were in for a long crawl.

The commandeered Uzi slung over his back, Schwarz crawled on. Here and there, the soil was wet. A nearby spring, perhaps? His hands were soon caked with mud.

As he crawled through the darkness, his mind drifted back to his tours in Vietnam. In addition to his training in electronics and explosives, Schwarz had been trained as a tactical and guerrilla warfare expert, which meant he had done a stint as a "tunnel rat," moving through the underground labyrinths armed only with a .45. He had encountered several of the enemy in the close quarters beneath the jungle, and it had never scared him more than any other facet of war.

But the chance of a cave-in and being buried alive had kept him alert to every particle of dust that had drifted through the air.

A loose dirt clod fell from above, striking the Able Team warrior on the head; reminding him once more that death came not only from enemy fire, but from any of the variable forces of nature.

He moved on, the ground getting damper and the mud moving up his wrists. After what Schwarz estimated to be a hundred yards, the team came to a halt. Lyons's voice drifted back through the narrow tunnel. "We've got a turn," he whispered. "Stay put. I'm going to chance the light again."

Schwarz reached back, pulling the Uzi around to his front and hitting the safety. A second later, the light flashed on and he saw Lyons leaning around a corner in the dirt passageway. The light died again. "Another twenty yards or so," the Able Team leader whispered. "I see a concrete wall with a door in it. That's the good news."

"There's bad?" Blancanales's voice whispered in the darkness.

"Maybe. Somebody's lying in the middle of the tunnel about halfway there. Might be dead. Might not. Let's go find out."

Schwarz followed the other two men around the corner. A moment later, Lyons switched on the flashlight again. The Able Team leader had moved past the body stretched out on the tunnel floor. Schwarz looked past Blancanales to see the open, pain-stricken eyes of a man of around thirty. A tiny trickle of blood still oozed from the stomach wound just above his navel.

He looked down at his hands. The mud covering them was a dark reddish brown. The dampness he'd felt in the earth had been from the trail of blood, rather than the underground spring he'd imagined.

The big ex-cop turned away and crawled the last ten yards to the concrete wall. Blancanales and Schwarz moved over the body and followed.

Lyons and Blancanales were studying the steel door in the wall when Schwarz came to a halt on his hands and knees. A simple padlock secured the door to the bolt. Easy to blast apart with a bullet. The electronics man raised a hand to the side of his head. His ear still buzzed from the shotgun blast.

They'd all need hearing protection when they blew the lock if they expected to come out of the narrow passageway with their eardrums intact.

Schwarz pulled a small black plastic case from his pocket and removed a pair of corkscrew earplugs. He stuck them into his ears as he watched Blancanales and Lyons do the same.

Lyons turned to his men and got two nods of readiness. He pressed the barrel of his Calico against the padlock, the gun angled so the bullet would ricochet off the steel door and into the dirt.

Schwarz looked down to the approximate spot where the 9 mm round should hit, his stomach suddenly growing queasy as something caught his eye. He started to speak, but before he could get the words from his mouth, Lyons pulled the trigger.

The next thing Gadgets Schwarz knew, the world was falling in on him.

Romania

THE HARD BONY KNEES struck Katzenelenbogen on both shoulders and felt like they'd driven the bones down to his ribs. A sharp pain cut through him like the blade of a knife, then his left arm went as numb as his right prosthetic limb.

Katz fell to the mountain trail amid a tangle of arms and legs, the back of his head hitting the packed earth with a crack. His vision blurred, and he saw the fuzzy image of the rifle-toting man roll off him as if under water. Rolling to his belly, the Phoenix Force leader got his arms under himself and pushed up. His arms collapsed, and he fell forward again. He rolled to his side in time to see the other man bound to his feet.

The former Mossad agent struggled to his knees. The nerves in his shoulders had gone dead, paralyzing his arms. He tried willing the limbs to rise, but they refused the order.

The man holding the rifle stepped forward, sticking the barrel into the Phoenix Force leader's face. Katz looked down the .30-caliber hole, his arms still frozen. He saw the butt of the rifle come around in an arc as if in slow motion.

THE FEELING HAD RETURNED to Katz's arms—the pain assured him of that. But they still refused to move. He looked down through half-open eyes and saw that his wrists were bound with a rough hemp rope. That rope, in turn, had been fastened to another that circled his waist. He was sitting in a hard wooden chair, bound further by more rope that strapped him to the rungs digging into his back.

A voice behind him spoke harshly in what Katz took to be Czech. Bees buzzed through his head. The voice spoke again, this time in broken English. Katz nodded.

"I ask who you are? How much men with you?"

Katz didn't answer. He closed his eyes again to the pain.

Something hard slapped across the back of his neck and sent the bees wings flapping. Bile rose from the Israeli's stomach to his throat, and for a moment, he thought he'd throw up. Then his belly settled again, as the voice repeated, "Who you are? How much men?"

Katz opened his eyelids and stared foggily at the figure that moved around in front of him. As his vision cleared, he saw a bearded man, well over two hundred pounds. The man stared down at him, expressionless. He wore a white open-collared shirt, khaki work pants, and held a brown leather police "slapper" in one hand, spanking it lightly against the palm of his other hand as he awaited Katz's reply.

The Phoenix Force leader closed his eyes again. He let his head fall to the side, as if he'd passed out.

The ruse didn't work.

The man used the edge of the slapper this time, opening a gash over the Israeli's left eyebrow. "Who you are!" he screamed. "How many men! What you know about what we keep here?"

The last question wasn't lost on Katz. It sounded as if the castle lab might also double as a storage site.

When he opened his eyes again, Katz saw that another man in jeans and T-shirt had joined the first. Katz's radio and headset hung at the end of his arm, explaining how the Israeli's tormentors knew he wasn't alone.

The former Mossad agent's vision had blurred once more, both from the slapper and the blood now dripping into his eyes. But between the two men, behind them on the wall, he could make out a clock.

It had been almost twenty minutes since the dark figure had descended from the boulder on top of him. By now, the rest of Phoenix Force would have tried to contact him on the radio, received no answer and realized something was wrong.

Another blow from the slapper split his lip. Though he hadn't thought it possible, the pain in his head intensified.

James, Manning, McCarter and Encizo would even now be preparing to hit the castle. Maybe they'd guessed what had happened to him, maybe not. But in any case, they'd carry on with the mission, which meant the thing to do now was stall, give out as much disinformation as possible.

The man in the white shirt had raised the leather bludgeon again by the time Katz spoke. "Many," he whispered.

The man stopped the slapper above his head. "What?"

"Many," Katz repeated. "There are many more."

"*How* many?" the man demanded.

Katz waited until he saw the man's fingers tighten around the slapper once more. Every second, every fraction of a second, he could stall might help. As the man cocked the truncheon to strike, he said, "Two hundred."

The steel-filled leather came painfully down on Katz's kneecap. A grunt escaped his lips as new misery shot through his leg.

"You are lying!" the man shrieked. He raised the club once more and brought it down on Katz's other knee.

Agony flooded both legs now, mixing with the pain in his head and shoulders to make the Israeli feel as if every inch of his body had been tortured. He fought the scream that threatened to burst from his throat, instead willing his lips to say, "Yes...I lied. There are more. Perhaps three hundred."

The man in the white shirt stepped back, eyeing Katz with a mixture of anger and respect. "You are tough," he said. "But we will find out just how tough." He moved in again, bringing the slapper back behind his back and swinging it into the Israeli's midsection.

Katz heard a crack as the edge of the leather-covered steel struck his rib cage. He coughed uncontrollably as the man in the white shirt drew the weapon back again. Slowly, methodically, wearing the expression of a chemist staring at a test tube and curious as to the outcome of his experiment, the man in the white shirt set about breaking the rest of Katz-enelenbogen's ribs.

Then, just as the sanity was about to be driven from his brain by a suffering far greater than Katz had ever dreamed possible, he heard glass break somewhere above and behind him. A split second later, the distinctive sound of an AK-47—fired semiauto—blasted his ears.

The man with the slapper looked over Katz's shoulder, his face changing to a mask of shock.

Through the pain racking his entire body now, Katz felt himself grin. That pain was about to end. One way or another. Perhaps he'd survive the attack, perhaps he wouldn't. Perhaps he would die of internal bleeding before the rest of Phoenix Force could get him to medical help.

But he had succeeded in what he'd set out to do. He had survived so far, and he hadn't given Ryba's men any information that would help them against the attack.

The smile stayed on the Israeli's lips, even after he'd lost consciousness.

Prague, Czech Republic

THE FACES of the three Czech cops on the sidewalk at the end of the alley changed from confused to curious as Bolan and Hammersmith continued to walk toward them. The officer in front, with hair as red as Hammersmith's sticking out from the sides of his cap and looking strangely out of place on a Czech, suddenly spoke.

"He wants to know what division we're from," Hammersmith whispered. "He doesn't recognize us."

Bolan turned to her, smiling, as if she'd just said something humorous. "You know any of the police divisions here?"

"No."

"Well, tell him something," the Executioner said as they continued to close the gap.

"My accent will never pass," Hammersmith replied.

"Do it." They were less than ten yards away now. He didn't need Hammersmith's words to be accepted. He just needed another few seconds to get within arm's reach.

Hammersmith spoke, and Bolan saw the eyes of the man with red hair open wide as he realized what was going on. His hand shot down to the flap holster on his belt, but by then the Executioner had drawn Sergeant Hromas's CZ-75 from his own leather and slid the last few feet to the sidewalk.

Bolan jammed the weapon into the red-haired cop's gut, at the same time reaching up and circling an arm around the man's head. With a quick glance up and down the street, he jerked the cop back out of sight into the alley.

Hammersmith had stopped at the sidewalk, and now aimed her own CZ at the other two police officers. She spoke again, and the men raised their hands before following Bolan between the buildings.

The warrior tightened the headlock, holstered his

weapon, then ripped the red-haired man's gun from his holster and shoved it back into his belly. "Get their guns," he ordered Hammersmith, who stepped forward and relieved the two cops of their pistols.

The Executioner let up on the headlock and allowed the cop to stand. The man's face was as red now as his hair, and he breathed hard, staring at his gun in Bolan's hand. The warrior motioned toward a large trash bin twenty feet deeper into the alley. "Tell them to walk that way quietly and they won't be hurt." He paused, staring into the red-haired cop's eyes. "And tell this one to quit looking at his gun. It's mine now, and if he doesn't stop thinking what he's thinking, I'll put the first round right through his nose."

Hammersmith barked the orders.

The red-haired cop jerked his eyes away from the CZ-75.

Bolan stopped the three men just short of the trash bin and leaned them forward on the metal. Quickly he removed their handcuffs from the pouches on their belts, then said, "Tell them to get inside and turn their backs to each other."

The woman spoke harshly. The three men struggled over the edge of the trash bin.

The Executioner cuffed them together, then forced their heads down below the opening.

"We need gags," Hammersmith said. "They'll start screaming to high heaven the moment they think we're gone."

"You happen to bring any gags with you?" the Executioner asked.

"Uh, no."

"We'll be out of here before anybody comes along," Bolan said. "But just to be sure, tell them to keep quiet for ten minutes after I close the lid. You might add that if they don't, and we hear them, we're going to empty their own weapons into the side of this thing." He tapped the metal wall of the trash bin.

After the British woman relayed the new orders, Bolan dropped the lid, and he and Hammersmith walked quickly down the alley once more.

"Where to now?" the MI-6 agent asked.

"To check in with my base of operations," Bolan replied. "We've been out of touch for several hours. They might have broken the codes, in which case we're going after the storage and launch sites."

"And if they haven't?" Hammersmith asked as they exited the alley and started down the street.

Bolan felt the burns on his arms again as they scratched against the woolen tunic. He shrugged. "More of the same, Ms. Hammersmith. More of the same."

Nixa, Missouri

LYONS PULLED the Calico's trigger. The resulting explosion in the narrow confines of the tunnel thudded through the earplugs into his ears.

A moment later, the tunnel started to reverberate. He turned in time to see the earth swoop down and swallow Gadgets Schwarz.

Lyons froze where he knelt, waiting for the avalanche of dirt to subside. Directly behind him he saw Blancanales do the same. Then dust filled the tunnel like the smoke from a burning oil well, blocking out the light and casting the shaft into darkness in spite of the flashlight. The Able Team leader pulled a handkerchief from the pocket of his coat and tied it over his nose and mouth.

Gradually the dirt settled and the light returned. "You all right, Pol?" Lyons asked.

Blancanales had tied his own handkerchief over his face. He nodded. "But Gadgets—"

"I know. I saw. Let's get busy. He might be unconscious and we'll have to move slow." Lyons pointed overhead. "It's still rumbling."

Carefully the big ex-cop squeezed in next to Blancanales. Together, they began sifting the earth off the pile where Schwarz had to be. Every shift and sound from above brought a deep breath from the two men, and each time they wondered if that breath might be their last.

"He can't be that deep," Pol said, coughing as a cloud of dust floated under his handkerchief. "The tunnel wasn't that deep."

Lyons continued to dig, clawing the dirt away and trying to walk a fine line between speed and serenity. They had to work fast enough to keep Schwarz from smothering under the mountain of earth. But they needed to remain passive enough to keep from starting another cave-in.

Finally Lyons's hand struck an arm. He dug faster, ignoring the still-shifting earth above his head. A minute later, the two Able Team warriors pulled Schwarz's head from the dirt.

"He's breathing," Pol said, digging on, trying to

get enough of Gadgets's body uncovered to pull him free.

Two minutes later, Schwarz lay prostrate on the tunnel floor. Lyons tore the handkerchief from his face, wiped the dirt from his teammate's eyes, then slapped him lightly.

Schwarz's eyes opened. "Thanks," he said, grinning. "I needed that."

Lyons and Blancanales helped him to all fours.

"First I get a crew cut from a shotgun," Schwarz complained, "then a tunnel caves in on me. My mother told me there'd be days like this."

The three men crawled back toward the door. Lyons stopped and turned back, staring past the two men to the solid wall of dirt behind them. For all he knew, the cave-in might extend all the way back to the house, and another avalanche of earth could come down on their heads any second.

There was only one way out—straight through the door. He turned back, pulled the broken lock off the bolt and dropped it into the dirt. As he reached for the handle, he felt a hand grab his arm.

"Ironman, wait!"

Schwarz had crawled past Blancanales and now squeezed in next to Lyons, his eyes glued to the ground. Gadgets's grime-covered eyebrows fell almost to his nose in concentration. He pointed toward the bottom of the door.

Lyons followed his finger. There, peeking out from beneath the door, he saw a thin blue wire.

"I saw it just before you blew the lock." Schwarz

dropped the Able Team leader's arm and moved forward. "It's wired."

Without speaking, Lyons moved back to give Schwarz room. He and Blancanales waited silently as the electronic expert fell to his belly, looking under the door. He dug through the dirt, finding two more wires. Green, red and blue, they all ran to the dirt wall adjacent to the concrete around the door.

Gadgets scratched lightly into the dirt on the side of the tunnel. With painstaking slowness, he began to uncover a dark brown object.

"Any way to speed this up?" Pol asked, coughing. "We're not only risking another cave-in, we're going to run out of oxygen down here before long."

"Speed up and we'll *blow* up." Schwarz dug more dirt from the wall. "Dynamite," he said over his shoulder. "Hold on. I think I see how it's rigged."

After what seemed like an eternity to Lyons, Schwarz finally turned around. "There's six sticks of dynamite in here, set to a timer. They must have started it when they passed through earlier."

Lyons nodded. "So? Where do we stand?"

Schwarz rubbed dirt from his forehead with the back of his hand. "We still playing the good-news-bad-news game?" he asked. Getting no response, he looked at Blancanales. "The good news is, you're wrong, Pol. We're not going to run out of oxygen." He paused, then went on. "The bad news is that we won't have time to. We're scheduled to be blown apart in a little less than three minutes."

"So what do you suggest?" Lyons asked. "You're the demo man."

"I was hoping you wouldn't ask. That's the worst news of all." He drew another breath, then coughed when dust followed it into his chest. "This device is so simple, it's hard. Three lines lead directly to the dynamite. One's the real fuse, the other two are dummies. But there's no way to know which is which."

"So pull them all," Lyons said.

Schwarz shook his head. "One of them's bound to be a trip wire," he said, "and if we pull it, we all go up ahead of schedule."

CHAPTER TWELVE

Romania

Gary Manning peered at the east side of the castle from behind the trunk of the tree. He was forty, maybe fifty yards away from the rough eight-foot stone wall that surrounded the courtyard, but it was as close as he dared to get.

There were bound to be guards outside the wall. He'd already encountered two while still coming up from the mountain. They now lay where he'd found them, never to move again.

Manning had climbed halfway up the tree only moments earlier, high enough to see the courtyard on the other side, an open area that stretched to the living quarters.

He was close enough, Manning reasoned. Even with his AK, pack and other gear, he figured he could cover the distance, including the eight-foot wall, in ten to fifteen seconds, tops. He'd run the forty-yard dash in sub-five-second times ever since his rugby days at McGill University.

He stared at the enigmatic structure in the distance. In a few more minutes, Katz would give the word and he'd prove his speed. The big Canadian moved back behind the tree and bent his right leg, stretching the left out straight to loosen his hamstring. Yeah, he was as fast as he'd been in college, but he'd noticed one other change, too, and it wasn't quite as positive.

At McGill, he'd been able to go into a rugby game stone cold and be just fine. Now, if he didn't warm up, he stood a good chance of pulling a muscle. Limping through the rest of this mission wasn't exactly what he had planned.

Manning shifted his weight to the other leg, stretching slowly. His head moved out from behind the tree and he saw the castle once more. It really did look like something out of a vampire or werewolf movie. He could almost see the frightened villagers with their pitchforks and torches mobbing the gates.

The big Canadian stood upright again, placed his hands on his hips and began to twist back and forth to loosen his oblique muscles. Stretching had a good effect on his mind, as well as his body. It kept the normal prebattle butterflies under control.

He finished stretching, looked at his watch and frowned. It had been fifteen minutes since Phoenix Force had split up. Everyone should be in place and ready to strike. With a quick glance around, he adjusted the headset over his ears and whispered into the face mike. "Phoenix Four, Phoenix One. Come in, One."

He waited for the reply, but got only static.

"Phoenix One, Phoenix Four, come in Katz," he said. Again, only a crisp series of clicks and buzzes met his ears.

"Phoenix Four, this is Two. Come in, Four" finally sounded over the two-way.

"I hear you, Calvin," Manning whispered. "Where's Katz?"

"Your guess is as good as mine," James replied.

Encizo's voice came on the air. "Phoenix Five to Four and Two. I had to sneak past a sentry on the way up. Katz might be too close to the enemy for radio traffic."

Manning nodded. It made sense. None of the men of Phoenix Force were armed with sound-suppressed weapons on this one, and a blade went only so far. If Katz had stumbled onto sentries, he might have chosen to hide rather than tipping the castle off with gunfire.

The big Canadian squatted next to the tree, waiting. Five minutes passed, then ten. The sureness he had felt that Katz was all right began to fade. The Phoenix Force leader would have heard them in his headset, even if he'd chosen to maintain his own radio silence. By now, he'd have called in.

But he hadn't, which meant he wasn't.

James voiced Manning's fears for him. "Two to Three, Four and Five. Something's wrong, guys."

Three voices whispered affirmation over the airwaves.

Phoenix Force had no official second-in-command. They didn't need one. Each of the men from Stony Man Farm was a leader in his own right, or he wouldn't have been at the Farm to begin with.

Manning now took charge, and no one questioned the big Canadian's authority any more than if Encizo,

James or McCarter had decided to take the lead. "Phoenix Four to Two, Three and Five. Proceed with the plan. Katz is either in a hole he won't get out of for a while, or he's been taken prisoner." He paused, the next words coming hard. "Or he's dead. The only way to find out is to go on. Everybody ready?"

Three more affirmatives.

"Then let's do it."

Pulling the bolt back on the AK-47, the big Canadian sprinted from behind the tree and crossed the open area to the castle, slinging the weapon over his shoulder as he ran. His boots left the ground ten feet from the wall and he flew through the air, his fingertips finding purchase at the top of the stones. Another second and he had pulled himself up and over the top and was dropping to the courtyard below.

Manning saw the guard thirty feet to his right, near a large building that had to have once served as the castle's stable. The man turned his way, but the Phoenix Force warrior didn't fire.

By the time he had pulled the AK-47 from his shoulder, he was already crashing through the window into the main living quarters.

Stony Man Farm

AARON KURTZMAN CLASPED his hands, popped the knuckles, then rubbed his fingers together. He had been typing for hours, and his brain might still be alert but his hands felt like they were in their death throes.

He leaned forward, lifted his coffee cup from the console next to the computer and took a sip of the liquid that had lost its warmth hours earlier. He set the cup down, clasped his hands behind his head and stared at the screen.

The Czech version of ACCESS DATA INCOMPLETE flashed on and off in yellow letters, with the same maddening persistence it had with every other attempt he'd made to break Joseph Ryba's code. Tapping a button, Kurtzman cleared the entry and returned to the deciphering program.

The same baffling symbols appeared on the screen.

Kurtzman closed his eyes. Breaking computer codes differed little from breaking codes on paper, as men had been doing since the birth of warfare. On paper, you wrote, and on the computer, you typed, but both involved a process known as cryptanalysis, which simply meant the analysis, or breakdown, of coded writing. That process was almost identical to the principles used by investigators who pieced together the clues and leads in a crime. Clear, systematic thought was essential, with persistence, tolerance and an optimistic attitude that ignored failed attempts being as essential to a positive outcome as the computer itself.

The computer wizard looked over his shoulder at Louis Tuma. The FBI man had discarded his coat and tie hours earlier, rolled up his sleeves and begun to offer his own original ideas as well as translating from Czech to English. His ideas had been good.

But they hadn't worked any better than Kurtzman's own.

Lifting his coffee cup again, he drained the remainder and turned back to Tuma. "Do you mind?" he asked, handing him the empty cup and pointing toward the coffeemaker down the ramp and against the wall. "It'll be faster than me rolling down."

Tuma smiled wearily, took the cup and walked down the ramp.

Kurtzman turned back to the screen, to the jumble of signs he saw before him. Somewhere, right in front of his eyes, was all he needed to know to break the codes and turn the confusion into coherent words that would identify Ryba's biochemical storage and launch sites. Some system had to have been used to encode those words.

But that was the missing link. *What* system? The clutter of shapes he saw made it clear that a cipher, with each letter of the alphabet being assigned a corresponding symbol, had been used. Eventually he would break the cipher.

What worried him now was what he suspected lay beneath the cipher—a true code, in which entire words or phrases had been assigned different meanings. That code could be anything.

"Apples" might mean Frankfurt, with "oranges" meaning Germany. "Hot dog" could stand for Liverpool, and "shoe" might really be Denmark.

True codes didn't need the rhyme and reason necessary to a cipher. Figuring them out without a "key" was possible, but might take years, years the Stony Man crew didn't have.

"But first things first," Kurtzman mumbled under his breath, "and the cipher comes before the code."

"Aaron?"

Kurtzman turned and almost spilled the cup of coffee Tuma was holding out to him. "Just thinking out loud, Louie," he said, taking the coffee and setting it down. "Okay, let's regroup again. So far, we've tried position codes, code wheels and multiplication codes. I'm convinced it's a position code. Every time I've tried one, a few of the symbols have changed to letters. So what we're looking at is a position cipher…but with one or more exceptions."

"Has to be," Tuma agreed, taking a drink from the cup of coffee he'd brought back for himself. "It's figuring out those exceptions that's going to be a bitch."

Kurtzman's fingers returned to the keyboard, tapped buttons, and four lines resembling a ticktacktoe board appeared on the screen. He filled the spaces in with the letters *A* through *F,* then drew an *X* beneath it. *J, K, L* and *M* went into these spaces before the computer man drew another ticktacktoe board and *X.* He filled in the squares and triangles with the remaining letters of the alphabet, but added a line over each one.

Letters are represented by the shape of their corresponding space, Kurtzman entered into the machine. Then, *"A" = backward "L"; "C" = "L"; "E" = SQUARE,* and *Letters "N" through "Z" include bar over symbol.* He tapped ENTER and sat back as the computer digested the information.

A moment later, as it had before when he'd tried the same process, several of the symbols became letters. But ACCESS DATA INCOMPLETE again flashed on as well.

Kurtzman shook his head. Again, close but no cigar. But he was on the scent. So close he could almost taste it.

A position code with exceptions. What were those exceptions?

The phone buzzed on the console, and Kurtzman lifted it to his ear. "Aaron," Huntington Wethers said, and Kurtzman turned instinctively toward the far side of the room where the man sat. "I tapped into the BATF lines and found out several AR-15s and .45s left through the back door of the Safari Arms factory in Olympia, Washington. You might pass it on to Kissinger in case Phoenix Force or Bolan need more cover weapons down the line."

"I'll tell Barbara," Kurtzman replied, turning to glance through the glass wall into the mission control room. Price was busy talking to someone on her own phone, and scribbling furiously on a notepad. Turning back to Wethers, Kurtzman said, "Thanks, Hunt."

Wethers nodded. "I'll get back on the Ryba psychological profile now. The more I learn about him, the less I like. That man is one egotistical bastard."

"Most megalomaniacs are, Hunt."

The anxiety started in Kurtzman's stomach the moment he turned back to the screen. What had Wethers said? Something had stuck in his subconscious mind and was now trying to surface. More stolen weapons? No, that wasn't it. Safari Arms? Olympia, Washington? Neither the firearms manufacturer nor the city seemed to have any bearing on this mission.

Ryba. Sure. It had been something in the passing comment at the end of the conversation, something about Ryba.

Excitement mounted in Kurtzman's soul as he grabbed his coffee cup and took a drink. Wethers had said something they knew already. Ryba was an egotistical bastard. Okay, fine.

Setting the coffee cup back down, Kurtzman looked at the screen. So what would be the ''exceptions'' in a position code created by an egotist? What letters would he change to confuse the code?

The letters of his name.

His fingers flying once more, Kurtzman entered the information that the letters *R, Y, B* and *A* be excepted. A few more of the symbols changed to letters.

He typed in J-O-S-E-P-H, then hit ENTER.

More of the cryptic message became clear.

Kurtzman snatched the phone from the cradle and tapped Wethers's extension number. A second later, Hunt said, ''Yes, Aaron?''

The computer ace looked down from the ramp into the face of the man on the other side of the room, barely able to contain his excitement. ''What's Ryba's middle name?'' he demanded.

''Uh…'' Wethers glanced up to his own screen. ''Jurgin. It's German, I think. Usually spelled with an *E* after the *G,* but Ryba uses an *I.*''

Kurtzman hung up. The letters *J* and *R* had already been entered with the first and last name, so he typed in only *U, G, I* and *N.* He hit the ENTER key again, and the rest of the symbols changed to letters.

Tuma leaned over his shoulder. ''You've got it, Aaron! That word at the top, that's Czech for 'storage.'''

Kurtzman's eyes flew down the screen. The names

of the cities and addresses were also in Czech, but they were close enough to make out. A smile broke over his face.

It changed back to a frown as he worked on down the list and came to a word that couldn't be a city.

Tuma leaned in closer. "It means 'flute.' It makes no sense."

"I'm afraid it does," Kurtzman replied. "We've hit a true code, Louie. 'Flute' has to mean 'launch,' or something equivalent in Czech." He looked on down the list. "Read them in English."

"Organ, Piano," Tuma said. "Guitar, Cymbal and so on. They're all musical instruments common to the music of classical Czech composers like Smetana and Dvořák."

Kurtzman grabbed the phone once more and buzzed Price. As he waited for her to answer, he tapped more buttons on the keyboard, sending the decoded sites of the storage facilities onto her screen in the next room.

"I'm picking it up, Bear," the mission controller said as soon as she answered his ring. "I'll get it to Striker and Katz as soon as they make contact. What's this…flute and—"

"The hard part," Kurtzman said. "The launch sites. I'll get back to you." Replacing the receiver on the console, he looked back at the screen.

"SOUNDS LIKE you've had a real time of it," Price commented into the crackling phone. The Stony Man Farm mission controller had barely hung up on Kurtzman when the phone buzzed again. This time, instead of coming from the next room, the call had been from a pay phone in Prague, Czech Republic. She had immediately switched the scrambler to both ends of the line.

"The bad part is how little we're accomplishing, Barb," Bolan said. "We've thrown some monkey wrenches into their works, but I've got a sneaking suspicion we've barely touched the tip of the iceberg. And Ryba's bound to be suspicious. We need the storage sites. Even more, we need the launch sites."

"Your timing is impeccable," Price replied. "At least for storage. Bear's got them. He's gone to work on the rest. It's a true code, using musical instruments."

"That could take time," Bolan said after a pause. "Okay, at least we're one step farther up the ladder. Any storage sites near here?"

Price looked down at the hard copy of the list she'd printed off her computer screen. "Affirmative, Striker. A couple."

"Give me the closest. And I'm changing battle plans. Like I said, unless Ryba is a complete idiot—and you don't get where he's gotten by being a fool—he's figured out that something's going on. Too many coincidences at the labs. I'm going to heat things up. Hard probes from here on out. Maybe we can get him to force his hand."

"I hear you," Price said. "The closest site is the old Hotel Spilberk in Brno. That's in Moravia." As she read the address, she pictured Bolan writing it down. "I've got Grimaldi circling between you and Romania, ready to pick up whoever needs him first."

"Romania?"

"Yeah. Phoenix Force."

"Okay," Bolan said. "Tell Jack to land and we'll meet him at the airport."

Barbara Price pictured Mack Bolan getting on the plane. She and Bolan had had a sort of relationship for some time. On the rare occasions when the Executioner actually appeared at Stony Man Farm, they seemed to find their way into one or the other's room to spend the night. In each other's arms, they found at least a momentary break from the war in which they were both engaged the rest of the time.

The picture in Price's mind's eye changed, and she saw Bolan standing in the phone booth. Behind him, she saw a red-haired woman whose name she knew to be Jonine Hammersmith. But the woman's face wouldn't come into focus.

"You say Phoenix Force is in Romania?" Bolan asked, breaking into her thoughts.

"Right," Price said quickly. "Transylvania."

"I'm signing off now. Get back to you when I have a chance."

"Affirmative, Striker, and be careful."

"Always," the warrior replied and hung up.

Price looked back at her computer screen, glancing down the list to determine the best place for Phoenix Force to strike when they'd finished in Transylvania. The mission controller did a double take. They wouldn't have to go far. According to the list, the castle they were in right now also doubled as a storage facility.

Giving in to a rare whim of curiosity, Price rolled her chair to the computer screen next to her desk. She tapped into the Stony Man intelligence files, then typed in Hammersmith's name, followed by Great Britain, and MI-6.

A moment later, a photo of the British agent appeared on the screen. Price studied the picture, noting the short red hair and smooth skin. The face was pretty, bordering on beautiful.

Though she knew Bolan would more than likely be attracted to the woman, Price felt no pangs of jealousy. She and Striker had no commitment to each other.

A moment later, the phone buzzed again. Price wheeled back to her desk and picked it up.

"Barb?" Hal Brognola's voice said from the other end.

"Go ahead, Hal." Price picked a pen out of the holder on her console and dropped it to the notepad.

All thoughts of Bolan and Hammersmith faded from her mind as Barbara Price, the consummate professional, returned to work.

Prague, Czech Republic

BOLAN HUNG THE TELEPHONE back onto the hook and stepped out of the phone booth. Hammersmith sat on a green wooden bench on the other side of the sidewalk.

"Naughty, naughty," the British woman said, grinning.

"What do you mean?" Bolan asked.

"You were talking to a woman," Hammersmith said. "A special woman."

"And just how can you tell that?"

Hammersmith stood. "Your voice sounded different. I can tell. I'm a woman, too, you know."

The Executioner smiled. "Yes, I know." He studied Jonine Hammersmith. She had changed into blue jeans and a T-shirt that they'd taken a few minutes earlier from a clothesline suspended between two apartment buildings. They'd also found a pair of green slacks and white shirt that almost fit Bolan. In any case, they'd come close enough to get rid of the police uniforms that were bound to work against, rather than for, them once they were out of the area the cops were still searching.

Bolan walked to the curb, flagged a cab and ten minutes later they arrived at the airport outside of Prague. Grimaldi had already landed, and they hurried on board.

"Brno," Bolan said after a brief greeting.

Grimaldi tipped the visor on his suede cap. "I know. Barb told me."

The Executioner led the way to the rear of the plane.

"This a Company plane?" Hammersmith asked.

"Not really," the warrior replied, his tone telling the British woman that was all she'd find out.

The warrior contemplated the mission. They were going in hard, this time. But they'd need concealment for their weapons until the firing started. And the time was long past when there was any point to using Eastern European weapons. Pulling the two CZ-75s from under his shirt, the Executioner set them on the table next to his seat and stood.

He walked to the row of lockers on the wall and opened the first. He pulled a black leather grip from inside, turned back and placed it next to the CZs. Unzipping the bag, he pulled the shoulder-holstered Beretta 93-R out, slipped into it, then reached into the bag again to withdraw a .44 Magnum Desert Eagle.

After adding two magazine carriers to his belt—one for the Beretta, the other for the Eagle—Bolan dropped the bag back into the locker, closed the door and opened the one beside it. He pulled a short square hard case out and set it on the table next to the CZs.

Lyons, Schwarz and Blancanales had been raving about the new Calico 9 mm subguns all week long during testing. Well, it was time he found out for himself. When it hit the fan in Brno, reloading would be the last thing he'd want to mess with. The high-capacity Calico might just get him around that.

The Executioner slipped the Calico's shoulder harness over that of the Beretta. The machine pistol, with 50-round drum attached, rode on his strong side opposite the 93-R. He dropped the 100-round backup drum into its holder in front of the Beretta.

The 93-R might be a little harder to get to if he needed it, but it was still accessible.

Hammersmith stood and walked to his side. "I've got my .22 and the P-7, but I could use something more substantial, too."

Bolan pulled a light Windbreaker from the locker and slid his arms inside. He frowned at the small woman. With his size, he could easily conceal the Calico under the midthigh-length jacket. Hammersmith's small frame provided a problem, though.

As he zipped up the Windbreaker, the Executioner glanced down to the emblem on the breast. It was another garment in the wardrobe of role camouflage he and the others kept on the plane, and the patch read Seattle, Washington Country Club. It brought an idea to his mind and a smile to his face.

Opening the last locker in the row, Bolan found the golf bag. He had left it there several weeks earlier when he'd used it to conceal an M-16 from customs officers in Scotland. The M-16 was still in place, fully loaded, with six extra 20-round mags hidden in a concealed pocket inside.

Hammersmith approved.

"In fact, we'd be better off with the complete tourist look," Bolan said. He unstrapped the guns and other equipment and began changing into the slacks and golf shirt he'd worn with the bag.

Hammersmith dug through the lockers and found a denim skirt and blouse. "They're a little big," she said, holding them up to her, "but they ought to work." She shrugged out of the clothes she was wearing.

Bolan replaced the weapons over his golf shirt and pulled the jacket back on.

"Two minutes," Grimaldi called from the front of the plane.

The Executioner sat down and prepared for the landing.

The wheels of the plane hit the ground and Bolan and Hammersmith stood. As an in-country flight, there would be no customs problems to deal with.

Shouldering the golf bag, the Executioner followed the British agent off the plane.

Hammersmith glanced at the bag. "Race you to the links," she said as they hurried across the runway to the terminal.

Five minutes later, they were in another cab, on their way to downtown Brno. So far, his probes had been soft. But before they left the city, the Executioner intended to destroy every trace of the biochemical agents that threatened the free world.

War had officially been declared.

Nixa, Missouri

ROSARIO BLANCANALES had never felt more helpless as he stared at the dynamite half-uncovered from the dirt wall.

Lyons was Able Team's leader; Gadgets was the explosives expert.

Well, they needed a leader right now, and they damn sure needed a demolition man. But at least for the moment, there wasn't much call for a specialist in psychological warfare or undercover work.

"Three minutes?" Lyons asked.

Schwarz nodded.

"What's to prevent us from just opening the door, walking through and closing it behind us. The door's steel and unless I miss my guess, the dirt ends here." He pointed toward the corner of the concrete. "We should be protected from the blast."

"Right." Schwarz nodded. "But there might be another trip wire linked to opening the door. I can't be sure. We're just lucky there wasn't one on the lock itself.''

"Can you see anything running to the door?" Blancanales asked.

Schwarz shook his head. "No, but that doesn't mean there isn't anything. It could run from the back of the device, into the concrete and around. Or it could be an electronic impulse activated when the door opens. Or—"

"Okay, okay," Lyons said. He sounded calm, though mildly irritated. "There's only one thing to do, guys. Gadgets, get down there and study that thing for the remaining time. Maybe you'll see something you've missed. If you don't, I'll call out the time at fifteen seconds and we'll open the door. At that point we won't have anything to lose."

Schwarz dropped to his belly in the dirt, his eyes fixed on the dynamite and related components making up the bomb.

"Give me a time," Lyons said, holding his wrist up in front of his face.

"Two minutes, seventeen seconds."

The Able Team warriors lapsed into silence as the seconds slipped by. Blancanales would have sworn he could hear Lyons's watch ticking as the tension mounted. He followed the countdown on his own watch.

With forty-five seconds left to go, Schwarz broke the silence. "Hey!"

"What is it?" Lyons asked anxiously.

Schwarz blew air from between his closed lips.

"Sorry. False alarm." His face sobered as he continued to contemplate the mechanism.

With twenty seconds left, Lyons looked at Blancanales and indicated that he should move toward the door. Pol moved in behind him, ready to dive out of the tunnel as soon as Lyons opened the latch.

If Able Team hadn't all been blown to kingdom come first.

"Gadgets," Lyons said, "get ready."

"Wait." He frowned, still staring at the dynamite. "I think...maybe..."

"Fifteen seconds," Lyons told him. "Let's go."

Lost in deliberation, Schwarz gave no response.

"Gadgets, damn it! Let's go!" Lyons yelled.

Schwarz didn't move.

Blancanales dived for Schwarz as Lyons threw the latch and opened the door. Gadgets was still on his belly, studying the bomb, so focused on devising a way to dismantle it that he'd lost contact with the rest of the world.

"Five seconds!" Lyons yelled.

Blancanales grabbed Schwarz by the collar of his jacket, hauled him to his knees and shoved him through the door onto his face. Lyons followed, diving over the electronics man. Pol hurled himself through the opening and slammed the door, dropping the latch back in place as the dynamite detonated in the tunnel.

The explosion was like a volcanic eruption. The concrete wall, behind them now, shook like paper. The steel door sounded as if someone had struck it with a jackhammer.

But the blast stayed behind the steel and concrete.

Blancanales had fallen over Schwarz. He stared down at his friend as Gadgets said, ''Now that's what I'd call lucky. It wasn't even wired to the door. Maybe this day isn't so bad. First the shotgun, then the cave-in, but the bomb—''

Lyons interrupted, his words reverberating off the concrete walls with a distant hollowness. ''Before you start calling it lucky, you'd better turn around.''

Blancanales rolled to his side and saw Lyons raising his machine pistol away from the door. The concrete room they were in was roughly half the size of a one-car garage, but it opened into a huge, underground cave—complete with dripping stalactites on the roof and razor-sharp stalagmites pointing up toward them.

None of that concerned Rosario Blancanales. He and the other members of Able Team had found their way out of caves before. What made him understand why Lyons questioned Schwarz's statement about luck, were the dozen or so men spaced throughout the cavern swinging their submachine guns toward the new arrivals.

CHAPTER THIRTEEN

Romania

As he listened to Gary Manning through his headset, David McCarter pulled the bolt back on his semiauto Chinese AK-47.

"The only way to find out," Manning said, "is to go on. Everybody ready?"

McCarter worked the rifle sling over his shoulder as he whispered an "affirmative" into the mike along with the other members of Phoenix Force.

"Then let's do it," the big Canadian said.

McCarter rose from the shallow ditch in which he'd been lying and sprinted toward the castle wall thirty yards away. The wall rose higher on this side of the fortress—nearly fifteen feet, he judged—probably because of the fact that cover extended closer to the castle, giving the enemy a shorter area to cross before striking.

Knowing he'd never be able to leap to the top, McCarter had picked out a path of hand-and footholds in the rugged stone as he'd waited. Now, as he neared the wall, the Briton slowed slightly, then jumped to the first outcropping he'd selected. The sole of his combat boot held firm on the narrow stand as he reached up and grasped a sharp edge of rock with both hands. One leg at a time, praying he wouldn't be spotted in such a vulnerable position, McCarter made his way up the wall.

Pulling himself up and over the top, he had swung his legs over the side when he heard the first rounds on the other side of the castle. Then explosions nearer his position sounded, and sparks flew as a stream of bullets chipped pieces of rock beside him.

The former SAS officer threw himself forward, dropping to the other side of the wall as his eyes turned toward the muzzle-flash that had winked to his left. As his boots hit the ground, he found the sling of the AK-47 and swung the weapon in front of him, reaching out to drop the cumbersome Kalashnikov safety to fire.

Another burst of rounds drilled into the grass next to his feet. McCarter squeezed the trigger, sending a 7.62 mm softpoint back at the flash. He heard a grunt, then saw a figure drop to the ground.

McCarter raced away from the wall toward the living quarters, spotting a small side door as he ran. A servants' entrance, perhaps. Impossible to tell.

That was one of the difficult aspects of this attack. Old castles didn't follow the rhyme or reason of modern buildings. They twisted and turned with the whims of the masters who'd had them built, and the three stories of this stronghold might be in any configuration imaginable.

Phoenix Force had no idea of the floor plan—where

the biochemical experiments might be conducted or where the guards might be.

And more important, they had no idea where they might find Yakov Katzenelenbogen.

Where the hell was Katz? He was the most responsible leader McCarter had ever served under, and he'd have answered their radio call unless...

He forced the sudden nausea from his stomach as he neared the door. All he could do at this point was to continue with the mission and follow the orders Katz had given him—enter quickly, find a way down to the cellar and clear it while James and Encizo did the same on the main floor. The Phoenix Force leader had ordered Manning on the main floor, too. It had been Katz's own job to go "high," but that would have to be covered by the big Canadian now.

A flash of shadow caught McCarter's eye ten feet from the door. Twisting to his right, he saw another figure running toward him.

Positive target identification was impossible in the darkness, and the Briton hesitated. Then he saw the gait of the shadowy form.

No member of Phoenix Force ran like that.

McCarter swung around the AK and fired, the 7.62 mm round striking the shadow in the chest.

A man wearing black fatigues fell at the Stony Man warrior's feet. A Czech Model 25 submachine gun rolled across the grass.

McCarter lowered his shoulder as he sprinted the last ten yards to the door, striking the wood with a hard rugby block. The rotting door splintered at the frame and swung inward. He ran through, almost doubling over an island sink in what appeared to be a kitchen.

The modernly outfitted kitchen was well lighted but empty. The overhead track lighting, stainless-steel sink, dishwasher, microwave and other appliances, looked out of place inside the ancient stone walls. As McCarter made his way toward a doorway on the other side of the room, he heard more gunfire booming from other parts of the castle.

Then a rifle barrel poked tentatively around the doorway toward which the Briton was headed.

McCarter studied the barrel. He couldn't identify it, but it wasn't an AK-47. He waited until a face followed the barrel, then blew it off with a pair of semiauto rounds.

Leaping over the fallen corpse, McCarter saw a constricted hallway winding away from the kitchen. The ceiling was six feet high at the most, and the Briton had to duck as he moved cautiously forward. He wondered briefly what the average height of a man had been when the castle was built—had to have been shorter to have made the ceiling this low—then he rounded a corner and a sudden burst of fire washed the brief thought from his mind.

McCarter's mind focused totally on the man in black fatigues who was firing another of the Czech Model 25s. The two men traded shots down the narrow hallway.

The man in black's wild full-auto blast sailed over McCarter's left shoulder, while the Phoenix Force warrior's carefully aimed semiauto round caught the machine gunner square in the "X-ring" on his chest.

A soft cough burst from the man's mouth, followed by a trickle of blood.

Pushing past the gunner even before he'd hit the stone floor, McCarter stopped in his tracks, turned back and looked down at the fallen Model 25. He could readily see why Barbara Price and Cowboy John Kissinger had wanted Phoenix Force to use the AK-47s—it provided another false lead, however small that lead might be, as to who was behind the attack.

But the semiautos put Phoenix Force at a definite disadvantage, and the Model 25s were already here.

McCarter dropped the AK-47, scooped up the Czech Model 25 and pulled three extra magazines from a carrier on the fallen gunner's belt. Checking the chamber to make sure the subgun was primed, he moved down the winding tunnel.

The former SAS officer saw a door ahead in the rock and walked cautiously forward as more sporadic gunfire met his ears from other parts of the castle. He stopped at the entrance to a large anteroom, the yellow caution light in his brain flashing on.

McCarter inched his head around the corner of the stone doorway. The room reminded him of the kitchen, in that it was a blend of old and new. Modern furniture—chesterfields, settees, end tables and electric lamps—was spaced about the large two-story expanse in several small conversation areas. Two other doorways, similar to the one in which he stood, were scattered around the room. Directly across from him, a staircase built from heavy boulders led both upstairs and down. A short rock wall circled the open floor above, topped by a more recent wooden railing decorated with carefully carved cherubs, seraphim and other angelic figures.

The gunfire around the castle had momentarily died down, and the overall ambience of the anteroom was one of peace. Which made the hair on the back of David McCarter's neck stand on end. The yellow light flashed brighter.

McCarter moved back against the wall, considering the situation. As he did, a shadow moved quickly against the wall in one of the other doorways.

The Briton waited, the flashing yellow light turning red. He trained the barrel of the Model 25 that way, his index finger lightly pressed against the trigger.

The shadow advanced again, closer to the door. Another burst of gunfire from somewhere down the third hallway stopped the furtive movement momentarily, then it resumed again, and half a face glanced suddenly around the corner before disappearing.

The Briton spotted the shadow of a Model 25 against the stone.

McCarter raised the subgun to his shoulder and sighted down the barrel on the spot where the face had appeared. His finger moved a fraction of an inch on the trigger.

Then Gary Manning stepped cautiously into the doorway and started to cross the room, his own appropriated Model 25 slung over his shoulder in battle-carry mode.

McCarter let up on the trigger instantly. Almost as quickly, he saw another movement on the floor above. At a forty-five-degree angle from Manning, the top of a head bobbed up over the railing. On top of the head was a floppy boonie cap that matched the black fatigues the other guards had worn.

The barrel of a subgun slid over the rail, aiming down toward the unsuspecting Manning.

McCarter swung his weapon up and out, dropping the sights just below the boonie hat. Without hesitation, his finger moved all the way back on the trigger and the blowback weapon sputtered a burst of autofire past the rail and into the hardman's face.

The boonie hat flew off, taking the gunner's scalp with it. The corpse fell back behind the stone wall.

Out of the corner of his eye, McCarter saw Manning turn toward him, aim down the barrel, then freeze.

"Go ahead," McCarter said in his best Clint Eastwood impersonation, "*ruin* my day."

Manning walked forward. "Damn," he said, "I saw the gun first. I thought—"

"I know. I almost shot you, too. Things are getting a little confusing, aren't they."

The conversation ended abruptly as two black-clad figures suddenly appeared on the floor above. McCarter swung his weapon upward, rattling off a stream of fire that caught the man nearest him in the upper chest and throat, while Manning did the same with the other gunner.

Both men toppled over the railing to crash onto the stone floor.

"Let's go!" Manning said, racing toward the staircases.

The Briton followed, dropping the magazine from

his Model 25 and replacing it with one of the spares just as he reached the steps.

Manning disappeared up the steps as McCarter moved down.

The lighting grew dim as the former SAS officer neared the bottom floor of the castle. He paused on the last step, letting his eyes adjust to the gloom. Then, warily rounding the corner, he slid silently through another of the narrow rock-walled halls.

An aged oak door stood at the end of the hall. McCarter reached it, balanced the subgun in his right hand and reached for the knob. Twisting quickly, he threw the door open and pressed his back into the stone, the Model 25 pointing into the next room.

Other than the continued intermittent outbursts of gunfire on the floors above, the castle was silent.

McCarter dropped to one knee, peered around the corner and saw what had once been a wine cellar. Wooden framework lined the walls and ran in columns through the middle of the room like the shelves of a library, their empty diamond-shaped centers gaping in disuse.

The Briton scanned the room. He had started to turn back when he discerned the faint glow of light at the bottom of the opposite wall. Moving with painstaking slowness, McCarter slid through the wooden labyrinth toward the light.

A sliding door almost blended in with the wall.

McCarter stood to the side, his eyes searching through the dim light for a switch, a lever, whatever it was that opened the semihidden passageway. But before he could find the mechanism, the door slid open.

Light shot out into the wine cellar as McCarter pressed his back against the wall to the side of the door. Then the barrel of a subgun poked through the opening.

McCarter let his weapon fall to the end of the sling, and reached out and grabbed the barrel with both hands. Pulling and twisting at the same time, he ripped the Model 25 from surprised hands as he stepped out in front of the doorway.

The man who had held the gun wore a blue T-shirt and jeans. The shocked look never left his face as McCarter jammed the barrel of the subgun into his gut and unleashed a burst of autofire into his intestines.

The hardman died as he fell to the ground.

McCarter looked past the falling corpse and saw a starkly furnished room. A figure sat facing away from him in a straight-backed wooden chair, and just beyond that, a man in khaki pants, holding a leather police sap in one hand, was frantically trying to draw a pistol from his belt with the other.

Another burst from the newly aquired Model 25 caught the man in the chest, throat and face. The sap fell to the stone floor, to be covered by the remains of the hardman.

McCarter scanned the rest of the barren room, then walked forward. The man facing away from him slumped forward, unconscious. He walked around the chair and stared into the face of Yakov Katzenelenbogen.

Or what was left of it.

Brno, Czech Republic

As THE CAB PASSED Brno's Cathedral of Saint Peter and Paul, with the cabbie running a free, nonstop tour narration of the drive, Bolan sat back against the seat.

Hammersmith nodded and smiled politely, occasionally answering the driver in Czech, but mercifully not translating the onslaught of words to Bolan.

The cab passed a long row of commercial buildings, and the warrior saw signs in Czech that he took to read Spilberk Plumbing, Spilberk Hardware and the Spilberk Restaurant. The signs brought a smile to his face. The Czechs had only recently thrown off the yoke of communism, but they were learning the ways of capitalism quickly, and cashing in on the name of the city's most famous attraction.

Hammersmith spoke to the driver as they passed an old, run-down hotel on the right. He answered quickly, shrugging.

"Says the place has been shut down since the Communists were in power," Hammersmith told him. "The Communists didn't know how to run a hotel."

Bolan nodded. "Let him drive another block or two, then tell him to stop in front of the next hotel that's still open."

The cabbie drove on. Then, as they passed a recently built American Holiday Inn, Hammersmith leaned forward, tapped the man on the shoulder and spoke a few words.

The cabbie shook his head and answered as he slowed.

"He says they are always full. But his brother-in-law owns a place where—"

"Tell him we had reservations."

Hammersmith did, and the driver resignedly stopped.

Bolan paid the man from the money supply he'd picked up aboard the plane, then turned toward the sidewalk. Just as he'd suspected, the city was alive with a mixture of native Moravians and tourists taking advantage of the new freedom and sight-seeing the country offered. At least twenty percent of the people strolling up and down the sidewalk were dressed similarly to Hammersmith and himself. A few of the men, like the Executioner himself, even had golf bags over their shoulders.

Bolan and his companion walked unhurriedly back down the street toward the Hotel Spilberk. "We can afford one walk-by," the Executioner said. "That's all. After that, we'll draw attention from any curious eyes inside the windows, so make sure you see everything you can the first time. And let's do our best to look like a happy husband and wife on vacation."

Hammersmith grinned. "We'll be from Cleveland," she announced, then hooked her arm under his as they strolled along the sidewalk. Two blocks later, they crossed the street on the other side of the hotel and slowed their pace slightly.

At the end of a four-building complex of square, three-story structures, the hotel shared a common wall with what appeared to be a medical clinic. The windows had been boarded over with plywood, and the front door in the middle of the edifice looked as if it hadn't been opened in years. A yellow legal-looking document had been posted in the middle of the door.

"I recognize the paper," Hammersmith said. For the benefit of anyone watching, she smiled as she spoke, as if she'd just spotted the most quaint sight she and her golf-playing husband had seen since they left Cleveland. "It's a Czech closure order. The building's been condemned and ordered to be torn down."

"What department does that fall under here?" he asked.

"Conveniently under the department of the interior," Hammersmith replied.

Bolan nodded. They moved past the medical building and a clothing store at the end of the complex. The Executioner led the way around the corner, and they began to circle the block.

An alley ran between the row of buildings and a similar set of structures behind it.

"You suppose that's where they come and go?" Hammersmith asked.

"Has to be. The front door would draw too much attention, being condemned." They crossed the next street, then picked up their pace around two more corners, finally drawing abreast to the side of the hotel. Eight windows ran along each of the three floors between the bricks—twenty-four rooms, assuming that each window accounted for one room. Add another two dozen on the other side of the door, the lobby, an office, and any other areas they found inside the Hotel Spilberk, and the Executioner and Jonine Hammersmith would have over fifty places to check for the chemicals.

After the battle.

Bolan turned back toward the Holiday Inn as they reached the corner. "It'll be dark in a couple of hours. I want to wait until then to recon the alley. Then we'll strike."

Hammersmith nodded, still holding on to his arm as if she and her husband had finally taken the dream vacation they'd planned since their marriage. "Where to in the meantime?"

"Let's try the Holiday," Bolan said. "We need someplace to plan, and I've got to make a call. The cabbie told us they were full so his brother-in-law would get the business."

"You sure?" Hammersmith asked.

Bolan shrugged. "The vacancy sign was out."

Hammersmith squeezed his arm, and in the corner of his eye the Executioner saw the grin return. "I didn't mean are you sure about the vacancy," she said coyly. "I meant do you think the Holiday's a good idea?"

The Executioner looked down at her, puzzled.

She stood on her tiptoes and kissed him on the cheek, looking for all the world like a happy wife caught up in the romance of one of eastern Europe's oldest cities. "The planning for this thing isn't going to take two hours," she whispered in his ear. "And all manner of bawdy things can happen when a happy husband and wife on vacation check into a hotel room."

Nixa, Missouri

THE FIRST BURST of gunfire from the underground cavern flew into the entryway, struck the hard concrete and ricocheted around the small enclosure as if the men of Able Team had stumbled upon a hive of giant wasps.

Carl Lyons felt something strike the middle of his back with the sting of a pebble launched from a slingshot. He knew what it was and thanked God the ricochet had lost most of its velocity by the time it found him.

"Get out of here!" he yelled to Schwarz and Blancanales as he unleashed a burst of 9 mm rounds from his machine pistol. "We're sitting targets!" He tapped a stream of cover fire as Gadgets and Pol dived from the entryway, ignoring the ladder that led down into the cavern.

The Able Team leader followed a split second later, jumping from the concrete floor into the cave as the Calico continued to sputter in his hands. Looking down as he fell, he saw the floor of the cave ten feet below.

A pencil-pointed stalagmite rose up directly under him.

Gadgets had fallen just to the side of the sharp stone. He looked up, then rose to his knees as Lyons feet neared the spike. Dropping his Uzi, the electronics man shouldered the Able Team leader's boots to one side and sent Lyons tumbling away from impalement.

Lyons twisted in the air, landing hard on his side as gunfire blew past him. The air rushed from his body as he struck the hard rock floor. He opened his mouth to bark more orders and felt his lungs create a vacuum as they desperately tried to replace the lost oxygen.

The Able Team leader rolled to his back, tightening his abdominal muscles to equalize the pressure. Next to him, he heard Schwarz and Blancanales returning the fire from Ryba's men. Rolling onto his belly, he rose and joined the battle as the air returned to his lungs.

All three Stony Man warriors ducked behind large boulders and stalagmites as the battle continued. A man in mud-stained white Levi's jeans threaded his way toward them, dodging from cover to cover, the Uzi in his hands blasting. Condensation dripped from the stalactites on the ceiling, raining over Lyons's face as he inched around the cover and popped a 3-round burst into the gunner's chest.

The man screamed and went down.

Schwarz and Blancanales each dropped a man before Ryba's gunners suddenly realized they were in for more of a fight than they'd counted on when they'd seen the three dirty and disheveled bodies dive from the exploding tunnel.

They found their own cover.

Lyons had a second to estimate that about twenty of the enemy hardmen survived before the Czechs disappeared.

The roar of gunfire died down in the cavern as the men settled in. With it went the ringing in Carl Lyons's ears. He glanced around the side of his rock.

A face poked tentatively around a boulder ten feet from the Able Team leader. A gun followed, and a round was snapped wildly in his direction. It struck the rock three feet above Lyons's head.

The former LAPD detective pulled back behind cover, flipped the selector to semiauto as he counted to three, then swung the machine pistol back around the edge of the rock. Just as he'd known it would, the face and Uzi, having met no immediate resistance, had edged away from the boulder once more.

Lyons tapped the trigger of the M-950A and sent a 9 mm round into the foolish man's nose.

A mortal game of hide-and-seek, cat and mouse, now began, with both Ryba's men and Able Team lurching from cover, taking a shot, then diving back behind the rocks. Lone rounds sang a song of death through the cave.

Lyons adjusted his face mike, then said softly, "Keep it down, guys. We're not doing any good. Let *them* waste the ammo. Just an occasional shot to let them know we're still here."

Taking his time, Lyons waited thirty seconds before firing again. Schwarz took the cue, waiting another thirty, then doing the same. Blancanales took nearly a minute before firing.

But the men on the opposing side of the cavern were no fools. They realized what was happening, and that they were doing no better than the men of Able Team.

Lyons heard a voice suddenly shout orders in Czech. He didn't understand the words, but he knew what they had to mean.

Whoever was in charge of Ryba's men knew that they had one big advantage. Manpower. They had the men from Stony Man Farm outnumbered six to one, but they weren't utilizing that advantage by staying behind cover, trading potshots.

Schwarz and Blancanales knew what was happening, too. "I think he just ordered a rush, Ironman," Blancanales said in Lyons's ear.

Mildly dissenting voices answered the orders the leader had given across the cave.

"Doesn't sound like they're just overjoyed about it though," Pol added. "Maybe—"

The leader of the hardmen barked louder and meaner, and the unhappy voices quieted.

"No, but I think he won the argument," Schwarz whispered into the radio.

A moment later, it sounded like the entire Czech army was crossing the cave with their weapons blazing.

Lyons rose over the boulder and fired a 3-round volley into the nearest gunner. Behind that man, at least fifteen more sprinted toward Able Team, Uzis blazing.

Romania

RAFAEL "PESCADO" ENCIZO felt a presence behind him and turned, bringing the semiauto AK-47 around in front of him. He lowered the barrel when he saw Calvin James standing in the stone doorway to the bedroom.

"Your end of the floor clear?" James asked, looking down at the two bodies behind Encizo.

Encizo nodded. "Yours?"

"Yeah."

The two men made their way back down another of the narrow passageways that made up the main floor of the castle. Entering the anteroom, they saw Gary Manning coming down the steps from the top story.

"Anybody left up there?" Encizo asked.

Manning reached the landing and shook his head. "At least nobody who'll be giving us any trouble."

"Anybody seen David?" James asked. "Or Katz?"

Manning turned the corner and started down the steps to the cellar. "Last I saw David, he was heading this way." He paused. "Katz…no."

Encizo fell in behind the big Canadian, with James bringing up the rear. There had been no gunfire anywhere within the castle since Encizo had found the last two of Ryba's men hiding in the bed chamber. But the operative word was "hiding."

There could always be more.

Drawing abreast of Manning as they reached the wine cellar, Encizo saw the open door that led into the next room. The body of a man wearing a blue T-shirt and jeans lay to the side of the door. He broke into a jog, threading his way between the wine racks, then stopped in his tracks when he saw McCarter and Katz.

The Israeli lay on the cold stone floor, his eyes closed. Blood covered his face from a gash over one eye. McCarter knelt next to the man, alternately pushing on the Phoenix Force leader's chest with cupped hands, then breathing into his mouth.

A straight-backed wooden chair stood a foot away,

and behind it, the body of a man in a white shirt and khaki pants. A long black police slapper lay next to him. Freshly cut strands of rough hemp rope were still tied to the chair, and McCarter's Sykes-Fairbairn commando knife rested on the seat.

Encizo moved forward cautiously, afraid of what he might see once he looked closely at his leader. The chair, rope and knife told the story all too well.

Katz had been captured, tied to the chair and tortured. McCarter had found him, killed the men in charge of his torment and cut him loose.

McCarter looked up as Encizo reached him. "Help me. He's not coming to."

The little Cuban dropped to his knees, taking his comrade's place next to Katz. McCarter moved up to the Israeli's head. "Careful. Half his ribs are broken."

Encizo pressed his hands together over Katz's sternum, pumping up and down as McCarter tried desperately to breathe life into the Phoenix Force leader's lungs. Encizo sensed Manning and James, standing over them.

Finally Katz opened his eyes. But they were dull, glazed.

"Yakov!" Encizo said, leaning in close. "Yakov!"

The Israeli's eyes cleared somewhat, and he forced a smile. "And my…Timex…is still ticking," he breathed, then began to cough.

McCarter stood. "We've got to get him to hospital," he said.

Katz reached up to grab McCarter's pant leg. "Did you find …the chemicals?"

"What chemicals? This is a lab—"

The Israeli shook his head, the movement bringing a grimace to his face. "Storage...too..." he whispered.

Encizo leaned in closer. "We'll come back. First you need to be—"

The Phoenix Force leader grabbed his arm with a steel grip. "Find them first," he ordered, then returned to his coughing fit.

"Katz," Manning said, kneeling down, "you need—"

"Do it!"

Manning stood. "You heard the man. The sooner we do it, the sooner we can get him out of here." He looked at James. "Stay with him."

Encizo sprinted through the wine cellar and up the stairs, followed by McCarter and Manning. They were racing the clock, now. Katz was right—if the castle was a storage as well as research site, they had to destroy the chemicals before they left. Thousands, if not millions, of lives depended upon it. And one life couldn't take precedence over that fact.

Even if that one life belonged to the best commander Rafael Encizo had ever served under, and one of the finest human beings he had ever known.

The three men of Phoenix Force split up at the anteroom, each taking a separate hall. Encizo hurried down the path he'd already cleared. Entering the first door he came to he stepped over the bodies of men he had killed only minutes earlier. A quick search of the room produced nothing, so he moved down the hall, repeating the procedure in every room to which he came. When he reached the library where he'd come crashing through the window, he turned and sprinted back down the rock tunnel to the anteroom.

Manning and McCarter were already there. The expressions on their faces told Encizo they had fared no better than he.

"Okay," Manning said. "Spread out across the grounds. It's got to be here somewhere. And be careful. There still might be a straggler hiding out there."

Encizo left via the nearest exit and found himself in the castle bailey. Racing past a Justice mount, he entered a dark building next to the wall, which happened to be the stable. Though it was empty now, the building still smelled of horses and hay. The Phoenix Force warrior kept the AK at the ready as he pulled a flashlight from his pack and began systematically checking the stalls.

He found the sealed canisters in the fourth compartment he came to. Piled waist high, there had to be at least forty containers of death.

"Phoenix Five to Four and Two," he said into his face mike. "I've found it, guys. Gary, it's in the fourth stall in the stable. You can't miss it."

"Affirmative, Five," Manning's voice said in his ear. "Go back with McCarter and help James get Katz ready to move out. I'll come take care of it."

Encizo spun on his heel and sprinted back into the castle. He met McCarter on the steps. The two men hurried down to the cellar.

Several of the wine racks had been torn down in the wine cellar, and Encizo saw why as he burst into the next room. James had fashioned a stretcher out of the wood and clothing from the dead men on the cellar floor.

"He's bad," James whispered as he stood up from the Phoenix Force leader's side. "His nose and half his ribs are broken. Not to mention the gashes on his face." The medic wiped the sweat from his brow. "I can't be sure, but I think he's got a concussion."

Encizo looked down. Katz's eyes were closed again. He and McCarter helped James place the Israeli's body on the stretcher. Lifting him into the air, they began maneuvering out of the room, between the empty wine racks, then up the stairs. Encizo was surprised at how light Katz felt.

Courage, honor and loyalty were intangible qualities, the Cuban-born Phoenix Force warrior reminded himself. They couldn't be measured in pounds. If they had been, he, James and McCarter could never have lifted Yakov Katzenelenbogen off the ground.

The Israeli's eyes were still closed when they met Manning coming out of the stable. The big Canadian held a remote-control detonator in one hand, one of the Czech Model 25s in the other. "It's set," he said, then moved in to help the others carry their leader.

"What was the stuff, Gary?" Encizo asked. "I didn't look closely."

"An anthrax compound," Manning replied as they headed out.

"It won't get loose with the explosion?" James asked.

"It will, but we're a long way from the village. It'll dissipate and deplete before it reaches a populated area. The only people who might be affected are those still hiding here on the grounds.''

''Sounds good to me,'' McCarter commented.

Phoenix Force struggled down the trail to the tree line. The lights of the village shone brightly through the foliage. Moving out into the clearing, they stayed close to the trees as they circled the village once more.

When they reached the trail in the woods where they'd started, Manning stopped them. As the others redistributed Katz's weight, the big Canadian pulled the remote from his pocket and turned toward the castle.

A weak voice spoke suddenly. ''Wait,'' Katz said.

The warriors turned to look at the man on the stretcher. His eyes were open again.

Katz struggled to a sitting position, his face a mask of agony. ''Okay, go ahead.''

Manning pushed the button. The explosion lighted the sky on top of the mountain.

Yakov Katzenelenbogen smiled wearily.

Then the Phoenix Force leader closed his eyes and collapsed back on the stretcher.

CHAPTER FOURTEEN

Plzeň, Czech Republic

"I am a spy, I am small, and I am a woman," Skrdla muttered. So, he pondered as he pulled into the parking lot outside the lab, where would the woman go after she fled this place? After her partner had just been killed?

The trail had grown cold over the past two days. The scent was gone, and Skrdla didn't know the answer to his question. He knew only two things: that the trace of blood and lipstick on the wall was his only lead and the lead would take him to the informant within Ryba's organization.

For the second time that day, Skrdla descended the steps to the lab in Plzeň where it had all begun. That meant the informant worked here. He had to. Where else would he, or she, take a foreign agent to prove that diseases were being perfected?

Skrdla rang the buzzer with one hand and knocked on the door with the big fist of his other.

A moment later an eye appeared in the peep slot, then the door swung open.

The same frightened man who had answered the

door earlier did so again. "You are back?" he said, pushing his spectacles up on his nose nervously. He stood back to allow Skrdla to enter. "I will have the others clear the lab."

Skrdla entered the hallway and started toward the lab. "You will do no such thing. I wish to watch them work."

The lab researcher's footsteps pattered on the concrete behind him. "But we are not allowed—"

Skrdla turned and looked at the man.

Something the scientist saw caused him to stop speaking, open the door to the lab and step back again.

The heads around the lab tables looked up anxiously as Skrdla entered the room. He stepped to the side of the doorway and crossed his arms behind his back.

"Go on about your business," said the researcher who had answered the door. "It is all right."

Fearful men and women bent to their tasks.

Skrdla reached out to grab the chief researcher's arm as the man started to return to work. "Is anyone absent today? Ill, or gone for any other reason?"

The man in the lab coat glanced to a chart on the wall, then turned back and shook his head. "No. They are all here."

"Then I wish to make an announcement," Skrdla said in a loud voice.

The faces jerked back up.

"There is a traitor in our midst," the hardman stated simply. "You may return to work."

The man in the gray suit knew that what he had

said would be enough. All they needed to know was precisely why he was there. They, themselves, would do the rest.

Skrdla began watching the researchers. He ignored the work being done, knowing full well he wouldn't understand it even if he tried. No, this type of work took intelligence, intelligence of the type measured on tests.

He also ignored the faces of the men and women. Other investigators he knew looked for fear in their suspects; fear that came from guilt. But Skrdla had learned long ago that looking for fear wouldn't work for him. Everyone, the innocent along with the guilty, showed fright when he watched them. All deer feared the wolf.

What Skrdla paid attention to was the movement and mannerisms of the men and women who went on about their duties, occasionally casting a furtive glance his way. Body language, they called it in the West. He had read of it long after he had been using it. Skrdla himself had no name for the mannerisms of people that led him to believe they were guilty. He had no idea how it worked for others, or even for himself.

But he knew that it worked. He knew that sooner or later, if he watched long enough, he would narrow the field of possible informants to two or three.

And he had other methods of narrowing it further to the guilty party.

Skrdla's gaze fell on a tall fat man who looked more like a shot-putter than a scientist. The man glanced up as if feeling the wolf's hot gaze. Just as quickly, he looked down again.

No, not him.

Moving to a slender woman whose gray hair had been tied up in a tight bun, Skrdla studied the way she poured some chemical from one test tube into another. Her hands shook slightly, her gaze locked to her task.

This woman wasn't involved, either.

Skrdla's eyes moved on around the room, studying each man and woman in turn and gradually weeding them out. A little more than half an hour from the time he'd first rung the doorbell, he had narrowed the field of possibilities to two: a short, pretty woman with blond hair and thick sensuous lips, and a taller, square-shouldered man with straight brown hair and the high cheekbones of the pure-blooded Czech. The two worked side by side at the second table to Skrdla's left.

A thin smile crossed the hardman's lips as he walked to the side of the chief researcher. "That man," he said, pointing to the man with the high cheekbones. He shifted his finger to indicate the short woman. "And that woman. What are their names?"

The researcher cleared his throat before answering. "Vincent Hlupnek," he replied, his voice shaking, "and Anna Berilka."

"They are to come with me."

The researcher nodded quickly, crossed the room and spoke briefly to the two scientists. The two heads snapped toward Skrdla as if on the same neck.

Skrdla stepped up to the couple. "Come," he said

smiling. "You have nothing to fear. But we must talk."

Brno, Czech Republic

"JUST HOW BAD IS HE?" Bolan asked into the mouthpiece of the phone.

"They aren't sure," Barbara Price's voice said from halfway around the world. "He keeps losing consciousness. But Gary said they worked him over hard, and Calvin says he needs more attention than he can give." The Stony Man mission controller paused. "I've sent Jack to pick them up."

"That explains why I couldn't reach him on the radio." He glanced at the headset on the bed of the Holiday Inn. "The relay to the satellite is somewhere over Transylvania."

"Right. I can send Jack back to pick you up after you've hit the hotel."

"Do that," Bolan agreed. "I can use the rest of Phoenix Force on the next leg of this thing. And I want Jack taking Katz to the first hospital he finds when we land in Prague."

"Those kind of wounds will bring the Czech cops," Price warned.

"So tell Hal to get on the horn and contact somebody. CIA, State Department, I don't care what it takes." He paused, his voice softening. It wasn't Barbara's fault that Katz had gotten hurt. "How about the final code—the musical instruments, Barb. Bear got anything?"

"Negative. And it doesn't look good. Oh, he'll get

it eventually. But he says that without the key, it could take weeks.''

"We don't have weeks.''

"I know. This 'next leg' of things you mentioned with Phoenix Force. Want to let me in on it?''

"We're going after Ryba,'' the Executioner said.

"But—''

"No 'buts' about it, Barb,'' Bolan interrupted. "Maybe it's what I should have done in the first place. In any case, we're running out of time. By now the man knows for sure we're onto him, and if he's got enough disease put together, he'll speed up his program. Cut his losses and go for broke. The only way to stop him is to break the code and hit the launch sites before he can do that. There's got to be a key book, and it's got to be with him.''

"It's a hell of a risk,'' Price said.

"High risk is part of my job description,'' Bolan answered. "I'm signing off now. We'll be at the airport by the time Grimaldi gets back with Phoenix Force.''

Bolan hung up and turned toward the woman on the bed. Jonnie Hammersmith was slipping back into the denim skirt and blouse. She shook her head in awe.

"I've thought all along that you were CIA,'' she said. "You had to be, just saying you weren't because America didn't want to get directly involved.'' She hooked the skirt around her waist and reached for her belt. "But you aren't, are you.''

"No.''

Hammersmith stood. She asked no more questions,

her expression showing that she knew she'd get no more answers.

"You ready?" Bolan asked.

The woman nodded.

Bolan lifted the golf bag and led the way out the door, down the steps and out of the Holiday Inn. The night was cool, crisp, and his Windbreaker didn't look out of place.

Five minutes later, they cut down the alley behind the Hotel Spilberk. They had gone fifteen steps when the man wearing a trench coat stepped out of the shadows. His hand disappeared into his coat pocket as he spoke in Czech.

"He wants to know if we're lost," Hammersmith said.

Bolan nodded to the man, pulled a tourist map from his own pocket and stepped up under the light from the rear of a store. The man stepped in cautiously.

The warrior wrapped both arms around the man's neck and twisted. A sharp snap echoed down the alley.

"You sure he was a bad guy?" Hammersmith asked skeptically.

The Executioner dragged the body into the shadows, reached into the coat pocket and pulled out a Hungarian-made copy of a Walther PPK. He tossed it to her. "Aren't you?"

Two rear entrances led from the hotel. A panel van had been parked between the two doors. Bolan and Hammersmith moved to the nearest entrance.

The Executioner set the golf bag against the wall, produced the M-16 and extra magazines and handed them to his companion. Then he turned back to the door, raised a foot and kicked.

The Hotel Spilberk had never been rated with many stars, and it had deteriorated further since it had "officially" been closed. The wood around the hinges splintered, and the entire door went flying from the frame.

Bolan swung the Calico out on the shoulder sling and led the way into a dark hallway, racing past several numbered rooms toward the lobby. The hotel had four main halls—he had seen that from the street— with the lobby at the front. He and Hammersmith made no effort to conceal their footsteps. This was a storage site rather than a lab, so he didn't expect to find every room occupied. But there had to be a base of some type, someplace where the guards gathered for coffee, cigarettes and intelligence updates.

The Executioner knew the best way to find it was to let the guards find *him*.

It didn't take long.

As they neared the lobby, one of the doors to a room swung open. A man wearing one of the familiar Jablonec Security uniforms stepped out to check the commotion, his pistol still riding in its flap holster.

Bolan dropped him where he stood with a 3-round burst from the Calico.

The guard slithered down the wall at the side of the doorway. The warrior pushed him aside and started to enter when he heard Hammersmith's M-16 chatter behind him.

Glancing over his shoulder, he saw the British

woman mow down a pair of guards who'd come out of a room they'd already passed.

The Executioner dived through the doorway into a small apartment, probably the home of the hotel manager when the Spilberk had operated. In any case, it had been turned into a combination break room-headquarters for Ryba's Jablonec men.

Four men who had been playing cards at a table in the center of the living room now went for their side arms.

Bolan stitched a figure eight back and forth across the room, spraying it with 9 mm fire from the Calico, drilling twenty rounds into the four men. They fell, one by one, to the carpet.

The last man to go down, a burly guy with tattoos running up and down his arms beneath his rolled up shirtsleeves, took three rounds in the chest, yet still managed to get off a shot.

The round flew high over the Executioner's shoulder and lodged in the doorframe.

Bolan tapped another three rounds from the machine pistol. The first struck a colorfully inked dragon on the man's wrist. The next joined the bullets already in his chest, and the third added a star-shaped red "tattoo" to his forehead.

The Executioner leapt over the falling bodies, rounded the table and entered a small kitchen. A Jablonec man had added an apron to his uniform while he boiled cabbage on the stove. He grabbed for his weapon, but the cloth stopped his hand.

Bolan took his time, firing a carefully placed round into the man's sternum.

The Executioner turned and hurried out of the kitchen, moving into the apartment's small bedroom. It appeared empty at first, then he saw the shoe sticking out from under the bed.

Bolan leaned down and saw the leg attached to the shoe. It wore the uniform pants of another Jablonec guard.

Standing back up, the Executioner tapped two rounds into the shoe. A loud howl came from under the bed as a wiry man with a bushy mustache rolled out. He held a CZ-75 in his hand as he struggled to make it to his knees.

The Executioner made sure that he didn't get there.

Bolan saw two doors in the bedroom wall. Moving cautiously to the first, he swung it back and stepped to the side.

A burst of gunfire flew into the room.

From the angle at which he found himself, the Executioner could see clothes hanging from a rod. The man behind the weapon was somewhere behind the clothing.

Dropping to one knee, the warrior poked the muzzle of the Calico around the door, held the trigger back and sprayed the hanging garments floor to ceiling. Shirts, pants and jackets danced on their hangers as 9 mm holes drilled through sleeves and legs.

As the Executioner stood, a wide-eyed body fell forward onto the floor.

A volley from an M-16, mixed with a variety of other weapons, still came from the hall as Bolan turned to the final door. With the same plan of attack, he stepped to the side as he pulled the knob.

Silence.

Bolan edged an eye around the corner.

A terrified man sat on the toilet, his Jablonec pants around his ankles. He held a revolver in both shaking hands, aiming it out the door.

The Executioner slid the Calico around the doorjamb and unleashed another burst of fire. The revolver fell to the floor on one side of the toilet, while the man fell to the other.

Bolan heard the steps behind him and swung around the Calico.

Hammersmith leaned to the side, looked past him into the bathroom, and said, "All clear?"

"Yeah. Anybody left in the hall?"

The British agent shook her head.

"Then let's go. We've got three other halls to clear. I suspect they were all centered here, but we have to make sure. And we've got to find the chemicals."

"I've already found them," the MI-6 agent said. "The other room—the one the other guards came out of—in there."

Bolan nodded. Sprinting past Hammersmith, he led the way through the deserted lobby and up the stairs. The rest of the halls, both downstairs and up, had been closed off. The Executioner broke through the plywood barricades to make sure.

Nothing.

Returning to the room where Hammersmith had found the chemical storage, Bolan saw a white sheet covering what looked like a pile of gallon paint cans.

He ripped it away to expose the black metal canisters.

"We're going to blow up all that?" Hammersmith asked.

"No, not with all the people in the vicinity. I brought C-4, but it's useless. We'd kill everybody on the street below."

"So…"

"So we take it with us," Bolan said.

Hammersmith looked at the fifty-odd gallon cans. "I suppose I should start filling my purse, or what?"

Bolan smiled. "Unless I miss my guess, we'll find in someone's pocket the keys to the panel van out back."

"Then we load everything into the van and go to the airport."

"Right. We'll dump this stuff over the Atlantic on the way back. It'll dissipate in the air."

"No dead fishies?" Hammersmith asked.

"No dead fishies."

Bolan and Hammersmith raced back downstairs and began searching the bodies for keys. They had almost given up when the Executioner remembered the man in the trench coat. Moving out the back door, he returned to the shadows.

The keys were in the coat pocket opposite where the gun had been.

Bolan looked at his watch as they started back into the building for the cans. "Let's go," he said. "The next stop is Ryba himself. And I've been waiting for this one."

Nixa, Missouri

LYONS TAPPED the Calico's trigger again, ripping another triburst into the chest of an Uzi-bearing man wearing a green tank top. He swung the subgun to the right, held the trigger back and cut a figure eight between two more of the men rushing between the boulders and stalagmites that covered the cavern floor.

On either side of him, behind their own cover, Schwarz and Blancanales opened fire with their appropriated Uzis.

Lyons glanced down at the Calico's indicator window, seeing he was down below nine rounds. As more fire ricocheted off the rock wall in front of him, he dropped back behind cover and ripped the 50-round "carry" drum from the Calico's well.

He had tugged the 100-round backup from the carrier when he saw the Uzi barrel flash to his side. A split second later, he felt it jam into his ribs.

Instinctively he used the big cylinder in his hand as a club, knocking the barrel of the other weapon down and to the side. A 3-round burst chattered against the stone floor next to his combat boot.

Lyons looked up at the face of the man holding the Uzi—round, hard, with square cheeks and cold eyes. Thick lips smiled obscenely as the man behind them saw that the drum mag was off the Calico.

The big ex-cop smiled back as he brought up the Calico, jammed it into the fat lips and sent the 9 mm round still in the weapon's chamber crashing through the teeth and up into the brain.

As the fat-lipped gunner fell over the rocks, Lyons dropped back behind cover, snapped the drum in place, then worked the bolt to chamber a new round.

Fire from Ryba's advancing men zinged off the rocks, flying through the cavern like deadly insects gone wild. A fine rain of limestone flew up, then back down through the air, giving the underground room a mysterious, misty haze.

With an even hundred rounds now in place, Lyons moved to the side of the stalagmite. Peering out into the cavern, he could see the men crossing the room had lost much of their enthusiasm.

Lyons erased two men who had changed their minds about the advance and now tried to dive behind cover. Holding the trigger back, he stitched a steady stream of 9 mm rounds into both men.

From the corner of his eye, he saw Schwarz roll from behind a boulder, leap to his feet and pound a double-tap of fire into an advancing man with moles covering his face.

Gadgets had set his Uzi on semiauto. Good. He and Pol were still limited on firepower. They were saving their rounds, making each shot count.

Lyons ducked back below an assault of fire, then rose again to hammer more Parabellum rounds into the chests of two men in coveralls. More of the painters they'd seen outside the house?

There was no time to wonder. He saw Pol drop a man with long hair tied back in a ponytail, then the final four men in the assault suddenly realized the odds had changed and had a simultaneous change of heart. They leapt behind cover.

There was a moment's reprieve as the explosive sounds died down around the cavern. Then one of the men screamed out in Czech. Another moment of silence followed.

"He's trying to talk to us," Pol said.

Lyons heard Schwarz's voice boom across the cavern. "Speak English if you can!" the electronics man said. "If not...die!"

A few seconds later, the same voice said, "We... capitu... capitala...."

"I think 'capitulate' is the word he's groping for," Schwarz said into the radio.

"Be careful," Lyons whispered into the mouthpiece. "If they're serious, great. They might have info on other sites. But if not..." He let his words trail off, knowing his partners would understand the danger. Men who'd been willing to rush across the cavern in a near-kamikaze attack a few minutes earlier didn't seem likely to suddenly lie down and quit.

It was a little too easy.

Lyons rose slightly behind the stalagmite. "Throw down your weapons, raise your hands and stand up."

Metal clanked against stone as the men obeyed the first order. Then first one head, then two, three and finally four appeared above cover from around the cavern. The hands followed, and then the men were walking slowly toward the Able Team warriors.

The nearest Ryba man wore blue jeans and a white T-shirt with a red-white-and-blue American flag across the chest. "Blasphemous," Schwarz said sarcastically. "I ought to shoot him just for that."

The man heard and stopped in his tracks.

Lyons rose slightly higher. "Come on!" he ordered. "And keep those hands up!"

The man in the flag shirt moved cautiously forward again. Lyons saw Schwarz and Blancanales creep out from behind boulders.

Then, just as Lyons had feared they might do, the man in the T-shirt suddenly barked orders in Czech.

In his many years under fire, Carl "Ironman" Lyons had experienced the phenomenon before. "Tachypsychia," psychologists called it—the visual effect in which everything appeared to be happening in slow motion.

As if moving under water, the man in the T-shirt reached behind his back. What seemed like minutes later, the snubby barrel of a S&W Model 19 began to move around his body.

As he pulled the Calico's trigger, Lyons saw the other three men reach sluggishly behind their backs, and in his peripheral vision, Schwarz and Blancanales responded with equally torpid movements.

Lyons could almost see the 9 mm rounds slide from the Calico across the twenty feet that separated him from the man in the T-shirt. They struck the flag, sent blood dancing up into the air and changed the expression on the gunner's face slowly from fear to pain.

The .357 Magnum in the man's hand seemed to hang in the air before floating to the ground and bouncing across the rocks as if on the moon.

Tachypsychia disappeared as quickly as it came, and suddenly Lyons, Schwarz and Blancanales were moving with the speed of light again. Lyons swung the Calico toward a man in green slacks directly behind the leader, pulled the trigger and the man went down. He turned to the other two.

Schwarz and Blancanales had already dropped them in death behind the rocks.

"So much for interrogation," Schwarz said, rising.

The Stony Man warriors moved cautiously through the maze of rocks, making sure no more survivors waited with pistols or other weapons. When they were satisfied that none of Ryba's men posed a further threat, they spread out through the cavern to search for the biochemical stores.

"Over here!" Blancanales called from a corner of the cave, his words echoing off the rocks.

Lyons and Schwarz hurried to his side. Gallon paint cans were stacked in a small room off the main cavern. Pol had pried the lid off several, revealing the black canisters inside.

"This explains painting the house and all that," he said, nodding. "They just mixed this stuff in with the real paint and smuggled it in. All part of the cover."

"Are we going to blow it, or what?" Gadgets asked. "There's probably some more dynamite around here someplace. I could—"

Lyons shook his head. "No sense in it. It's as safe down here as anywhere. We'll notify Stony Man and let the blacksuits cart it out." He rigged the Calico back into his shoulder harness. "In the meantime, let's find a way out."

Pol pointed across the cavern. "It's this way. I saw light coming down a crawl space." He led the way back across the cavern and into a narrow rock passage forged by the elements of nature over the ages. The men of Able Team climbed up and over more of the craggy boulders toward the light, emerging in a wooded area of thick pines.

"Anybody got a compass?" Schwarz joked.

A car horn honked off to the right. Lyons, Schwarz and Blancanales moved toward the sound and came to a blacktop highway.

A small country gas station stood on the other side of the road, and the three men hurried across.

A Chevrolet van with New Hampshire plates pulled off the highway and up to the pumps as Lyons led the way toward a phone booth just outside the service station's door.

The gray Justice Department suits the men from Stony Man Farm had worn were ready for the rag bin. Mud, topped off by limestone dust, covered their faces, hands and every square inch of cloth over their bodies.

The van doors opened and a young couple with a four-year-old boy got out. The father unhooked the hose from the pump as the mother led the little boy toward a sign marked Rest Rooms.

As Lyons opened the door to the phone booth, the child broke away from his mother. Running up to Gadgets Schwarz, the little boy said, "You're supposed to change clothes before you go play after Sunday school, mister." The child frowned. "Boy, are you gonna be in trouble when your mom sees *you*."

Prague, Czech Republic

JOSEPH RYBA DROPPED the handset of the telephone back in the cradle on his desk. He had no more than raised his hand away when the instrument rang again.

Ryba clenched his other fist as he ripped the phone up again. "Yes!" he shouted into the receiver. He listened briefly, said, "Stand by for orders," then slammed the black plastic down again.

He stared at the map of Europe on the wall across the room. The phone hadn't stopped ringing for the past twenty minutes. First had come the report that the local sheriff in Missouri had stumbled upon the storage base, mistaken it for an illegal drug lab of all things, and destroyed his men. The extent of the damage, and whether the anthrax supply hidden in the cavern near the house had been discovered, wasn't known.

Ryba had been willing to accept this as another of the strange coincidences presently plaguing him until the phone rang again. Armed men had taken out the castle lab and storage site in Transylvania. And this time, the cans of anthrax *had* been found and destroyed.

The Czech minister clenched his fists again. That supply had been scheduled for transportation to the launch site nearby in the morning. With it, he could have held an ax over the heads of Romania, Bulgaria and Ukraine.

Then had come this last call from the Deliverance Squad man in charge of inspecting the sites here in the Czech Republic. Someone had wiped out the storage site at Brno's old Hotel Spilberk.

There was no longer any doubt whatsoever that the

West was onto his plan, at least in part, and Ryba mentally kicked himself for not realizing it sooner.

Lifting the receiver and tapping the buttons, he spoke out loud to himself. "It is time to go with what we have. And if the countries of Europe, and the United States, do not respond—" he paused as the line rang "—they will die."

The line connected, and Ryba said simply, "Make the final preparations and await launch orders," then hung up. He repeated the call again to another site in Europe, then called the U.S. with the same order.

Ryba sat back, feeling better as the adrenaline rushed though his veins. It was all so simple, really, and he thanked fate he had caught on to what was happening early.

If he *did* have to launch the anthrax now, he wouldn't destroy as many people as he would have, had he been given a little longer to prepare.

The Czech smiled. But he would kill enough to ensure that the world followed his orders afterward. The body count would still be high, perhaps in the millions, enough to convince the other countries that they not only should, but *wanted* to become part of the New Kingdom of Bohemia.

The minister lifted his pipe from the holder on his desk, filled it with tobacco and stuck it in his mouth. He lighted it with the gold lighter and drew the smoke into his mouth.

It had never tasted sweeter.

Ryba grinned ear to ear. Within a few hours, the launch preparations would be in place. In the meantime, he had more calls to make, then something to do.

He let smoke drift from the corner of his mouth as he tapped the buttons to connect him with the chief of the Deliverance Squad. "The men at the president's office," he said. "Send them in. It is time." He held the button down on the phone, disconnecting the line. The armed men of the Deliverance Squad would have no problems breaching security at the president's office.

They were the security.

Ryba let up on the button and tapped more numbers into the instrument. A moment later, the secretary to the president of the Czech Republic answered.

"This is Joseph Ryba. I must urgently speak to the president."

"Mr. Ryba!" the secretary nearly screamed. "There are men here! They are—"

"Tell them who is calling. They will let him answer."

Ryba heard the line transferred. Then the president said, "Hello."

Ryba's smile widened even further. The Czech leader had been on shaky ground since taking office. He was typically weak, like all of the Czech leaders who had allowed their land to be overrun by invaders for centuries. What Ryba had planned should not be difficult.

Without preliminaries, he said, "Hello, Mr. President, or I suppose I should say Mr. Ex-President." He outlined his plan.

The Czech president gasped, and Ryba could almost see the rifle barrels in the hands of the Deliverance Squad poking him in the ribs as he sat behind his desk.

"One more thing," Ryba added. "Be so kind as to have your press aide—no, I should say my press aide—inform the media that I will hold a conference at 7:00 p.m. sharp. Make sure CNN is there. I can think of no better way to inform the countries of Europe that they are about to be honored by becoming a part of our new empire."

Ryba pressed the disconnect button again. Two more calls. The first was a return call to the chief of the Deliverance Squad. "Go to my home," he said. "I will be arriving there in another hour or so. I want Mrs. Ryba to have disappeared by then." He paused, thinking of the world-changing events that were about to take place. After the press conference tonight, he would need far more protection than the three bodyguards he was presently using. "And arrange for twenty more of the Deliverance Squad to be at my side on a permanent basis," he ordered. "We will need an appropriate number of vehicles, as well."

As Joseph Ryba placed his final call before going to his home to await the press conference, and the beginning of the New Kingdom of Bohemia, the smile returned to his face. He tapped the button on the intercom, and said, "Marja, please come in."

The woman who had borne two of his children opened the door, resplendent in the short black leather miniskirt and skintight blouse. She started to sit, but Ryba shook his head.

Marja stopped half in, half out, of the chair in front of his desk.

"You have no time to sit down," Ryba said. "You have work to do."

"Yes?" Marja smiled. "And what is it?"

Ryba rose, rounded the desk and took her in his arms. Looking down into her eyes, he said, "You must pick out a wedding dress, my dear. One that is fit for a queen."

CHAPTER FIFTEEN

Joseph Ryba knew that things were about to start happening, and when they did, they would happen fast.

Led by a burly Deliverance Squad bodyguard, and flanked by two more, Ryba marched down the steps of the Interior Building, his spirits soaring. He had awaited this day ever since meeting Boris Stavropek and the other former Soviet Biopreparat researchers who were desperately seeking employment anywhere, doing anything. Much like soldiers returning from a war that had ended, they were desperate to put their skills to work for them.

And he had given them the opportunity to do just that.

Ryba reflected over the past couple of years as one of his men opened the rear door of the limousine. There had been times when he was filled with doubt. Would it ever really happen? Would the project ever reach a state where he could not only threaten the powers of Europe with genocide if they didn't succumb to his will, but at the same time hold the World Watchdog at bay?

That had been the Soviets' plan. But they had been unable to make it happen. They had been trying to

work within a politico-economic system that was not
only doomed from the beginning, but had reached its
death throes by the time Biopreparat was initiated.

Yes, Ryba thought as he slid into the back seat of
the limo, communism had been doomed since its in-
ception. Dictatorships and monarchies, on the other
hand, had proved themselves since the dawn of mankind.

Ryba settled back against the seat as his bodyguards got in around him. A moment later, they were
pulling out of the underground parking lot and onto
the street.

The Czech minister opened his briefcase, pulled out
several pages and began riffling through them. He
stared down at a list of names for Department of Ag-
riculture officials, mentally crossing several off the list
and replacing them with men who had been loyal to
him during the project. As the limo pulled down the
street, he moved on to a list of judges on the Czech
Republic's Supreme Court.

Ryba sighed. So much to do. So little time.

He heard the sudden sound of screeching tires, and
was thrown forward against the seat belt. His eyes
jerked up in time to see a flash of blue through the
windshield.

The next thing he knew, the screech of metal
against metal filled his ears and the limo squealed to
a halt. Through the windshield, Ryba saw the dented
front fender of a blue Oldsmobile Toronado. The automobile had been knocked several feet away from
the limo by the collision, and now the driver was exiting the car.

Ryba saw the man. A black man. He watched as a white woman with short red hair got out of the car on the passenger's side. Ryba shook his head in disgust. More mixing of the races—like the Slavs. The sight brought nausea to his stomach. He would soon put a quick stop to such nonsense.

The Deliverance Squad man behind the wheel opened the door and started to get out.

"Handle this quickly," Ryba instructed him. "There is much I must do." His eyes returned to his papers. But suddenly the illness in his belly returned as well. The woman. Red hair. Where had he heard of a red-haired woman recently?

Skrdla. The answer came simultaneously with the first gunshot.

Ryba looked up to see the black man pump two rounds into his driver. The red-haired woman had drawn a pistol of her own.

The other two Deliverance Squad hardmen leapt from the vehicle, frantically trying to pull their Skorpion submachine pistols from under their coats. Ryba froze in his seat as a short Hispanic man with grizzled black hair appeared from out of nowhere and calmly shot the bodyguard who had ridden in the passenger's seat.

More gunfire came from the side, and Ryba turned to see two tall Caucasians team up to fire bullets into the bodyguard who had sat next to him in the back seat.

Before Ryba could react, the car door next to him flew open. He turned as a tall man with dark hair and chiseled features slashed through his seat belt with a long knife and lifted him from the car as if he were a baby.

Ryba raised his fist to punch the man. Did a thin smile of amusement cross the man's face? Before he could decide, the big man had caught his fist, twirled him around as if they were dancing and jammed a huge forearm into his throat.

The Czech felt the pressure of the man's other arm on the back of his neck. He closed his eyes.

His last thought before he lost consciousness was that he had been right. Things *were* happening. And fast.

But they weren't happening at all the way he had planned.

THE LAIR OF THE WOLF was modest. He needed little, for hunting was his only pastime.

The bedroom was bare except for the throw rug on which he slept. The living room too, had no furniture. In the kitchen, there were no plates or utensils in the cupboards, and the stove and refrigerator hadn't been used since he'd taken the apartment. A bare light bulb glowed in the ceiling, and the only other furnishings in the small living quarters were a scarred wooden table and four matching chairs. They had been positioned directly below the light bulb.

Skrdla had purchased the dinette set at a used-furniture store. He had never eaten at the table, nor had he ever used it or the chairs for anything other than what he was using it for now. But in the manner in which they were now being used, the table and chairs had seen a plenitude of use over the years.

Three feet away from the man and woman across from him, Skrdla stared into their horrified eyes. He felt no emotion—emotion wasn't part of his job. The closest thing to passion that ever filled his soul was the thrill of the hunt.

Of course torture was sometimes part of the hunt.

A quick and unusual flash of self-examination entered Skrdla's brain, and he wondered for a moment if his psychological makeup would have allowed for normal emotion if he'd chosen another path in life. The moment passed without furnishing an answer.

The wolf returned to the task at hand—determining which of the two research scientists had helped the red-haired British woman enter the laboratory.

Skrdla studied the man. Vincent Hlupnek. His eyes showed fear far past what had been evident while he worked in the lab. That, of course, was normal. Anyone in Hlupnek's position now would exhibit fear.

Stripping a man naked, binding and gagging him, had that effect on a man. As it did on women.

Skrdla turned his eyes to the woman with the long blond hair. The ropes across her chest divided her nude breasts, forcing them out to the sides. The pointed pink nipples reminded Skrdla of a walleyed boy he had known at the orphanage. He glanced down to the thatch of dark pubic hair between Anna Berilka's legs. So. Blond wasn't her natural hair color.

The hardman sat back, studying the horror in the woman's eyes. Yes, she was wondering if he would rape her. She had no idea that such activities offered no appeal to him. He had torn the garments from her body for the same reason he had stripped Vincent

Hlupnek—not to purge her of her clothing, but of her dignity.

He wanted her mind and soul bare. He didn't care about her body, at least not in the way most men would have cared about the shapely curves and mysterious crevices. He did feel a certain lust to see how those places responded to pain, but Skrdla suspected his lust was different than other men's, as well.

Rape? No, he wouldn't rape Anna Berilka. But by the time her ordeal was over, rape would have seemed pleasant compared to what he had done.

Skrdla rose and stepped forward, seeing the terror rise in both sets of eyes. He moved toward the man. His instincts had told him that Hlupnek was the more likely suspect as soon as he'd tied the two to the chairs. He wasn't sure yet, however. And even if he was correct, bringing the woman along might still prove valuable.

Lifting the gag from Hlupnek's mouth, he said, "This can be easy, you know. Tell me the name of the British woman, and where I can find her. Then I will return you to work."

Hlupnek didn't speak.

It had been worth a try, at least. It would have saved time in the hunt if Vincent Hlupnek had come clean at this point. But Hlupnek was smart. He was like the boys who had scored high on the IQ test at the orphanage. The scientist knew Skrdla was lying, and he knew that regardless of what he said, he would never leave the apartment alive.

But the wolf knew his prey. He knew the deer had to be hunted differently than the rabbit. And he saw instinctively in Hlupnek's eyes the course the hunt should take.

Skrdla sighed. "You know nothing of a red-haired British MI-6 agent, then?" he asked.

Hlupnek shook his head.

"Then it must be her." Turning to the woman, he pulled a long lock-blade folding knife from the side pocket of his gray coat. He opened it and ran the back of the blade slowly down the soft skin on Anna Berilka's right breast.

The woman's breast quivered as the cold steel stroked it. Skrdla noted that the nipple stiffened. Curious.

He turned the blade around to the razor-honed edge. The tooth of the wolf went to work. It bit slowly at first, then harder, deeper.

The woman's eyes opened wildly. Muffled groans came from behind the gag.

As Skrdla worked, he kept one eye on Hlupnek. The man's eyes grew as wild as the woman's. Tears flooded suddenly down his face. "No! Stop!" the researcher cried. "She is innocent! She knows nothing!"

"Then it is you?" Skrdla asked calmly.

He got no response and turned back to the woman.

"Yes! Please...I will tell you what you want to know!"

"The name of the British woman, and where she can be found. Do you know where she lives?"

Hlupnek closed his eyes in agony. He nodded.

"Tell me, then."

The researcher did as he'd been told.

Two minutes later, Skrdla closed and locked the door to his apartment behind him. He made a mental note to ask Ryba to send men from the Deliverance Squad to clean up and remove the bodies, then started down the steps to the street.

The man in the gray suit felt oddly cheated in the hunt so far. Hlupnek had been too easy, and he hadn't been able to spend as much time with the woman as he'd have liked. How odd, the way her nipple had responded to his blade. Much the same as a woman's breast reacted when stroked. Or so he'd heard.

Skrdla opened the hall door to the street, stepped out and started down the sidewalk. No matter, he told himself as he flagged a taxi and gave the driver the address of Jonine Hammersmith's apartment. If the red-haired woman wasn't home when he arrived, he would wait, wait as the wolf had waited for the deer. She would return eventually, and there would be plenty of time for his experiments then.

Prague, Czech Republic

"YOU WILL NEVER make it past the guards at the gate," Joseph Ryba warned.

Next to him in the back seat, Bolan pressed the muzzle of the big .44 Magnum Desert Eagle into the man's ribs. "You'd better hope we do, Joe," the Executioner said. "You'd better hope it goes smoothly, and that we get the code key. Because if we don't, the first round fired is going right through your heart. The second I'm reserving for your brain."

Bolan glanced to the front seat as the limo turned

a corner. David McCarter sat behind the wheel, with Gary Manning in the passenger's seat. Like Bolan, they were dressed in ill-fitting suits taken from Ryba's Deliverance Squad bodyguards. To add to the poor fit, all three of the suits sported bullet holes and bloodstains.

The Executioner knew the moment of truth was at hand. The holes and stains weren't obvious from inside the limousine, but if the guards at the gate looked closely...

Bolan let the thought drift away. The problem had no answer. There was no other choice but to go on with the mission, hope the guards paid them no attention and handle whatever came up when it came up.

The limo slowed at the gate. A man wearing a Jablonec uniform stepped down from a small guardhouse and walked forward, carrying a clipboard. He frowned.

Bolan jabbed the Desert Eagle into Ryba again and said, "Make it look real, Joe. Your life depends on it." He bent slightly to cover the gun from the eyes of the man outside the car.

Ryba spoke in Czech.

Bolan watched the guard as he waited. The man's eyebrows rose slightly.

The Executioner pushed harder on the Desert Eagle. The three Westerners didn't speak Czech, but Ryba didn't know that. "Careful," he warned.

Ryba glanced at him, then turned back to the guard, speaking again.

The Executioner had no idea what had been said either time. But it appeared that Ryba had chanced some clue the first time he'd spoken, then modified it when Bolan called his hand. In any case, the guard stepped back and the gate swung open.

The limo headed down a long winding driveway and into a three-car garage. Bolan hid the .44 under his jacket and nodded Ryba toward a door leading into the house, then closed the garage door and opened the trunk.

Jonine Hammersmith climbed out first. Rafael Encizo followed, with Calvin James bringing up the rear.

McCarter led the way through the door into the kitchen.

A woman wearing a maid's uniform looked up from the sink as the procession filed through. Her face showed mild surprise. She spoke in Czech, and Ryba answered curtly.

Hammersmith waited until they'd left the kitchen and started up a staircase at the end of a hall before whispering to Bolan. "The maid said his wife just left with several men who said she was to meet Ryba," the British woman stated. "Ryba said there'd been some confusion and not to worry."

Bolan nodded. Things had gone smoothly so far. Too smoothly? Ryba had seemed a little too cooperative, too ready to admit that the key book that would unravel the mystery of the biochemical launch sites was at home in his safe.

The Executioner couldn't quite believe that a man who had worked so hard for years to achieve his goal would give up so easily. No, Ryba had something planned. Some ace in the hole.

"This way," the Czech said, pointing down a hallway. He led the way to a door, into what appeared to be the master bedroom and up a short flight of stairs to another room.

Bolan followed him, stopping just to the side of the door so the others could pass. The room was paneled in knotty pine, with several closet doors on each side of the room. Prints of the portraits of famous world leaders lined the wall. The portraits hadn't been chosen at random, however. There was a theme—megalomania.

Napoleon stared back at the Executioner from directly behind Ryba's desk. On the side walls, he saw Stalin, Alexander the Great, and even Adolf Hitler.

McCarter whistled. "Nice company you keep," he commented. "Where's Saddam Hussein?"

Ryba ignored him, moving to the portrait of Napoleon behind the small PC on his desk. Bolan moved up behind him, cocking the Desert Eagle and resting the barrel just over the man's ear as Ryba swung the frame back to reveal a wall safe. "Be very careful, Ryba," he cautioned. "This has all gone a little too well for my liking."

Ryba shrugged. "I know when I am beaten."

"Do you?"

The Czech turned slowly. "You requested that things go smoothly. They have. Now you want me to make trouble? Please, make up your mind. You cannot have it both ways."

Bolan tapped the safe with the big .44. "Go on," he said. He stepped to the side where he could see into the safe the minute Ryba opened it. For all he knew, the man had watched too many movies and hidden a pistol inside.

Ryba spun the dial several times and the tumblers clicked into place. He opened the safe to reveal several manila file folders and a plastic box. Through the box's opaque lid, the Executioner could see floppy computer disks.

The Czech minister moved slowly as he removed the box, turned and set it on the desk. He opened the lid, dug through the contents, then pulled out one of the disks. "Here you have it," he said, smiling.

Hammersmith moved forward and took the disk from his hand. She looked down at the label, then back up at Bolan. "It's labeled Flute Sites," she said, frowning. She pushed the button on the PC behind her and stepped back as the computer warmed up.

Bolan felt the hair rise on the back of his neck. Something was wrong. It had all gone far too easy. A man like Joseph Ryba, with dreams of dominating all of Europe and maybe even the world, didn't just lie down, play dead and give up that dream like this.

The computer stopped humming and Hammersmith inserted the disk. A moment later, a list flashed on the screen. "This *is* it," Hammersmith said in awe. "The word 'flute' means launch. 'Organ' stands for Bonn, and 'Piano' means Germany. There's more that follows—a more exact location in Bonn probably, but it's in the same code as the storage sites." Bolan watched her scan down the list. "Thank God, only three of the sites are ready to launch. 'Guitar, Cymbal'—that's Kiev, Ukraine and...let's see. Kansas City, Kansas." She turned toward the Executioner, smiling triumphantly. "All it'll take now is to get this to your computer man and—"

Bolan cut her off in midsentence. Turning back to Ryba, he grasped the man by the collar of his coat and almost lifted him into the air. "Okay, Ryba," the Executioner growled, "what's the catch?"

Ryba smiled. "The 'catch,' as you put it, is this. Opening the safe without deactivating the alarm—a button on the other side of my desk—alerted my men to come up the rear stairs." His eyes flickered toward a wall, and suddenly the doors of what Bolan had taken to be closets flew back.

Deliverance Squad men armed with Model 25 submachine guns burst into the room, covering the men from Stony Man Farm.

"So," Ryba said, grinning still wider, "I suppose you could say that the real catch is that although you have the information you wanted, it will do you no good."

The Executioner's eyes swept the room. Ten men stood evenly spaced around them, their submachine guns aimed at him, Hammersmith and Phoenix Force. They were outnumbered and outgunned.

There was one way out, and one way only. Maybe.

Bolan made his decision as the smile on Ryba's face was suddenly replaced by a scowl. "Kill them!" the would-be King of Bohemia shouted.

Before the Deliverance Squad could fire, the Executioner swept a foot up and against Ryba's knees, knocking the man's legs out from under him. The minister fell to a sitting position behind the desk.

Bolan was on him in a heartbeat, forcing him onto

the floor and shoving him into the desk well out of sight. The Executioner clambered in after the man, pushing Ryba's back against the front of the desk.

Murmurs of confusion came from the guards. But without being able to see where Bolan and Ryba were positioned, none of them dared shoot through the wood.

Bolan shoved the barrel of the Desert Eagle under Ryba's chin, forcing the Czech's face against the top of the desk. "You move, or speak when I don't tell you to, and I'll kill you," he whispered. "You got it?"

"You will die," Ryba mumbled almost incoherently against the wood. "You will all die."

"We're used to that idea," the Executioner growled. "The question is, are you?"

Ryba didn't answer.

Bolan's voice boomed from under the desk. "Can you hear me?"

A voice answered in Czech.

"I don't have the time or inclination to play games!" the Executioner yelled out. "Get me somebody who speaks English or you'll be chanting 'The King is Dead.'"

Another voice spoke immediately. "We are listening."

"What's your name?" Bolan demanded.

"Shimanek," said the voice. "Lieutenant Shimanek."

"Well, Shimanek, let me explain the ground rules to you. The woman you see out there is going to send some information over the computer modem. You do anything to stop her and there'll be a .44 in Ryba's brain. Clear so far?''

There was no answer.

Bolan pressed the gun barrel harder into Ryba's chin. His face flattened further across the wood and his lips spread out. "You better tell him yourself, King." He let up on the gun slightly.

"Do…as he says," Ryba mumbled.

"Rule number two. The same goes for the rest of my men out there. Get in their way, do anything to harm them. Bam." The Executioner paused, then went on. "Number three. If I see anything move behind the desk, head, arm, whatever, it'll get the third bullet out of this gun. I've already promised Ryba the first two. You understand all that, Shimanek?''

"Yes."

Bolan frowned beneath the desk. Hammersmith wouldn't know how to link things up to Stony Man. "David," he called out, "set the modem up for her."

"Aye-aye."

For the next several minutes the sound of tapping keys was the Executioner's only contact with the world above the desk well. Then Manning's voice said, "Striker, it's me. I'm coming back so don't shoot."

"Come on," Bolan said.

A second later, Manning's head poked into the desk well. "They're all behaving themselves, but what do we do after Hammersmith's finished?"

Ryba snickered, his face still against the wood. "Good question," he mumbled. "Just how do you plan to get out of here?"

"The same way we got in," Bolan replied. "With you."

Manning shook his head. "There are too many of them, Striker. You try to wrestle him out of here and back down to the car, someone's going to get a clean shot."

"Go get me a blanket, Gary," the Executioner said.

Manning looked at the Executioner as if the man had lost his mind, then slowly the big Canadian's face changed to one of understanding. He crawled back out of the desk well, rose to his feet and disappeared.

He returned a minute or so later, said, "It's me again," then dropped a fuzzy king-size bedspread under the desk. He sat beside Bolan.

Ten minutes later, Hammersmith said, "I'm finished."

The Executioner turned to Manning. "Once this thing starts, I won't be able to talk. You'll have to explain things to Ryba's men."

Manning nodded and stood.

Bolan pulled Ryba's face away from the desk and pulled the bedspread over the man's head. Then, sliding under the cover himself, he shoved the gun back under the man's chin and said, "Keep quiet."

Slowly, the bedspread concealing all but their feet, the two men scooted out from under the desk and stood. Bolan pressed his chest against Ryba's back, wrapped his arms around the Czech's shoulders and shoved the Desert Eagle back up under his chin. He pressed his head to the side of the man's neck to make sure one head was indistinguishable from the other beneath the bedspread.

Manning's voice penetrated the cover. "You gentlemen listen, and listen good. You can see feet, and you can see ankles. And you might think you can even figure out which head is which. So whichever of you heroes wants to be the one who takes the chance on shooting your boss...be my guest. Otherwise, stay the hell out of our way."

Blind beneath the bedspread, Bolan waited. The scent of stale pipe tobacco and Ryba's nervous sweat filled his nostrils. Then someone—Manning again, Bolan assumed—grabbed the front of the bedspread and began to lead them out of the office area. Footsteps fell in behind them, and when they reached the bedroom, Encizo's voice said, "Watch the steps." The Executioner and Ryba shuffled down the short staircase and through the bedroom.

The procession continued slowly downstairs, through several rooms, and out of the house. Bolan heard a car door open and McCarter's voice said, "Okay, get in." Still hugging Ryba tightly, the Executioner pushed the man into the back seat of the limo.

Bodies crowded into both of their sides. The front doors opened, and the engine started. "If anybody follows us out of the gate, Ryba's a dead man," Calvin James warned the hardmen Bolan assumed had followed them out of the house.

A moment later, the limo pulled down the drive and onto the street.

"Anybody following us?" Bolan asked a minute later.

"Don't think so," James said next to him. "Go ahead."

Bolan pulled the bedspread from over his head, leaving it on Ryba. "Just stay where you are," he ordered. He saw James on his right side, with Manning squeezed in against the other door. McCarter was behind the wheel, with Encizo and Hammersmith in the front seat next to him.

Hammersmith spun around in her seat. "I couldn't tell you before with all of them around, but whoever it was I sent the code key to sent a message back. He said that by the time we could get to a phone, he'd have the launch sites pinpointed."

Bolan nodded. "Then we'd better get to a phone."

JONINE HAMMERSMITH turned back in her seat and looked out through the windshield as the limo raced down the streets of Prague. Things were winding down. Soon, it would be over. All it would take now was for the man on the other end of the modem to identify Ryba's operational launch sites, then they would destroy them. How, exactly, would they destroy the sites? She had no idea.

But she didn't doubt for a minute that the man in the back seat would have a plan.

Hammersmith pulled the visor down in front of her and caught a brief glimpse of Rance Pollock riding next to that degenerate excuse for a human being still covered by the bedspread. Pollock. Sure. His name was Pollock about as much as hers was Fergie.

Just exactly who was Pollock, and who were his friends? She didn't know. But she did know that the man was a combination of all the attributes she felt it took to make a man with a capital *M*. He was tough, smart, fast and strong. But there was another side to him, as well. He could be sensitive, kind and gentle.

She glanced into the mirror again. How about the others—who were they? They all weren't Americans. The black man was from somewhere in the Midwest, she'd guess. But the one they called McCarter was as British as she was. His accent gave him away as a Cockney. And the other big gentlemen, she'd guess him as Canadian. He might be from Montana or one of the other northern states, but she doubted it.

And they'd spoken in hushed tones of a fifth man— Cats. A nickname, probably. He was hurt, and although Hammersmith had never met this Cats, she felt a pain in her heart for him as if they'd been partners themselves.

What it all boiled down to was that Jonine Hammersmith didn't know who these men were, and she'd given up trying to figure it out. All she knew was that they were the good guys, as Pollock had once said, and she was proud to be working with them.

The limo turned onto Prague's Resslova Avenue, then crossed the Jiraskuv Bridge. A service station appeared on the right-hand side of the street, and McCarter pulled in.

In the mirror, Hammersmith saw Pollock turn to the covered lump in the bedspread. "Be a good boy while I'm gone," he told Ryba, "so my friends don't have to kill you." He got out of the limousine and walked to the phone booth at the front of the service station.

Hammersmith continued to look into the mirror, but

now her eyes focused on herself. Good Lord, she was a bloody mess. Her hair was filthy, her makeup had long ago been rubbed off, and her eyes looked as if she'd been on a two-week bender. She could use a five-minute break in the rest room.

Hammersmith watched a beaten and battered Chevy Cressida pull up to the gas tanks as she folded the visor back up and turned to the side window. Two tough-looking punks with shaved heads, black leather jackets and enough chains to sink them to the bottom of the Thames got out and began to fill the gas tank.

It was then that Hammersmith realized where they were. The corner of Resslova and Zboravska? She kicked herself mentally. They were less than three blocks from her apartment. They could have all gone there and used the phone, and she could have freshened up a bit. Too late now.

Bolan returned to the limo and got in. "Bear's ID'd the sites," he reported. "Two in Europe—Bonn and Kiev—and Kansas City."

Ryba spoke for the first time since entering the limo. "And they are set to launch by midnight if they do not hear from me. You will never stop them."

Bolan pulled the cover off the man's head. "I don't suppose you'd care to call it off?" he asked.

"I don't suppose so," Ryba said defiantly.

The little man Hammersmith guessed to be Cuban pulled out a long thin-bladed knife. "We could possibly persuade you to do so," he said softly.

Bolan looked at Ryba and shook his head. "No. There's no way of knowing what type of verbal code they might have for a situation like this. For all we know, Ryba saying 'Call it off' might mean 'Launch immediately.' We can't take the chance.''

He turned back to the others. ''We'll just have to call this off for you, King Joe. We're splitting up, guys. Hammersmith and I are going to Kiev. Grimaldi's on his way to pick us up. The rest of you are heading to Bonn. Barb's already contacted GSG-9 and you'll be working with them. Their plane is waiting for you at the airport now.''

Hammersmith turned in her seat. ''How long before our plane arrives?'' she asked.

''He's an hour or so out. Why?''

''I live only three blocks from here. Could we stop off on the way to the airport? Let me tidy up and get a change of clothes at least? It won't take five minutes.''

Bolan glanced at his watch. ''GSG-9 is waiting—''

''We can find other transportation,'' Manning said, looking through the window at the two punks in the Chevy. He grinned. ''Give the gal a break, Striker. She's been through a hell of a lot.''

McCarter turned around behind the wheel as an Oldsmobile Cutlass pulled up to the pumps. The driver got out wearing a short red skirt.

One of the skinheads walked over and pinched her on the behind.

''Yes,'' McCarter agreed, ''we can find other transportation and save a young maiden in distress at the same time.'' He slid from behind the wheel as the others got out of the limo.

Hammersmith watched as the muscular Canadian

walked up behind the punk hassling the girl, grabbed one of his ears and guided him down to the concrete.

The Cockney pulled his pistol and shoved it under the other youth's nose.

The girl in the short skirt got back in the Cutlass and drove away.

A moment later, the American's friends did the same in the Cressida.

"You drive," Bolan instructed. "And hurry. I'll baby-sit while you go up and get what you need."

CHAPTER SIXTEEN

Still in the back seat of the limo which Hammersmith had hurriedly parked on the street, Bolan watched the British agent ascend the steps of the apartment building and disappear through the door. Cars passed by on the busy thoroughfare as the Executioner turned to Ryba. "Got any hobbies, Joe?"

Ryba looked at him, puzzled. "What do you mean?"

The Executioner shrugged. "Just wondering what you'll do to kill time behind bars for the rest of your life."

The man snorted. "I will never go to prison. Do you remember the bomblets your own country used during the Gulf War?"

Bolan didn't answer.

"I have the same bomblets. Only mine will dispense anthrax," Ryba bragged. "How can you stop them? You cannot. And when your attempt fails, you will need me to negotiate a settlement. Do not try to fool yourself, American. The New Kingdom of Bohemia is the world's destiny."

"Well, we'll do our best to see that doesn't happen," Bolan said with only a trace of sarcasm.

The warrior glanced at his watch, noting that five minutes had gone by since Hammersmith had entered her apartment. He waited silently, facing the front, but keeping one eye on Ryba.

The man showed no signs of wanting to escape. That could be a ploy on his part. Or perhaps in his megalomania he really did believe the West would fail to stop the biochemical launches and that he would step back into the role he had created for himself.

A sinking feeling suddenly turned the Executioner's stomach. Depending on what happened in the next few hours, Ryba might just be right. Oh, this Kingdom of Bohemia would never come about. That was the dream of a madman. But stopping the bombs was certainly no done deal, even with GSG-9, the new Ukraine military and the U.S. Air Force already on alert.

The Executioner looked at his watch again. Ten minutes. What was keeping Hammersmith? Her makeup? That didn't seem likely. So far, she'd been the consummate professional with no problem sorting out priorities. And with a million people scheduled to die in the next few hours, Bolan couldn't believe she had now decided to take time out to get her lipstick just right.

The Executioner looked out the window at the apartment building. Something was wrong. Pulling two sets of plastic handcuffs from his pocket, he turned to Ryba and said, ''Turn around.''

The Czech smiled. ''Afraid I will overpower you?''

Bolan didn't have time to waste on wisecracks. Pulling a fist back to his shoulder, he sent it crashing into Ryba's jaw. The man slumped forward, unconscious.

The warrior cuffed Ryba's hands behind his back, secured his ankles together, pushed the man to the floor of the limo and covered him with the bedspread.

Locking the doors of the limousine, the Executioner stopped at the curb, waited for a break in the heavy traffic, then sprinted across the street and up the steps into the building. Stopping just inside the door, he realized suddenly that he didn't know which apartment was Hammersmith's. The building contained four units, two upstairs and two down. Turning to the mailboxes, he saw four names. Three were obviously Czech. The fourth read Chamberlain, an English name.

The Executioner's mind traveled back to the alley behind the hardware store, when Hammersmith had worried that even through she spoke fluent Czech, her accent would never fool the cops.

The British agent's cover would never have included trying to pass herself off as a native. Chamberlain it had to be.

Bolan mounted the stairs quietly, wincing when they creaked. Something was going on inside apartment number 3 upstairs, and he didn't want his approach announced. Reaching the door, he twisted the knob slowly. Unlocked.

The Executioner inched the door partway open and peered inside, seeing a short hallway that led to a living room. Empty. He slipped inside and closed the door behind him.

Bolan moved silently across the carpet to the end

of the hall. He stopped, looking into the living room. Two other doors led out of the modestly furnished room, one into what appeared to be a kitchen—he could see the edge of a cabinet. The light was on.

The Executioner had taken two steps into the living room when he saw a huge gray bulk rise from its haunches to the side of the door. The shiny blade of a large folding knife slashed down in an arc at his shoulder.

Bolan twisted out of the way and turned as the knife came at him from the side. His arm shot out, blocking the wrist of the man in the gray suit as the Executioner backpedaled across the living room.

The tall man paused, letting a smile creep over his face. Bolan had a split second to wonder who he was before the knife came at him again, this time in a thrust toward the Executioner's heart. Bolan stepped to the side, parried and caught the man in the face with a back-fist as he shuffled farther across the room.

A painful shout erupted from deep in the throat of the gray man. His face took on the look of some wild and wounded animal as the Executioner reached for the Desert Eagle under his jacket. But before he could draw the big .44, the blade was slashing again.

Bolan stepped to the side of the man, grabbed the wrist that held the knife and twisted his other arm under it. He looked down at the blade and saw blood.

The sinking feeling he had gotten in the car returned. The blade hadn't touched *him*. The blood on the knife had to belong to Hammersmith.

The Executioner tightened the arm bar around the other man's elbow. The sound of snapping bone rocketed against the walls of the small flat. The growl of a wounded beast followed as the Executioner dropped the arm and caught his opponent with an overhead hammerhand to the head.

The hardman stumbled, then fell to one knee. Bolan stepped back, catching his breath.

The enemy turned toward him, screaming in pain and hatred, his right arm hanging limply at his side. He dived forward, circling his other arm around the Executioner's knees and throwing him to his back.

Bolan's head struck the carpet. Spiked teeth circled his lower calf, sinking deep into the Achilles tendon. The warrior rose to a sitting position, hammering another fist on top of his crazed attacker's skull. He heard a crack, but his adversary hung on like a dog to his favorite bone.

The warrior reached out, grasping his enemy's shirt collar. With a fistful of shirt in his left hand, he drove his right fist into the man's temple. The collar ripped away in the Executioner's hand, and with it came what appeared to be a string of animal teeth that had hung around the man's neck on a rawhide strip.

The Executioner drove another fist into his adversary's nose. When the man turned his head, growling, Bolan rolled to one side and scrambled to his feet.

The gray man rose to his knees, stuck his hand under his coat and withdrew a flat-black Russian Tokarev pistol.

Bolan stepped forward, kicking the hand. The toe of his shoe caught the barrel of the gun, knocking it upward as a round exploded. The man howled, looking up at the bullet hole in the ceiling as if baying at the moon. Blood and a sticky white froth dripped from his mouth.

The Desert Eagle appeared in the Executioner's hand as if having a mind of its own. As the front sight fell on the man's face, the Tokarev came into play as well.

Bolan squeezed the trigger a microsecond before his enemy.

An ear-shattering blast exploded throughout the apartment. The .44 Magnum round caught the hardman just above the nose, drilled up through his eye and left a crater the size of the Executioner's fist when it exited.

The man in gray fell to his back on the floor.

Bolan stepped forward, the Desert Eagle trained down. The back half of the man's head was gone, but the eyes—flat, expressionless, yellow-tinted eyes—stared at the Executioner, looking strangely like those of a wolf.

Bolan turned toward the kitchen, afraid of what he might find.

Hammersmith sat gagged and bound to a wooden kitchen chair. Her clothing lay in a pile to one side, and a thin red line of blood ran down her neck.

The Executioner moved forward and removed the gag. "Are you hurt?" he asked.

Tears formed in the British woman's eyes. They ran down her face as she said, "It isn't bad. He was just starting."

Bolan pulled a combat knife from under his jacket and sliced through the ropes. Hammersmith bounded to her feet and threw her arms around his neck, her breasts heaving in sobs against his chest.

"Easy," the Executioner said softly. "It's over."

He held her quietly for several minutes, then Hammersmith pushed herself away and looked up into his eyes. The tears stopped, and her face took on a hardness Bolan hadn't previously seen in the British woman. "Not quite. We've got to stop the launches." She looked down at her clothes.

Bolan turned his back as she picked up her blouse.

Hammersmith laughed quietly, her confidence returning after the brief outburst of emotion. "Give me a break with the gentleman routine," she said. "You've seen it all before."

The Executioner turned back around. "Not really." He smiled, wanting to help her good humor come back. "It was dark."

The British woman laughed again.

"Still want your makeup?" Bolan asked.

"The hell with the makeup. Let's go get those sons of bitches." She led the way out of the apartment and down the steps.

They reached the outside door and walked onto the concrete steps in time to see Joseph Ryba hop out of the back seat. Still bound at the wrists and ankles, the minister stood wobbling in the center of the street. Car horns blasted the irritation of their drivers as the vehicles swerved past him.

"Help!" Ryba screamed. "I am the minister of the interior! I have been kidnapped!"

Bolan started down the steps, taking them two at a time.

"I am the—" Ryba screamed.

His words were cut short as the speeding Mazda Miata struck him broadside and sent him flying up over the hood and roof before he collapsed like a rag doll on the concrete.

Bolan and Hammersmith rushed forward as traffic came to a screeching halt around them.

Blood covered Ryba's face and body as the Executioner knelt next to him.

Joseph Ryba looked up at the warrior, his face a mask of pain. Then, slowly, the lips curled up into a smile. "I am...the King of the New Bohemian Empire."

Then he closed his eyes.

Kansas

CARL LYONS LOOKED DOWN through the windshield at the rolling plains as the Beechcraft Baron neared the private airport just west of Kansas City, Kansas. The flatland seemed to go on forever.

The airport had been the perfect cover for Ryba's launch site. Small privately owned planes—small, yet big enough to drop anthrax-laced bombs that could destroy hundreds of thousands of lives—landed and took off all the time. And you didn't get much more centralized within the U.S. than Kansas. From this vantage point, they could cover the entire country in a matter of hours.

Lyons glanced at the photograph in his hand, then shoved it into a pocket of his black combat suit.

Formerly owned by a conglomerate in Denver, the

airport had been sold a year earlier to a millionaire businessman in Chicago. He had paid an unreasonable price to get the small business, and it had been assumed by the happy company selling the property that the airport was to become nothing more than a rich man's plaything.

The man's name was Richard Kokojan. A first-generation American, his family had returned him to the old country for his college education. As it turned out, he had been a classmate of Francis Hunyadi and Joseph Ryba.

Amazing what Stony Man Farm could find out when it got on the right track, Lyons thought. Kurtzman had even tapped into an American airline's computer system and learned that Kokojan had been on the passenger list to Kansas City the night before. Meanwhile, a Stony Man "blacksuit" masquerading as a private pilot had refueled at the Kokojan airport, reporting back that there was little if any armed guard.

Lyons reached for the microphone, switched the radio to the USAF frequency and said, "Justice to Bald Eagle. Come in Eagle."

The coarse voice of Air Force Captain Dan Elliot, leading the squadron of F-104 Starfighters now hidden above the clouds, came back. "Go ahead, Justice."

"We'll be going down in…" Lyons looked at Charlie Mott, behind the controls of the Baron.

Mott held up two fingers.

"Two minutes, Eagle."

"Roger, Justice. We'll stand ready." Elliot's squadron would be ready to pounce on any aircraft that slipped past Able Team.

Lyons handed the mike to Mott, then switched it back to the FAA frequency. Mott spoke into the radio, getting clearance to land as Lyons turned toward the back of the plane. "Everybody ready?" he asked.

Schwarz and Blancanales both patted their Calico submachine guns.

Lyons checked the safety on his M-950A, then sat back as the Beechcraft began its descent. He whistled softly through his teeth. This one had been close, and it still wasn't over. If Striker hadn't located the disk with the code key on it in time, they'd still have been wondering where the launch sites were hidden when the planes below took off to spray biochemical death across the nation.

And Lyons didn't kid himself. The threat wasn't over. If a plane did get off the ground, Elliot and his men would have to hope they could force it down without a fight. If they had to fire, and ruptured the canisters of anthrax over a city, the resulting fatalities would be horrendous.

The wheels of the Baron hit the runway, and Mott slowed the plane, then taxied toward the hangar.

Blancanales opened the door, said, "See you guys later," and jumped to the tarmac.

Schwarz waited until they neared the hangar, then did the same.

As they drew abreast of the small office building to one side of the runway, Mott suddenly gunned the engines again and the Beechcraft left the tarmac and took off across the grass.

"Airport Control to Beechcraft!" came over the radio. "What do you—"

Lyons didn't hear the rest of the radio transmission. By then he had leapt from the aircraft himself, hit the ground and rolled back to his feet.

He sprinted through the open door to the office, the Calico leading the way. A surprised young man looked up from the desk just inside the door, then dived for the radio.

Lyons beat him to it with a steady stream of 9 mm rounds that took out the entire communication system. The man fell to his knees. "Please…" he pleaded. "Don't shoot me."

The former LAPD officer didn't. Instead he hit the man over the head with the barrel of the Calico and dropped him unconscious to the floor. He had started past the desk to the office behind it when a burst of gunfire outside drew him to the window. On the runway, he saw the subgun in Blancanales's hands jump as a stream of autofire tore the wheels from beneath a Piper Cub that was trying to take off.

The Piper screeched like a banshee as it slid to a halt on its underbelly.

Lyons started toward the office again, then heard Schwarz in his ear. "Send in the cavalry whenever you're ready," the electronics man said into the headset. "I've got a dozen of them backed up against the wall and ready to do time."

The big ex-cop finally made it into the office, stopping just inside the door.

Richard Kokojan stood frozen next to a desk against the wall. Another man had turned to face the door, equally cowed.

"Mr. Kokojan," Lyons said, swinging the machine

pistol up under the airport owner's nose, "this airport is officially shut down." He paused and let a smile creep over his hard features. "And I'm afraid that's going to be the least of your problems."

Above Bonn, Germany

"WE HAVE HAD intelligence concerning this Joseph Ryba," Dieter Kaufman said. "We suspected he was up to something, but had no idea what it was. Or that it was at this advanced stage."

McCarter nodded. He studied the German GSG-9 captain. Kaufman wore a one-piece dark green suit bearing the Bundesgrenzschutz insignia, and identical to those of the regular German border patrol police. The only difference was the Fallschirmjager jump wings. A Heckler & Koch MP-5 was slung over his shoulder in battle-carry mode, the barrel aimed forward.

The former SAS officer moved around inside the transport plane as it made its way to the farmhouse outside Bonn, just west of the suburb of Konigsvinter. The rest of the GSG-9 commandos were dressed identically, the only personalized equipment being their side arms. Hanging from the belts of the Germans, McCarter saw everything from Glocks to H&K "squeeze-cockers." A lot of SIG-Sauers and even a new Browning Hi-Power in .40 caliber. One man, a burly German with a close-cropped flattop, wore a Smith & Wesson double-action-only Model M-64 .38 revolver, made expressly for the New York City Police Department.

McCarter didn't ask where the German commando had come up with the weapon. GSG-9 commandos were not only famous for their counterterrorist strikes around the world, some were equally known for their off-duty escapades when they'd had a few beers. The Phoenix Force leader wasn't sure he wanted to know how the weapon had been acquired.

"The farmhouse is fairly isolated," Kaufman told McCarter, pointing to an aerial map on the table bolted to the floor of the plane. "Even if one gets into the air, we will have a few seconds in which our planes can shoot it down." He paused. "The chemicals should have dissipated by the time they reach the closest village, and the two farmhouses within…" He let his voice trail off. "How do you say it? The area where people could be killed?"

"Kill zone."

"Yes, the farmers in the kill zone have been evacuated."

"So we'll drop out of the plane under cover of darkness with a five-man squad of your men," McCarter said. "How many can you have on the ground?"

"Four more teams of five. They will hit the place from all four directions, with the ground forces covering the landing strip, hangars, and other outbuildings while we make our way to the main house." He paused, cleared his throat, then said, "That is, if this plan meets your approval. I have been instructed that you will be in charge. I do not like those orders, but I will obey them."

McCarter smiled. The man was used to running the

show himself. But like any good soldier, he could take orders as well as give them when told to do so. "It's a good plan, Dieter. Let's do it."

The GSG-9 captain softened somewhat. "There is one more thing I am not clear about," he said. "I was told you represented the SAS."

"Yes."

Kaufman glanced toward James and Manning. "These men are not British. I can tell by their voices." He turned to Encizo. "And who should I believe he is? A Mexican Gurkha?"

McCarter laughed. "I've got my own orders, Dieter, and they include a certain bit of secrecy. Even from you. I'm sorry."

Before Kaufman could answer, a voice from the cockpit spoke in German over the sound system.

"We jump in one minute," Kaufman translated. "Do not forget your gas mask." He grinned again. "Or your parachute."

McCarter felt himself smiling as he shrugged into his chute. Kaufman was a likable sort, making the best of being unseated in his command. Admirable.

The door slid back twenty seconds later. McCarter moved to the head of the line next to Kaufman and waited. When the red light went on, he was the first man out the door.

The Phoenix Force warrior could see lights moving on the farm below as he fell through the darkened sky. They were getting ready to launch—if they weren't prepared already. Probably putting the final touches on things before beginning a strike that was meant to kill millions of human beings in western and central Europe.

"They think," McCarter said out loud.

James's voice came back in his headset. "What David?" the black warrior asked.

McCarter realized he'd spoken out loud. "I said let's get this one for Katz."

Four voices affirmed the sentiment enthusiastically. McCarter watched the buildings below take shape as he thought briefly about the Phoenix Force leader.

Grimaldi had taken Katz to a hospital in Prague, where several Stony Man "blacksuits" were stationed in plain clothes. Doctors had found internal hemorrhaging among the broken bones.

The Israeli's condition was critical, and none of the doctors would lay odds on whether he'd make it or not.

McCarter forced his thoughts away from Katz. It wouldn't do to be worrying during the battle that lay ahead. He looked down as the buildings became more clear, seeing a large frame house, several outbuildings and a landing strip. He frowned. The place reminded him of somewhere he'd been before.

The Briton laughed out loud when he realized where that place was. Stony Man Farm itself.

His laughter ended abruptly as the first rounds of fire flickered below. Bullets whizzed up past him. Twirling the Uzi on the sling, he aimed downward.

McCarter opened fire on two men who stood aiming their Czech 25s into the sky. Two short bursts took them out as the ground below, and the sky around him, lighted up with muzzle-flashes.

The Stony Man warrior's boots hit the ground and he unclipped the lines, letting his chute fly back up into the sky. Holding the Uzi's folding stock to his shoulder, he dropped the front sights on a man wearing green fatigues who raced across the grounds toward him.

Another burst of fire from the Israeli machine pistol sent the man tumbling to the ground. McCarter swung the Uzi to his side and held the trigger back on a trio of men in fatigues as Kaufman hit the ground next to him. The German's MP-5 sputtered, sending death across a twenty-yard expanse into two more men in green.

One by one, the rest of Phoenix Force and the GSG-9 commandos hit the ground, their weapons blasting death to the men who were preparing to bomb the world with disease.

McCarter fought his way toward the main house as Kaufman fired next to him. Together, they dropped six more of the Czech hardmen.

GSG-9 troopers in green jumpsuits suddenly emerged on all sides of the farmhouse, spraying the air with 9 mm Parabellum rounds from their MP-5s. They spread out, some of them cordoning off the landing strip while others entered the hangars, taking out the hardmen they encountered.

McCarter reached the front door first, ripping it open. As he did, he heard the roar of a plane engine behind him. Turning, he saw a small airplane taxiing down the runway in defiance of the 9 mm rounds that spotted its sides with holes. Too far away and too dark to determine the make or model, the former SAS officer watched it speed away.

The plane left the ground. It had reached a height of perhaps a thousand feet when the Panavia Tornado F.2S came sweeping out of nowhere, its 27 mm Mauser gun chattering in the sky.

A mile away on the horizon, McCarter saw the white trail between the Tornado and the smaller plane. Then the Sidewinder missile found its mark and the skyline lighted up in flames.

McCarter patted the gas mask on his belt, making sure it was still there. He'd need it in a few minutes. He led the way into the house, and he and Kaufman swept through the rooms. All empty. Everyone inside had left to join the defense of the farm. They now lay dead in the yard.

The gunfire had stopped by the time they stepped onto the front porch. But on the horizon, they could still see the flames of the burning plane that had tried to escape with the chemical death.

McCarter turned to Kaufman. The big German smiled. "My wife and I," he said. "We have a Siamese."

McCarter was taken back. "Pardon me?"

"A Siamese cat. My wife and I have one named Greta."

McCarter knew that the stress of battle, even on seasoned warriors, sometimes caused strange reactions. But Dieter Kaufman didn't seem the type to have gone nuts. "Excuse me, Dieter, but did I miss something?"

Now it was Kaufman who looked confused. "You

and your men. You must like cats. Before we landed,
I heard you say so.''

McCarter suddenly remembered what he'd told the
other members of Phoenix Force as they prepared for
battle. *"Let's get this one for Katz."* He forced a
smile, but inside his guts churned with anxiety as he
remembered the Phoenix Force leader. "Yes, Dieter.
My men and I like Katz very much.''

Neither of the two warriors spoke as they pulled
the gas masks over their faces.

Ukraine

THE DNIEPER RIVER, the third-largest river in Europe,
flows through three of the republics of the former Soviet Union. From western Russia it runs south, passing
the Valdai Hills and Smolensk before entering Bye-
lorussia to run through Mogilev, Zlobin and Recica.
Then it flows into Ukraine, picking up force from its
various tributaries as it goes. The mighty Dnieper con-
tinues past Kiev, Dnepropetrovsk and Zaporozhye,
where its waters provide hydroelectricity with stupen-
dous dams and power plants.

The Dnieper has been the lifeline of that part of the
world for centuries.

Joseph Ryba had decided it would work just as well
as a death line.

"We sent agents as soon as your President contacted ours," Ukraine Intelligence Major Rotislav
Morovsky told Bolan, tapping the map on the wall of
the former Soviet Mil Mi-8 helicopter with a wooden
pointer. Morovsky's English was excellent, exhibiting

more of the British accent of his instructors than that of his native Ukraine, and his voice was loud enough to transcend the noisy blades of the chopper. "They were able to get close enough to report back that we are in luck, in some ways. In other ways…not so lucky."

Bolan nodded. He glanced around the inside of the Mi-8. Ukrainian special forces soldiers were conducting last-minute gear checks and preparing for battle. Their battle dress consisted of what had once been Spetsnaz cammies, and here and there the Executioner saw one of the old blue-and-white hooped T-shirts that had been worn by all Soviet special forces. The sight brought a hard smile to his lips. He had spent far more time shooting at those uniforms than with them. But Ukraine had to get its troops somewhere, and at least the uniforms, like the helicopter and other equipment being used, were now fighting for freedom rather than against it.

The Executioner took a quick look at Hammersmith, standing next to him. Like Bolan himself, she had changed into Ukrainian battle fatigues provided by Morovsky. Looking back to the map, Bolan said, "Go ahead."

"Their headquarters are in the boathouse I showed you when we flew over a few minutes ago. It was formerly owned and operated by the state, or course. A small airport with two landing strips lies a mile farther inland." He pointed to the glass porthole in the side of the chopper. "We should be passing over it about now."

Bolan moved to the round window, looked down and saw the two runways and a small building.

"The airport has always been used to make flight connections from air to river," Morovsky stated as the Executioner returned to the map. "It, too, was formerly Soviet-owned."

"Let me guess," the warrior said. "Sometime since the end of the Union, the government sold both places. And unless I miss my guess, they were bought by the same man. A Czech."

Morovsky was a tall man with a tight, angular face. But when he smiled, his entire body seemed to show his pleasure. He did so now. "You are close, Colonel Pollock," he said, tapping the map again. "A Czech consortium, actually. Do you wish to know the names?"

"Not now. Those men will enter into the 'cleanup' that goes on when this is over. But right now the number-one priority is to get down there and stop the anthrax from getting into the sky."

"Exactly," Morovsky said. "Now, the 'lucky' part I mentioned is that in order to preserve their cover, they have been limited to only a few small private aircraft. The part that will make this difficult is that we are talking about Kiev, a heavily populated area. If one of the planes does get into the air, we cannot shoot it down for fear that it will contaminate the entire city."

"Then we have to make sure none of them make it into the air."

"Correct."

"Where do we stand right now?" Bolan asked.

"At the moment, both the boathouse and airport are surrounded by special operational troops who are either hidden or masquerading as night workers. We have two boats on the river, disguised as cargo ships, in the event that there are biochemicals waiting to be shipped by water. And, of course, the Ukrainian air force is on alert and will take off just before the attack begins." He paused.

"If your men are in civvies, it's going to be hard to tell the good guys from the bad."

Morovsky shook his head. "The boathouse and airport have contracted to a Czech security company and all of the workers there will be wearing light blue jumpsuits with a shoulder patch. It reads…" He paused to glance down at the file on the table in front of him.

"Jablonec," Bolan said.

"Exactly," Morovsky replied, looking back up.

"How soon can everyone be ready to strike?" Bolan asked.

"We are ready as soon as you give the word."

The Executioner glanced at Hammersmith, then looked back at the Ukrainian major. "Let's do it."

Morovsky walked to the front of the chopper, took a radio mike from the console and spoke into it.

Several voices answered back over the airwaves.

Bolan slung the Calico over his shoulder as the chopper turned around and sped up. He checked the Beretta under his arm, the Desert Eagle on his hip, then turned back to Hammersmith.

The British woman looked no worse for wear from her close call with the man in the gray suit. Bolan

wondered briefly who he had been. At this point, it
didn't matter. Details of the mission would be run
down by Stony Man operatives after the fireworks
were over. He'd learn the answers then.

Hammersmith checked the thumb snap on the holster carrying her squeeze-cocker, then shouldered the
M-16.

"You ready?" Bolan asked.

An impish grin spread over the redhead's face.
"Like you Yanks used to say during World War II,
'Give 'em hell, Harry.'"

Bolan laughed. "You're too young to remember
that."

"You are, too." Hammersmith grinned. "My father told me."

A second later, the chopper dropped through the air
and the doors swung open.

Bolan and Hammersmith jumped to the ground, followed by Morovsky and the other special forces men.
Crouching beneath the rotor blades, the Executioner
led the sprint toward the boathouse.

Automatic gunfire broke out suddenly as the men
in the light blue jumpsuits realized they were under
attack. The barrage provoked an immediate response.

The front door of the boathouse swung open as Bolan leveled the Calico on two men who had turned
toward him firing Model 25s. A steady stream of fire
cut back and forth between the duo, dropping them to
the damp earth next to the door as a speedboat suddenly emerged. A white wake of foam trailed the boat
as it cut a sharp turn onto the Dnieper and tried to
pick up speed.

The Executioner turned toward the boat, quickly noting that the open deck held no cargo. If canisters of biochemicals were on board, there weren't many. Bringing the subgun up to eye level, he sighted down the top of the drum, then squeezed the trigger and sent a steady stream of gunfire into the gas tank.

The speedboat exploded in a fury of flame, fifty yards out on the water. Any compounds on board would be taken care of by the inferno.

Bolan felt a burst of fire zoom past his neck and turned the Calico toward a man in a light blue jumpsuit holding a Czech Model 58-P assault rifle to his shoulder. A 5-round dose of 9 mm death sent the rifle flying through the air as the man hit the ground.

The Executioner heard the familiar *rat-ta-tat* of an M-16 and saw Hammersmith drop another of the blue-clad hardmen.

Bullets of every caliber flew through the air as Bolan and the British agent fought their way toward the boathouse. Four men in blue emerged from a side door. The first, wearing a long straggly beard, whirled toward them with a CZ-75 grasped in both fists.

Bolan popped two rounds from the Calico into the man's gut, then finished him off with a shot to the head.

The second two men looked as if they might be brothers. Dark stringy hair fell over their ears. Both were short, squat and had big foreheads that shone under the lights around the boathouse.

The Executioner took the man on the right, peppering his body with a torrent of Parabellum rounds.

Hammersmith concentrated on the man's twin, firing two successive 3-round bursts into the lower abdomen, then the chest.

The American and Briton teamed up to put the last man—a tall gangly Czech who looked somewhat like Ryba himself—on the grass to one side of the boathouse.

Bolan led the way, vaulting the bodies and crouching as he leapt through the door to the small building. Three more speedboats floated in their slips between the planks of the dock. A dozen men were busy loading them down with wooden crates.

The warrior had no doubt what the crates contained—more of the canisters that held the anthrax. And he had a different situation on his hands with these boats than with the one that had sped by him into the open river. Here, he took a good chance of hitting the canisters themselves, rupturing the containers and setting the disease loose. It didn't matter that it wouldn't travel far on its own—it would spread far enough to reach him, Hammersmith and the Ukrainian troops within the area.

The Executioner raised the Calico to the end of its sling, flipped the selector to semiauto, sighted carefully down the drum and sent a lone round into the head of the nearest man.

The crate in his hand slid into the water.

Hammersmith had switched to semiauto, as well. She took out another of the men in the blue jumpsuits as the Executioner swung the submachine gun to the next boat, dropping two more of Ryba's hardmen with another pair of rounds.

The British woman switched to the boats themselves, carefully pumping a series of rounds into the hulls. The vessels sank lower into the water.

The three men around the last boat dropped their crates and turned to run. The Executioner flipped the selector back to full-auto, emptying the remaining 9 mm rounds until the weapon's bolt locked open.

Bolan let the weapon fall to the end of the sling and drew the big Desert Eagle from its hip holster. Hammersmith had finished dotting the speedboats with enough holes below the waterline to sink them. The threat from that arena had ended, and Ukrainian divers would retrieve the canisters from the bottom of the harbor.

Racing back outside, the Executioner and his companion joined the battle that was now dying down as the Ukrainians took control of the area from Ryba's men.

The Executioner fired a double-tap of .44 Magnum rounds into one of the remaining hardmen as he saw Morovsky drill a burst into a fat man to his right. Then the Ukrainian major frowned, spoke into his face mike and ducked back around the corner of the boathouse.

Bolan raced away from the boathouse, then turned the corner wide to make sure Morovsky recognized him. Coming to a halt at the Ukrainian's side, he said, "What is it?"

Morovsky shook his head in disbelief. "One of the planes at the landing strips. It was loaded and ready for takeoff when the assault began. Somehow, even with all our troops, it got off the ground."

"So where does the situation stand right now?" Bolan asked.

"Four of our MiG-25s are following it, ten klicks to the north."

"Have they established radio contact?"

"Yes. The pilot understands the advantage he holds and refuses to land."

"Let's go," Bolan said, turning to sprint back across the grounds to the helicopter. Morovsky followed, climbing up into the cargo area. They hurried to where the pilot still waited behind the controls. A moment later, they were airborne.

Bolan took a seat in the cabin with Morovsky and the pilot. He pointed to the radio. "Your Russian has got to be better than mine," he told the Ukrainian major. "You do the talking."

Morovsky lifted the mike. "And what do I say?"

"Order the MiGs to intercept the plane and form around it," the Executioner said. "Have them force it away from the populated areas and onto a path we can intercept in this thing."

Morovsky's heavy eyebrows rose, then he spoke into the mike.

Bolan sat back against the seat as the helicopter took off across the city to the north.

Ten minutes later, a voice spoke in Russian over the radio.

"They have closed in on the plane," Morovsky said. "The pilot is threatening to crash it."

"Where are they?"

Morovsky spoke again and received an answer. "They are less than two kilometers ahead of us, cutting back toward the east."

"How far from people?"

Morovsky looked at the radar screen, then consulted a map. "If we close in on them immediately, we will be safe. But on the course they are taking, they will be over Nezin in only a few minutes. There are several other small villages in the area, as well."

Bolan leaned forward, eyeing the controls for the Mi-8's 57 mm rockets. "Then we'd better do it now."

The pilot sped forward as Bolan and Morovsky watched the specks on the radar screen. Then, far in the distance, they saw more specks on the horizon through the helicopter's windshield. Coming from the west, the specks grew larger until Bolan could make out the four MiGs surrounding the smaller private craft.

Bolan worked the controls, locking in on the smallest of the dots on the screen. "Tell the pilots that when I count three, I want them to pull off, and they'd better pull off fast."

Morovsky issued the warning over the radio.

The Executioner took a deep breath, his thumb on the trigger button. He would have one shot, and one shot only. If he missed, the pilot of the small plane might well have time to reach the village and carry through with his kamikaze threat.

As the chopper neared the planes, the Executioner said, "One."

"*Adee'n,*" Morovsky said into the microphone.

"Two," Bolan said, his jaw tightening.

"*Dva,*" the Ukrainian translated.

The Executioner took another breath as he double-checked his target on screen. Then, letting half of it out as if this were nothing more than a final pistol shot on a target training range, he said, "Three!"

"*Tree!*" Morovsky cried.

Four of the dots on screen suddenly took off above and beyond the fifth.

Bolan gave it another count, then thumbed the button.

The 57 mm rocket thrust forth from the helicopter, leaving a trail of white behind it. A moment later, an explosion rocked the chopper, then the sky ahead of them lighted up with the fires of hell.

The Executioner glanced down at the screen. The dot had disappeared.

"Check the reading," Bolan said quickly. "How far were we from the villages?"

Morovsky frowned, punched several buttons in the control panel and stared at the Cyrillic letters and numbers that appeared on the screen. Then the frown became a grin. "The people on the ground are safe."

The warrior sighed in relief. "So is the rest of the world. At least for a little while."

As the big C-17 descended over Heathrow Airport, Jonine Hammersmith took a sip of her Scotch and water and leaned back against the stuffed lounge chair in the converted cargo area. She closed her eyes for a moment, then opened them again, letting them roam across the other faces on the plane one last time.

Hammersmith had known the men on board less than three days, but she felt as if they'd grown up together, as if they were her brothers. Well, all except Rance Pollock. She certainly didn't think of *him* as a brother.

Seated across the metal floor on one of the bolted-down bunks, was the man she knew only as Katz.

She had only met him when the other men had brought him on board from the hospital a few hours earlier. But she even felt as if *he* was her friend. He looked Jewish, but his accent sounded like a mixture of cultured Hebrew and French. Another mystery to which she'd probably never get an answer.

The big Canadian came walking into the cargo area from the cabin. "You feeling all right, Katz?" he asked.

The older man propped himself up on his elbows.

"Never felt better." He grinned, tapped the casts on both knees, then the tight bandages around his ribs. "Little hard to breathe, but I could still handle a battalion of wimps like you guys."

"How about the face?" the Canadian asked, referring to a dozen or so stitches.

"It's still prettier than yours."

The other men seated around the cargo area laughed. It was obvious that they all had the greatest affection for the older man, even though they were the type that only showed it through good-natured insults. But Hammersmith had seen the looks of relief in all their eyes when they'd learned that Katz would be as good as new in a couple of weeks.

The pilot's voice came over the loudspeaker from the cabin. "About there, Jonnie. You ready?"

Hammersmith rose. Lifting a small satchel that held her two pistols, she moved around the room giving each man a goodbye hug.

The plane hit the runway, then taxied to a stop. The woman turned to go when Mack Bolan suddenly appeared. The big man took the bag from her hand, and Hammersmith hooked her arm through his as they stepped off the plane.

Neither of them spoke as they crossed the tarmac. There was nothing much to say. The MI-6 agent knew she would never see the man again, would never even know his real name.

She smiled as she walked. Knowing his name wasn't important. She had seen his soul.

Bolan stopped at the gate. "We just got word from

our base. The rest of the launch sites, labs, they've all been neutralized. It's over.''

A sharp stab of pain hit Hammersmith's heart. ''Yes. I know it's over.''

''Jonnie, I think—''

Hammersmith held a finger to his lips, silencing him. ''No, don't think. Just remember.'' Then she was in his arms, kissing him. She turned around and walked through the gate. A tear formed in her eye, and she wiped it away with her hand.

When she glanced over her shoulder one last time, the big American was gone.

STONY MAN™

Embark on a new Stony Man adventure every
month as Mack Bolan and his teams battle new
dangers. Experience the fast and furious pace
of combat combined with new technology in
each exciting new book.

*A brand new Stony Man novel
is available every month from selected*

WHSmith
stores.

SM/RTL/GEN

STONY MAN ™

Ten tactical nuclear missile warheads have been hijacked from a Russian Convoy by North Korean communist hard-liners.

Phoenix Team corners the enemy in the Pacific, while Able Team hits Seattle where the gang is being financed by drug barons, in their mission to take down the hard-line gang.

WARHEAD

is published on 3rd November, and is only available through selected

WHSmith

stores.

SM/RTL/5

STONY MAN™

A string of brutal and indiscriminate terrorist attacks has rocked the world. No organisation is claiming responsibility but a pattern is emerging that suggests the targets were not chosen at random.

Stony Man launches a three-pronged attack, but this is merely the first step in tracking the source and collecting payment—in blood.

BLOOD DEBT

is published on 5th January, and is only available through selected

WHSmith

stores.

SM/RTL/7